SILENT SISTER

SILENT SISTER

MEGAN DAVIDHIZAR

DELACORTE PRESS

Visit us on the Web! GetUnderlined.com

Educators and librarians, for a variety of teaching tools, visit us at RHTeachersLibrarians.com

Library of Congress Cataloging-in-Publication Data is available upon request.
ISBN 978-0-593-70564-3 (hardcover) — ISBN 978-0-593-70566-7 (ebook) — ISBN 978-0-593-81524-3 (int'l ed.)

The text of this book is set in 11-point Sabon MT Pro.
White paper texture background art by Abbasy Kautsar/stock.adobe.com
Interior design by Cathy Bobak

Printed in the United States of America
10 9 8 7 6 5 4 3 2 1
First Edition

For all the girls left behind

CHAPTER 1

Grace: April 27

The face on a missing person poster is supposed to be a stranger. Those yellowed papers tacked up in grocery stores are children who disappeared fifteen years ago. Amber Alerts are kids from other states with parents fighting for custody. And yet the face staring back at me from the TV—the girl under the siren-red *MISSING* letters—

That's me.

If there's any face I should recognize instantly, it's my own. I've seen it a million times in every mirror and every photo I've ever appeared in. But I don't recognize the girl staring back at me from the hospital's flat-screen. It's like looking at someone else, not myself.

Whoever sent in the picture cropped our volleyball team photo where I'm wearing my uniform, and I have perfectly straight brown hair and a shiny smile. The image on the screen shows a happy Grace, one who laughs and charms and lives up to her name. Nothing like the Grace I am now: weak, bruised, and broken in a hospital bed.

The TV's volume is muted, but the dull hum of the AC suddenly roars in my ears. The photo is replaced by one of me and my sister, cheek to cheek. There are no captions, but I can imagine the news anchor's voice, cold and detached, updating the community on the status of the search: *Grace Stoll was found on the side of the road early yesterday morning, but the search for her sister, Maddy, continues.* As if on cue, the screen switches again, this time to a picture of Maddy.

We look as if we could be twins. She resembles me more in that photo than I do right now. My hair is still tangled and knotted, and while the dried blood's been washed away from my face, I spotted some flecks of it along my hairline in the bathroom mirror this morning.

I look exactly like you'd expect after being found on the side of the road.

But I'm not the one still missing. Maddy is.

It's only been a little over a day since I woke up and was told my sister is gone. I've been trying to convince myself it's still early . . . There's still time . . . It hasn't even been forty-eight hours yet. We'll find her.

We will.

Maybe it's a blessing that I look like this, that the reflection gazing back at me is a stranger, that I don't have to see a copy of Maddy's face in the mirror knowing she's still out there. Somewhere.

Mom comes in, carrying a bouquet of flowers in one hand

and wiping her puffy eyes with the other. Watching her pain is worse than feeling it myself. She tries her best not to cry in front of me, but the tears haven't stopped since she walked into the hospital yesterday. At first I thought she was only crying with relief that I was okay, but then Dad told me about Maddy.

Mom takes one look at the news update on the screen before grabbing the remote from my hand.

"Let's turn this off." She clears her throat, scraping away the tight hold of tears and worry. "Dr. Thelsman says the best thing you can do right now is rest, and they're not reporting anything we don't already know." She sets the vase of flowers on the table beneath the TV, along with the remote, far out of my reach.

"I have been resting." My voice is scratchy, raw, foreign.

A too-soft pillow swallows my shoulders, and stiff sheets cover the long scratch up my left calf. The police took the clothes I was found in. When the hospital gown slips from my shoulder, I gently adjust it, careful not to tug the IV taped to the back of my hand. I can barely get out of bed without someone helping to hold up my gown or untangle the IV, much less help Maddy.

"Someone from the school came by to deliver this," Mom says, ignoring me and pointing to the flowers surrounded by other colorful arrangements, cards, and gifts. The waiting room's been a revolving door of people stopping by, neighbors and friends, mostly, since my parents were both only children and their extended family isn't local. No one stays for long. I'm not allowed visitors yet. Plus, sitting in the lobby and wishing me good health is pretty useless when they could be searching for Maddy.

Mom hands me a get-well card with scripty gold writing. The inside's covered in student signatures: Mackayla, Jade, Nicole . . .

"Nicole," I say slowly. "She was on the trip with us."

"You remember it?" Mom's eyes grow wide—not with surprise. Something else. I shouldn't have said anything, because too late I realize what it is: hope.

"No, not exactly," I say. We stood outside the school before boarding the bus last Monday. Five days ago. It's the last thing I remember. We were all signed up, packed, and ready to endure the hour-long ride to Shady Oaks Lodge, and then . . . nothing. "Nothing new. Only before the trip."

"Oh." Her shoulders drop a fraction of an inch.

"I'll let you know when I remember something."

She smiles. A genuine smile. The first genuine smile I've seen since I woke up this morning.

But my heart sinks further because I said *when*, and I meant to say *if*. The doctors already said they can't predict whether those memories will return.

"Dad's bringing some of your things from home," Mom says.

"Does that mean I'm leaving?" I ask with hope of my own. The doctors ran every test they could yesterday. I was only awake for pieces of it. My eyes fluttered open when the ambulance siren screamed its arrival. The gurney jostled as they loaded me in. Doctors and nurses called my name. Someone asked me if I remembered what happened. I'm not sure how much time passed before my parents arrived. Mom cried into my shoulder, and Dad smoothed the hair back from my forehead to give me a kiss before I drifted back to sleep.

There were no flashes of nightmares or dreams, or what might have knocked me unconscious and landed me in the hospital in the first place.

There was nothing but darkness. Sleep. Silence.

But today, I'm awake. I'm fully aware of my reality: I can't remember anything from our weeklong senior trip. My sister and I went missing, but I'm the only one they found.

"Dr. Thelsman wants you to spend one more night for observation, and then if everything else comes back clear, he hopes to release you tomorrow morning."

Release me.

The doctors and hospital walls aren't the only things trapping me.

A quick knock raps against the door with a hushed "Ms. Stoll?"

A tall, middle-aged man swings the door open and enters with a clean-shaven guy. Both wear police uniforms. The first man's eyes move from my mom to me, and his face breaks into a soft smile. "Glad to see you awake." A few gray hairs speckle his dark goatee. "I'm Detective Howard, and this is Officer Jones." I shake his offered hand and nod to the younger officer, who waves. "I was hoping you might be able to answer a few questions for us."

"I don't know if she's ready yet," Mom says, her arm draped protectively over the back of my raised bed. "The doctor said—"

"The doctor said I'm fine," I interrupt. "Every test has come back clear so far."

"You're hardly fine if you—"

Officer Jones jumps in: "With all due respect, your daughter's eighteen and can legally make that decision on her own."

My mom's mouth drops in surprise, but Detective Howard speaks first. "It's all right. We understand this might be difficult." He talks to me, but his eyes flick to Mom. "We just want to get as much information as we can to help find your sister."

"I want to do this. I want to help." I should be searching for Maddy. I should be doing something to find my sister and make sure she's okay. And if I'm stuck in this room, if this is the only way to be useful, then nothing is going to stop me.

Mom swallows and nods her consent, legally required or not. Detective Howard pulls a chair over to the edge of my bed and lowers himself to my level.

"What do you remember from the trip?"

"Nothing, I—I can't remember anything."

Dr. Thelsman said memory loss is fairly common following a head injury or traumatic event. Even though no one knows exactly what this event was, it's pretty obvious it can be classified as traumatic.

Detective Howard pauses. "Do you know why you might have been on Oldham County Road?"

"No, I didn't even know the name of it until right now."

"That's where Trent Gutter found you yesterday morning."

"Your math teacher?" Mom asks.

"History," I correct.

"He was a chaperone on the trip," Detective Howard clarifies.

"Mr. Gutter was?" I ask. "But Mr. Holtsof and Mrs. Sanderson were the ones at the meeting." They were definitely the two staff members originally signed up for Senior Sabbatical. Then, at the surprised look on Detective Howard's face, I add, "I can remember everything from before the trip. All of it."

He nods and consults his notes. "We spoke to a Mr. Trent Gutter and Mrs. Katie Sanderson, both Forest Lane Academy staff members assigned to chaperone the trip."

When I neither confirm nor deny this fact, Detective Howard shares a glance with Officer Jones, who then types something into his phone, possibly a note to confirm that later. The detective asks slowly, "Can you think of anyone on the trip who might have wished you or your sister harm?"

"No, definitely not." No hesitation. Not even a moment.

Mom gives my shoulder a reassuring squeeze, but her fingers tremble.

Detective Howard waits as if he's attempting to watch the memories play like a movie across my forehead, but there's nothing else to say. We were with classmates, *friends*. No one who would hurt us.

"You're sure?"

"Yes, I—" I pause, longing to pull at any thread of memory. The effort ignites a flash of sharp pain. I rub my temples, wishing it away.

"Do you recall fighting with your sister or anyone else on the trip?"

"No," I say, shaking my head. "I—I don't remember anything after getting on the bus Monday morning."

Disappointment leaks into the lines on the detective's forehead, but I keep my eyes trained on him, because it's easier to watch him than to face my mom, who I know will be looking at me the same way. Maddy needs me. I can do this for her.

"Did you leave the lodge for any reason?"

"Not that I can remember." And then, in a desperate attempt to be helpful, I add, "Except, well, obviously I did at some point if I was found on that road."

"Do you remember it?"

"No. I only remember boarding the bus. Then . . . nothing. Not until I was loaded onto the ambulance." I scrape my hair away from my face, careful not to let the teeth of the hair clip bite the stitches on the back of my skull. The injury is under my hair, not visible—unlike the black eye, the scratch on my cheek, or healing bruises—and the gash at the base of my skull required seven stitches and hurts worse than all the rest of them combined.

"I think that's enough," Mom says, stepping forward with her hand toward the door. "My daughter needs her rest, so unless you have any updates on the search . . ."

Detective Howard ignores her. I can feel him looking at me, but I keep my chin raised, eyes focused on the pocked tiles covering the ceiling, willing the headache that's blossomed across my temples to disappear. I squeeze my eyes shut until I hear the scrape of Detective Howard's chair being returned to its place against the wall.

"It's all right," he says. "We've got enough for now. Be sure to call us if you remember anything about that night." He hands me a business card with the police logo on it.

I reach for it, but his last word sends another wave of throbbing through my head.

"Wait, I thought we went missing in the morning." I look to Mom, the only source of news I've had, for confirmation.

She nods, but her brows pull together in confusion. "The school called us yesterday morning to say the girls weren't accounted for."

"After talking with the staff chaperones and other students on the trip, the last report we have of either girl being seen is Thursday night, the twenty-fifth, around nine p.m."

Mom's chin crumples and her eyes water. Twelve hours. Maddy's been missing for twelve hours more than we thought. I swallow the rising panic. I know what they say about the first forty-eight hours. Everyone knows. And we lost twelve without realizing it.

"I don't understand," Mom says, her voice brittle, threatening to break. "The school said they started searching as soon as the girls were reported missing. That wasn't until Friday morning."

"Their roommates and another boy from the trip, a"—Detective Howard scrolls through his phone, checking his notes again—"Ryan Jacobs, first noticed the girls' absence at six a.m. on the morning of the twenty-sixth, and told the school staff members right away. They searched the lodge and its grounds, and then called us the same time they notified you."

"What time is it now?"

"Just after four," Officer Jones says.

That means if Maddy isn't found in the next five hours, then she's probably . . .

They don't say how important it is for me to remember.

They don't have to. Maddy is missing.

And I'm the only one who was with her when she disappeared.

CHAPTER 2

Maddy: April 20

Forty-two days until graduation.

Fourteen days until prom.

Two days until Senior Sabbatical.

Seven minutes (maybe) until my life (hopefully) changes forever.

I tap a pen relentlessly against the notebook in my lap and fight the urge to check my phone again. Nothing has changed. Probably. It's only been two minutes since I last hit Refresh on my email, but the results are supposed to be announced today. I need to stop thinking about it. I'll stop riiiiiight now.

Okay, *now.*

Stop, stop, stop, stopstopstop.

But I should probably check to make— My phone vibrates, and I nearly fall off my bed snatching it from the pillow next to me.

Not an email. A message from Erica pops up: a picture of

her cat looking mutinous. It's enough to make me laugh and forget my empty inbox long enough to reply.

Did you move when she was sleeping on you again?

Her response arrives immediately. *No, it's three minutes past when I normally feed her.*

I send a crying emoji and ask if she wants to come over tonight. All week long at school, she's avoided mentioning her plans today. But it's obvious why. She's my best friend—okay, my only friend—and we always surprise each other. It's our thing. We randomly get each other gifts, and they always have googly eyes. I'll bring her a cup of coffee in the morning with two big plastic eyes stuck on the lid. A few weeks later, she'll bring me a donut with a fresh pair of eyes on top. Bath bombs. Pencils. Phone cases. Make-up. Gifts big and small, all with a ridiculous pair of adhesive eyes to make the other laugh. But since I filled her car with googly-eyed balloons two months ago, she hasn't given a gift back. She's definitely been planning something big, and I predict the reveal will come tonight.

There's no lightning-quick response this time. I smirk. Fine, leave me on read. She has to reveal the plan soon. I heard her talking about the music festival when I walked into English on Tuesday. She stopped as soon as she spotted me, and I played it off perfectly. She has no idea I heard. It will take at least thirty minutes to drive to the city and another ten for parking. Plus, time to get ready together . . . I estimate she'll be forced to confess and send a picture of the tickets topped with eyeballs in the next hour.

Maybe by then I'll know if I can afford college next year. Too much waiting for good news all at the same time.

I can't take it.

I toss my phone back onto the bed and return my focus to the blank page in front of me. My portfolio for the Dorene Williams Memorial Writing Scholarship was submitted months ago, so it's not as if there's any pressure to fill this page in front of me. But poetry relaxes me. Usually. Not today, apparently.

Getting the congratulatory email would mean heading out of state and enrolling in any liberal arts school I want, but it's amazing how a major money announcement can suffocate all my creative abilities as swiftly as a rumor ruins a reputation in junior high.

My parents don't know I want to attend Trinity University. I could never show my dad the tuition costs. His eyeballs look best firmly attached to his head, thanks. But this scholarship would change everything. More than the money, it's the investment. It would mean someone reading my work and thinking, *She's worth it.*

Bzzt. My heart stops at the muffled vibration coming from the direction of my pillow. I reach for my phone but hesitate. It's probably Erica with plans for my surprise.

But maybe it's not. Maybe it's Dorene Williams's grandson himself—or one of the board members, more likely—notifying me that my writing absolutely blew them away and they've never been more excited to invest in a young writer. My mouth goes dry at the thought.

I clutch my phone to my chest. Close my eyes. Take a deep breath and—

"Eww." Grace races into our room, her eyes scanning the floor as she pauses to show her disgust. "What are you doing?"

"Nothing." I say, slipping my phone into my lap.

"With those?" She crinkles her nose and points to the bowl next to my notebook while craning her neck to peer around the other side of my bed.

"Eating." I pick up a thin slice of orange pepper and slather it in ranch dip. "Want one?" I ask.

Grace gags. "Do you *want* me to throw up on your bed again?"

"Nah, second grade after Alejandra's pizza party was enough, thanks." I snap the pepper with a satisfying crunch. She rushes to her side of the room, and I take a quick peek at my phone, still mostly expecting another text from Erica.

But it's not. It's an email. It's an email from the Dorene Williams Foundation! It'sanemailfromtheDoreneWilliamsFoundation!!!!

Grace flings up the skirt of her bed and groans. "Have you seen my volleyball jersey?"

"Huh?" I glance up, too terrified to click Open with someone else in the room. I need to be alone for this, whether good news or bad.

"My jersey," she repeats, wrenching open the closet door. "Have you seen it?"

"Nope." I silently pray she can't hear my heart hammering. "Laundry?"

"No, I thought I forgot it in my bag from last week, but now I can't find it." She scrutinizes herself in the mirror and scrapes her long brown hair into a high ponytail. "Coach is going to kill me if I don't leave soon and make it to the game on time."

"Here, let me." I lay my nerves down with my phone, bounce

up on my knees, and tug her arm away, forcing her hair to tumble behind her shoulders.

"You're a lifesaver." She assumes her usual position on the floor, and I drape my legs on either side of her shoulders, then swiftly pull a brush through her hair. We've had the same routine since I was seven. Grace was crying while Mom tried unsuccessfully to drag a brush through her snarls. I took over while Grace still had hair left to detangle. Under my touch, my older sister's sniffles turned to smiles.

Sixty seconds later, an inside-out braid climbs down Grace's back without a single bump or stray. And I've only had to suppress the urge to vomit from nerves approximately twelve times in the same span.

She stands and resumes her search, digging through drawers and then tossing aside her bedspread. "That writing foundation announces their scholarship selections today, right? Have you heard anything?"

"Oh, umm, I haven't thought to check," I lie. Grace and I share a room, a bathroom, and even some of our wardrobe, but I don't want to share this. I have this feeling, a kernel of hope, that all my hard work has paid off and the email waiting for me on my phone *right now* will be the news I've been longing for.

But there's a hazy cloud of doubt, too, enough to stop me from being honest.

"If you put yourself on the page, I'm sure they'll love you," she says.

I try to smile instead of cringe. Easy for her to say. Everyone loves Grace when they meet her. There's a reason she has plans with twenty different friends this weekend, and I'm still waiting to hear from my one.

Mom's voice echoes from downstairs. "Maddy! I mean, GRACE! Whoever you are!"

Grace rolls her eyes. Whenever Mom is stressed, she calls the wrong name, which causes more stress, and the cycle continues endlessly.

Mom pops into the doorway and tosses a blue shirt with gold numbers in Grace's face. "We have to be at the gym in twenty minutes. Let's go!"

Grace yanks the jersey over her head, ignoring my warning to not mess up her hair. "Where did you find it?"

"Dryer. Your dad washed it last night. Thank him later. Shoes, now!"

Grace sprints out our bedroom door. "Good luck," I call.

"Are you sure you don't want to come?" Mom asks.

"Yeah. Homework," I say by way of explanation and point to the notebook next to me in bed. My phone still sits, face-down, right beside me, moments away from a swipe and a click to open.

Having the finances to go to Trin U will mean moving away from home, creating a new version of myself, one based on who I want to be and not who others think I've been since middle school. I'll be my own person with my own accomplishments, no longer the quiet one next to Grace, effortless extrovert. My hard work will shine in my grades, not be dulled next to the pluses beside all of her As. I won't be *the sister of that volley-ball player.*

"Mom!" Grace yells from somewhere downstairs. "Let's go!" A door slams, signaling my sister's gone outside.

"Don't forget to let the dog out."

"I won't," I call as Mom leaves. I wait for the door downstairs to shut a final time.

Alone. Finally. I snatch my phone from the floor faster than a dropped Oreo. There it is, in bold letters in my inbox: Dorene Williams Foundation. It's here! It's actually here! It's here, here, here!

> *Madelyn Stoll,*
>
> *Thank you for submitting your application to the Dorene Williams Foundation for this year's scholarship. We regret to inform you the scholarship has been awarded to another poet—*

I don't need to finish. I know the rest.

The phone slips into my lap.

I'm not sure how long I sit here, but eventually Fizzy plods into the room and rests her shaggy brown head on my lap. I scratch behind her ears, and she gazes up at me like she knows my heart is broken.

"You're right," I tell her. "I shouldn't let this bother me." *But it does.* I give her ears a double-scratch before picking up my notebook and pen. Whether the poetry committee recognizes it or not, writing is the one way I can put my true self out into the world. "I'll make a list of all the reasons this scholarship doesn't matter."

Fizzy jumps onto my bed and curls up at the end while I write. When I finish, I read the list aloud to Fizzy.

- *Some other writer is really freaking happy right now.*
- *Senior Sabbatical still starts Monday.*
- *The community college is an option even without the scholarship.*
- *I didn't really want the stupid scholarship anyway.*
- *Dorene Williams's grandson is probably a sad, bitter man with zits on his back.*

Fizzy opens her eyes for a moment before closing them again. "What?" I ask. "That last one is completely valid." I reread the first item on my list, willing myself to find peace in it but failing.

I had a plan for next year. Things were going to be different. I dreamed of being independent, living on campus, writing in my notebooks at some college coffee shop or reading books on a park bench. Friends—plural—would recognize me from a distance and chat with me between classes. It was going to be sunny and quiet and everything I dreamed. But now those pictures of my future are replaced with a void, and the tears prick at my eyes.

"Nope. We're not doing *that*." I wipe my cheeks. The scholarship was a long shot anyway. I shouldn't have let myself dream it was a possibility.

I pop another pepper in my mouth and chew thoughtfully. Packing is a good distraction. Tomorrow is still wide-open to prepare for the trip, but I pull my duffel bag from the closet anyway.

Grace has a packing list stuck to the bulletin board above her dresser, along with her 4.0 report card, which she got despite never studying. Next to it hangs the official brochure advertising Senior Sabbatical as a chance to bond as a class, build teamwork skills, and make new discoveries about ourselves. Of course, they don't mention the few hundred dollars it costs until we come home with the permission slip. My science teacher complains about the weeklong absences every time a chunk of the class registers for the next trip, but the school remains adamant: Forest Lane Academy established this tradition over fifty years ago, and they're not about to end it now.

We get to miss the whole week of school. Four nights, five days at Shady Oaks Lodge. I count out a pair of underwear for each day and throw them in. Actually, better bring an extra just in case.

I'm not sure exactly what to expect. People say everything changes after Sabbatical. They can't tell us how, of course, thanks to some sacred commitment to keep the events a secret. You're only allowed to discuss Sabbatical with those who already attended Sabbatical. What happens at Shady Oaks stays at Shady Oaks.

Or at least that's the excuse Erica's been citing since October, when she went. The senior class is too big to stay all at once, so we have to go in groups of thirty. Erica and I were supposed to sign up for the first one together, but Grace had senior night at a volleyball game that week, so that wasn't an option. Even if

Mom hadn't made me, I would have gone with the family, walking her onto the court with posters and flowers. I'm sure Grace would come for me if I was ever recognized.

Erica didn't want to wait until the last trip of the year to go with me. I would've waited for her, but I can't expect her to do the same. That's not who Erica is. She's impulsive and random and funny, extroverted in all the ways I'm an introvert.

It's been the two of us since freshmen year. Maddy and Erica . . . or we were until Erica returned from the trip.

I grab my phone to ask her what else to bring for Sabbatical, and the rejection email glows up at my face again. Swipe—into the trash it goes. Close the inbox. Push all thoughts of it aside. I am not touching that little M icon for *days,* no matter how many notifications come through. When I open my chat with Erica, there's already a message waiting for me.

I can't tonight. I'm going to the music festival.

Knew it. Her confession is a small victory to help wash away the defeat of the scholarship. *With who?* I ask, forcing her to type my name. The ellipsis appears and disappears a few times. Would the green top be better tonight, or Grace's blue one?

But when I check my phone again, it's not my name lighting up the screen. It's Zoey's.

Zoey. Erica's roommate from Sabbatical. The girl who's turned our duo into a trio since they made a mysterious, incredible bond over some activity they can't even talk about. I've been telling myself all year that Erica's still my best friend. Things haven't truly changed. She's been busy, not forgetting me. She hasn't been pulling away. I've been too sensitive.

You can come too if you want.

The follow-up text punches me in the gut. It's not an invitation. It's a confirmation she's had this planned with Zoey all week. Or longer. My stomach hollows like someone's scooped it out and scraped the insides. Zoey's not the third wheel. I am.

I push a pair of sweatpants into my bag more forcefully than they deserve. If I got that scholarship, I could go to school for writing. I could start over with new friends and new people, be seen and have my voice heard.

But I didn't, so none of it matters anyway. I rip some shorts and leggings from my drawer and throw them onto the bed next to the dog. Fizzy hops off and paces next to me. Erica should've told me. She obviously felt like she had to hide it, which only proves we're not as close as we were before.

Focus on something else.

Sabbatical.

Packing.

Right.

I grab plenty of socks and shove them into my bag along with my emotions. Push them down and zip them up tight. If I let Erica know it bothers me, there's a chance I'll discover something worse: She doesn't care if I'm hurt or not.

It's safer to pretend than take that risk.

I just remembered I have to babysit tonight. Have fun though.

She'll probably detect the lie, but I can't worry about that.

On Monday I leave for my own Sabbatical. I'll have my own roommate and my own secrets. I grab a lime-green pen from the cup on Grace's dresser and remove the calendar from the wall.

Five days of no classes. No scholarship deadlines or results. No Erica and Zoey walking half a step ahead of me in the halls. I draw little stars around all five days.

When I check my phone again, I don't even open Erica's response, but there's another text from Grace.

Games are running late. Mom says to put a pizza in the oven for dinner. Did the poetry scholarship make their announcement yet?

I start typing the truth, but it's too painful to put my failure into words. I press the backspace key until the box is empty, with the cursor blinking once again. *Results come next week. Read the date wrong.*

Ugh. I hope the waiting doesn't ruin the trip.

I toss my duffel bag on the floor and flop onto my bed. I've already hit rock bottom and dug a little hole to hide in. Nothing could ruin this trip.

Lots of things—a lone set of car keys at the beach, a pair of glasses on top of your head, your GPA after a hard chem test, respect for your role models, a friendship that has too many secrets, a shoe in a messy closet, the one great toy from your childhood, a coin sliding under the passenger seat, your confidence after a rejection, a remote between the couch cushions, the person you love most in the world, your sanity, your grip on reality—can all be L ost

CHAPTER 3

Grace: April 28

"Home sweet home." Mom releases a tired sigh as we pull into the driveway the next day. The five hours after Detective Howard left my room passed quicker than any in my life. The first forty-eight hours came and went without any sign of Maddy. The K-9 unit picked up a scent outside the lodge where we stayed, but lost it at the edge of the woods. The drones dispatched around the mountain haven't delivered any new information either. Now it's been over sixty hours since anyone remembers seeing Maddy.

Maybe I saw her more recently than that, but unless my memories come back, it doesn't matter.

Detective Howard said the police canvassed the area around the lodge and asked residents near where I was found to review doorbell and other security camera footage for anything suspicious. Nothing helpful has been reported yet.

I need a list of everyone who was on the trip. Maybe looking at all the names will trigger . . . something, anything. Since the police still have my phone, I can't even look online or contact anyone for information myself.

Not yet, at least.

Detective Howard mentioned Mr. Gutter was the one who found me. If I can get in touch with him, ask him what he knows, maybe . . .

It feels dangerous to finish that sentence, to hope.

Mom's gaze hangs on me. I ignore the worry lines on her face and direct my attention to the chipped paint of the garage door, which is slowly rising. Dark bedroom windows loom above us with the blinds drawn. There are tulips in the front berms, but the leaves are yellowed, the petals faded and falling off. So much has changed in the last week.

"Dad's not home yet." Her voice is tight, like a trip wire set to trigger an explosion if nudged. "He said he'd be back by now. Here," she says, the frustration lifting from her eyes. "Let me grab your bag."

I expect the house to be different somehow, but the fridge is where it's always been, covered in free magnets and reminders of bills. The counter's still pristine, wiped clean by Mom, I'm sure. The floor is still scratched around the kitchen table from us ignoring Dad's repeated warnings to lift the chairs, not slide them. Fizzy still bounds to greet me at the door.

"Hey, girl!" I drop to my knees and scrunch my fingers in the goldendoodle's fur as she covers me with kisses. Her whole back end shakes when she wags her tail and jumps on me. She knows exactly what I need to feel at home again.

Fizzy, too excited to stop wiggling for me to pet her, rushes to reach Mom, then runs to the door like she's waiting for someone else to walk through it. Like she's waiting for Maddy.

"Come here, girl," I call, patting my knees so I don't crumble.

She whines and sits by the door.

"It's okay, Fizzy. I'm here," I assure her. Still, she whines. I drop to the floor and squeeze her in a hug. "I don't know when she's coming back," I whisper so only she can hear. "But I have to believe she is."

"You feeling okay?" Mom asks.

I stop petting Fizzy and stare at the door, wincing and dismissing her concern with a wave. "Just a little headache."

"Dr. Thelsman said that's to be expected." She mentions it as if I wasn't in the same room when we were given my discharge notes. Dr. Thelsman released me this morning when my final lab results came back indicating no lasting physical damage. He couldn't confirm that my memories will ever return.

"Why don't you lie down until lunch is ready?" Mom pulls open the fridge where, in true Midwest fashion, the contents reveal that every neighbor in a mile radius has dropped off a meal.

I politely ignore the tears that unexpectedly spring to her eyes. This might be our life now: crying when we don't want to and pretending no one else can see it.

"Do you know how long they're going to keep my phone?" I don't need to explain who *they* are. The investigation, Maddy, the police: They're all constantly swirling overhead, invisible context in every conversation. It seems pointless for the police to search a phone that was confiscated as soon as we arrived, but I'm not going to question it if they think it could help find Maddy sooner.

"They didn't say."

A small vase of yellow flowers sits on the counter. The card tells me they're from Erica's family and they're praying for us. If only the gesture from Maddy's best friend brought comfort instead of a hollow twang of emptiness.

"I was thinking of trying to get in touch with a few people. Dr. Thelsman said it's important for me to have support. Talking to some friends might help me take my mind off everything."

I leave out the part about using my phone to find my own information about the investigation. She's trying so hard to make sure I don't worry.

"We could get you one from Walmart." Her face shifts, like she's found the task she's been looking for, one to cling to that might distract her from agonizing over Maddy. "Something cheap to call and text. Or, hold on." She disappears into her room and comes back a few minutes later holding a pink Android I haven't seen in four years. "It'll be an old number, but we could bring this to a store and get it reconnected to our plan."

Our phone from junior high. I say "our" because Maddy and I had to share for two years, and we hated it. My parents said they wanted us to learn limits while being entrusted with the new responsibility, but we both knew it was because the cost of two new phones and two more numbers on their monthly plan was too much. They only bought us separate ones in high school. Even with the scholarships we earned for Forest Lane Academy, the tuition was so high Mom and Dad had to downsize. We said we'd rather share a room, so we moved into this smaller house but got two new cell phones.

Mom checks the clock. "I'm going to give your dad a call and see where he is."

As I grab my bag, Fizzy seems to instinctively know where I'm headed and races up the stairs ahead of me. She reaches the top and waits, panting, but I can't force myself to climb. I picture our bedroom: the unmade beds on either side of the big window, the TV above the dresser, clothes littering the floor. I imagine my pictures from middle school tucked into the frames on our dresser and old volleyball ribbons stuck to the bulletin board, faded from years in the sun. Every little detail of our room should bring me comfort.

But when I walk through that door, Maddy will still be missing.

As much as that fact anchors my feet to the ground, another piece of me hopes there will be enough of her—her notebooks, her Chucks, her books, *her*—in the room that I'll get to imagine, even for a little while, that she's not truly gone at all. If I don't push the thoughts aside, I may never move again, so I raise my chin and climb the fourteen steps to our room.

Opening the door makes me want to cry. Of course I was naive to imagine our room before the accident. Of course Mom zipped in and did all the laundry and made the beds and stacked the books as soon as we left for the week. Of course it wouldn't be the same as before.

I flop onto the bed. The pieces of Maddy in the room—her fantasy books on the shelf, her unscented lotion on the dresser, her pictures in frames—scream that she's not here. I wish I was the one missing and she could be left to comfort Fizzy. She could be the one to stand tall under Mom's concern or catch Dad staring vacantly into space. She could be the one to walk into the shell of a room with no life in it at all.

A tear slips down my face, running over the scratch on my cheek. I keep going over all the possibilities in my head, always starting with the most innocent—the story I can't stop clinging to: Maddy and I might have gone for a hike and gotten lost. I finger a particularly nasty bruise still visible on my shin and wince at the sudden pain. I might have gotten it while hiking, maybe from falling. Maybe I hit my head first, and Maddy went for help but got lost along the way.

But then, where is she?

As much as I want to believe this is all some terrible accident, a mistake, part of me knows that's only wishful thinking rooted in denial, not logic. The police, the questioning, the news—everyone on the outside peering in knows to search for something sinister, something I don't even want to consider. They know these things happen all the time. I know it, too, but not . . . not to my sister.

My friends will know why I left that night. I need to talk to Nicole.

I check the phone Mom gave me earlier, and it says fully charged, but from what I remember, it will drop to 80 percent in mere minutes. This phone's battery has always been awful, and it was one of the reasons Maddy and I fought so much about it.

I did *charge it like I promised.* Maddy's middle-school voice rings in my head. I squeeze the phone in both hands. I don't care if she yells or screams or shouts. I would do anything to hear her again. . . .

The lock screen shows a picture of us cheek to cheek, our

teeth covered in braces and our hair parted on the side. I try not to cringe too hard, remembering how great we thought the picture was. The nostalgia is intense. So many of the apps are games I haven't played in years. While I remember a couple of my friends—Nicole and Caleb—who went on the trip with us, this phone doesn't have their numbers.

I sprawl on my bed, connect to the Wi-Fi, and swipe through the apps, but the only social media app Mom and Dad let us download in junior high is basically obsolete, and I'm not sure anyone would still have it on their phones or even check it. It only takes a few seconds to download the apps everyone uses now, but after I type my name in the log-in screen, my fingers freeze.

All the apps are installed on my phone, so I never need a password, and—even worse—the phone number attached to the account is for the phone the police have. Email recovery is my only option. I log into my Forest Lane account. Or try to.

Username and password do not match.

I try again. And again. Cursing myself and the school's requirement to change passwords every ninety days, I close the browser with a growl. With no other options, I scroll through the apps to the mail icon. The inbox opens to the account Maddy and I shared as tweens: StollSisters4eva@mail.com.

The five-digit number of unread spam messages practically gives me hives, but even that thought is wiped away when I realize I don't know any of my friends' email addresses because (A) who uses email? and (B) on the rare occasion I've had to share a doc, the address populates on my school account when I start typing in someone's name.

I'm completely shut off from messaging my friends.

Fizzy seems to sense my urge to scream, because she jumps on the bed next to me.

I can't give up that easily.

I open another tab and enter Mr. Gutter's name in the search bar. Student email addresses aren't public, but teachers' might be, and if I can't get to my friends for answers, I can get to someone else, anyone else, who might give me *something* to go on, to jog my memory.

The school's website comes up first, but a headline below catches my attention: "History Teacher's Involvement with the Missing Stoll Sisters?"

I click on the blog. It's dated this morning and already has over one hundred thousand views. How far has our story spread? My stomach twists at the thought of people talking about us in their homes across the country like we're the subjects of the most recent Netflix serial killer documentary.

A banner across the top of the page says "Stoll Sisters Secrets and Theories" and four other posts are linked to the side.

> Trent Gutter has been teaching history at Forest Lane Academy for over twenty-five years, but could his relationship with his students be something more? As a chaperone on the senior trip, Gutter had access to both girls who disappeared on the night of April 25. However, Gutter was not originally assigned to chaperone. Some say he volunteered for the trip to be close to students after his colleague got sick. Others report the school questioning students about their relationships with

teachers during the week of Sabbatical, creating speculation that the school used Gutter's time on the trip to begin an investigation into possible inappropriate relationships.

Allegedly, he also found one of the sisters on the side of the road the morning they were reported missing. Just how did he know where to look? He's attended every search event since then. A helpful citizen in the right place at the right time? Or a pervy teacher injecting himself into the investigation?

I close the tab, my breakfast threatening to come up. Mr. Gutter's always been on the higher end of the weird spectrum, but what teacher isn't? I can't believe he'd ever be dangerous. People used to joke he was a pedophile, but there wasn't any real basis for that, was there? Most teenage girls are at least a little wary of single middle-aged men who spend their time alone with kids. But a real predator?

And "*Others* report the school questioning students about their relationships with teachers . . ." Who are these "others"? The school wouldn't let him chaperone a weeklong trip if they seriously suspected him. No way.

He did find me on Oldham County Road, though.

Another wave of nausea rolls over me. I want to go back to being convinced no one could hurt us, that it must have been a freak hiking accident that caused the gash in the back of my skull.

Oldham County Road. Switching tabs, I pull it up on Maps. The curvy road runs next to French Lake. I need to zoom out to find the lodge, though. How far is that? I pick a random house on Oldham County Road without not knowing exactly where I was found, type in the address to get directions to Shady Oaks Lodge, and wait for the app to load the results.

Over a mile, almost a thirty-minute walk.

And it was raining. Mom said I was found shivering in the rain, covered in mud.

We walked that far by ourselves, at night, alone. Supposedly. But even if that's true, it wouldn't explain *what* hit me so hard on the back of the head that I've forgotten the entire week.

Or *who*.

CHAPTER 4

Maddy: April 22

I would kill to get off this bus.

Not because of the cramped seats and bumpy road. Not because I haven't been able to fall asleep since we boarded at 6 a.m.

Not even because I'm sitting next to Tori Syblonski. I was, after all, the one who scooted over when she needed a spot to sit.

No, I want off this bus because I desperately need to pee. You'd think I'd be used to this by now, with a bladder the size of an acorn, but it somehow always manages to take me by surprise. Grace, who's basically a camel, always teases me about it on family road trips.

Her loud laughter floats up from the back of the bus, quickly joined by a chorus of her friends. I have no idea what they're laughing about, which is typical since she always seems to drift away when we get around her friends. Today was no different: Grace jumped to the back of the bus with Nicole as soon as we got on. They're in their own orbit, circling each other in a gravitational field. I'm more of an asteroid spiraling through space alone without a destination.

"I think we're almost there," I tell Tori, squeezing my legs and breaking the awkward silence that's been hanging between us for the last fifteen minutes. It wasn't until she sat next to me that I remembered one teensy problem: I'm horrible at making conversation.

Though, to be fair, Tori might be worse.

"Mhm," she mumbles, which is possibly an agreement or possibly a frog in her throat. In any case, she pushes up her glasses—which makes little difference as they still take up half her face—and resumes gazing dreamily out the window.

In the last hour, I haven't learned much about Tori from her mostly monosyllabic responses or long-winded stories featuring her cats, but I genuinely admire her confidence. She's wearing no makeup and her bushy-brushed hair could be straightened or curled, but she leaves it somewhere in between, content with her natural looks.

The bus follows the curving road, and the trees open up to a clearing ahead. The bright yellow letters of SHADY OAKS LODGE pop against the dark wood of the sign. At the top of the hill sits a big redbrick building with ivy covering most of the right side. White stone outlines the square windows on the first and second floor. The architecture evokes vibes from the fifties. Very vintage. Cracked concrete steps lead to the front entrance, but its dark windows betray nothing of its interior.

"Did you know it was going to be this big?" I ask.

"Nope," Tori answers.

"Pretty secluded."

"Yup."

"It looks like the kind of place serial killers bring their victims so no one can hear them scream."

"Oh." She shifts a smidge closer to the edge of the seat.

Oh, good. I found the line between making conversation and making it weird.

Ryan Jacobs's head pops around the back of the seat. "Nah," he says, perfectly suave hair flopping to the side. "If you think this is creepy, wait till you see the caves." He winks with a mix of cocky charm and arrogant humor. Which pretty much sums up Ryan Jacobs's entire personality.

Tori shrinks back down into the seat.

"You're not too scared, are you?" He goes back to laughing with the other football players, who have been obnoxiously loud most of the trip.

"I'm sure he's exaggerating," I tell Tori.

"Okay."

Two syllables, and neither one about cats. My small win comes as the bus lurches to a stop.

Outside, the morning chill gives the air a swift bite as a fresh breeze blows my hair across my face. The shiver running down my spine might be from the cold or my excitement.

"All right, seniors." The school's Sabbatical director, Mrs. Sanderson, stands by the front doors of the building, yelling with her hands cupped around her mouth. She's older than she appears, with kids in college but hardly a gray hair or wrinkle on her. She's swapped her pencil skirts and dress pants for jeans, making her seem more like a stranger than our teacher. Those of us nearest to her wait expectantly, but the rest of the group laughs and talks the same way they did on the bus. "ALL RIGHT, SENIORS!" she repeats.

Every conversation drops faster than our cell reception did once we hit the mountains. Clearly none of my cohort had Mrs. Sanderson in freshman algebra. She does *not* appreciate asking twice.

Her face softens. "Welcome to Shady Oaks Lodge." Ryan Jacobs and his friends, Caleb and Bryson, erupt in a round of applause. Grace and her friend Nicole join in across the circle. Mrs. Sanderson begins again when everyone grows quiet. "Over the next four nights and five days, you'll discover new insights about yourself and your closest friends."

I'll have to be satisfied only learning about myself. I have no friends here. Grace doesn't count. If my hour next to Tori is any indication, making new ones will not be easy.

Mrs. Sanderson brings my attention back to her. "You'll get to know so many other students in your class you never thought you'd be friends with. You'll walk away with new bonds that will last far beyond graduation!"

That feels impossible, but I don't need lots of friends. Maybe a few people. Maybe one. One person to connect with. Someone who's not related to me but will think to invite me first, not as an afterthought. Someone who will know *me*.

My phone dings in my hand, a message breaking through the poor service from the mountains surrounding the lodge.

A picture of Erica and Zoey pops up with their smiling faces pushed together and the words *Breathe the 5th*. I frown, not knowing what the phrase means, only that it's connected to the trip. Everyone comes back chirping it in class and posting it online.

I should be thankful they thought of me at all.

"Thank you for reminding me, Ms. Stoll," Mrs. Sanderson says, indicating my phone and reaching for a bag. "Before we begin," she calls to the crowd again, "some of you will consider this the hardest step of the week. Yup, that's right. It's time to surrender your phones for the entire five days."

Mr. Gutter, the other staff member assigned to chaperone the trip, steps forward with a bag for all our phones. He might be smiling, but if he is, the overly long, grizzled beard and beady glasses hide it. He would resemble a lumberjack if he wasn't so pasty white, skinny, and tall. More like an escaped prisoner.

"Drop 'em in here," he says.

"It's not like we're going to be AirDropping any horse pictures," Caleb mumbles loud enough for most people, including Mr. Gutter, to hear. Nicole lets out a noise halfway between a gasp and a giggle and playfully punches his arm, but Ryan practically falls over laughing.

I, myself, fight off a gag at the memory of the picture that rocked the school when it was dropped during lunch last week. Someone—and the very appalled administration has yet to figure out who—edited Mr. Gutter's face into a photo of a person proudly riding a horse. It wouldn't have been so bad if the body hadn't been practically nude. The caption read, "I like them young and wild."

Mr. Gutter's mustache meets his beard, like his lips are pressed together in a tight line, but he's proceeding as if he didn't hear Caleb's comment.

Mrs. Sanderson, on the other hand, apparently really didn't hear him and continues addressing the group.

"You all knew this when you agreed to the terms of this trip. There's horrible service out here anyway, and your SnapToks and TikFaces or whatever will still be waiting for you on Friday."

Several people roll their eyes at her attempt to be current, but her smirk makes me wonder if she relishes in the cringe.

"If there's an emergency," she continues, "there are plenty of reliable landlines in the lodge and no reason for concern. The forecast shows only a small chance of rain. If your parents need to get ahold of you, they can contact the school. You'll get your phones back when we board the bus again on the last day. Come on, drop them in. Yes, sure, power them off first, because Mr. Gutter and I have nothing better to do than snoop through your phones while we're here."

I ignore her sarcasm and shut off my phone, following everyone else dropping theirs into the bag.

"What if we want to take pictures?" Grace clutches her device in front of Mrs. Sanderson.

"We have disposable cameras at each table in the main hall."

"Disposable?" Grace's face falls with disgust as she reluctantly tips her phone into the bag. She pouts and gives it a dramatic wave. "They could've at least gotten Polaroids."

"Probably a tradition like everything else at Forest Lane," I tell her. She loops her free arm through mine and hikes up the duffel bag slung over her shoulder.

"Probably. I bet it's also so no one will post the pictures online. They're too worried about Sabbatical stuff staying secret."

"Yeah, probably."

It's surprising, though. A rumor exposing what Krista Hawthorne and Ryan Jacobs did over the weekend burns through the school like a forest fire, yet everyone who attends FLA's senior trip is able to keep the traditions and events a secret, only admitting vague hints in cryptic phrases like *Breathe the 5th*.

Before we walk through the dark-glass front doors, Mrs. Sanderson makes one more announcement.

"Senior Sabbatical is a privilege, and you will be trusted with this privilege. There are rules here to keep you safe. No swapping room assignments. No food or drink in the bedrooms. And absolutely no leaving the lodge without supervision. Especially after dark."

Her mouth is a hard line as straight as the finger she points at us. She sweeps the circle with a glare and says, "The other part of this privilege comes when your classmates tell their stories. Each and every one of you promised to keep the secrecy of our traditions and the confidence of your peers. This promise never expires, for the rest of your lives. Or you shall answer to me."

She's using hyperbole for dramatic effect, but it works. The group remains still. Every mouth closed. Every body on edge. Mrs. Sanderson doesn't need to convince us. All the other seniors keep this deal, and we aren't about to break the Forest Lane Academy Senior Sabbatical pact.

This week is about new opportunities. Fun. Excitement. Discovery. Senior Sabbatical is all about making memories that will last a lifetime.

The adventure begins.

An anagram
is when you take
the letters of a word and
scramble them around
like soup

then pull one letter
out and allow the rest
to follow behind

Some are simple like LIVE and EVIL
Some match as a pair like LISTEN and SILENT
Some are honest like CONVERSATION and
VOICES RANT ON
Some offer a problem and solution like
STRESSED and DESSERTS
Some strike a chord of irony like
TEACHER and CHEATER
Some predict the future like
REAL FUN and FUNERAL
Some reveal an unlucky truth like
ELEVEN PLUS TWO and
TWELVE PLUS ONE
Still equal thirteen

But there's no way to rearrange
the events of my life and have them
spell happiness

CHAPTER 5

Grace: April 28

Fizzy darts from the room and barks down the stairs. The door from the garage slams. Dad must be home. I close the map of Oldham County Road and the lodge on my old phone as Mom calls up from the kitchen.

"Your dad's home and lunch will be ready in a minute."

"Coming," I call back. A twinge of a headache sprouts again, like it has every time I've pushed myself to remember something useful in the last two days. Dr. Thelsman warned about that, and I may have to take some of that pain medication.

Gingerly, I trace the stitches on the back of my skull, along my hairline, as I traipse down the stairs, trying to shake off the disturbing suspicions of how I got hurt. The smell of baked cheesy casserole greets me first, then Dad's hug.

Mom's phone chimes, making us all jump. She pounces on it, but her face falls in an odd twist of relief and disappointment. "It's only Mary asking for an update."

Still no news about Maddy.

"They sent the dive teams into the lake first thing this morning," Dad reports while Fizzy wiggles around his ankles. "No word yet. How're you doing?" His question feels rhetorical, but it's better than trying to pretend we aren't all frayed threads hoping someone will braid us together again.

Before I can answer, Mom cuts in. "You'd know if you were at the hospital this morning like you said you'd be."

"I told you." He sucks in a breath. "I went back to help the search."

"You said they weren't allowing the public to help, that they cleared the area for the thermal cameras."

"I had to be *there*."

"But why? Why couldn't you be *here* with us?" Mom points at me. "She's still here. She still needs her dad's support too."

The declaration hangs in the air like a live grenade.

Dad's jaw tightens and Mom's shoulders brace for the explosion. I'd throw myself into the blast to protect them from the damage of this war, but the words stick in my throat.

The timer goes off on the oven, defusing the tension. At least for now.

Mom turns her back and picks up a sponge to wipe down the sink. Dad stops the beeping and pulls the meal out of the oven.

He serves me a sloppy square of something with chicken, cheese, and red and green flecks. Peppers. I want to point out that Maddy likes them, not me, but I don't because it seems wrong to complain about a warm meal while Maddy is still out there—somewhere.

"I'm fine," I say, accepting the plate and answering his initial question. "Tired, but—"

"That's to be expected," Mom chimes in with me.

I give Dad a weak smile to show I'm not hurt that he wasn't at the hospital this morning. I understand why he's keeping us at a distance. It's easier than succumbing to the pain. He was with me all day Friday once I was found, and he only left on Saturday to bring me clothes from home. But this is how they are. Dad wants to go *do* something while Mom wants to shelter in place, keep us together, protect what she has left.

Mom sets down her sponge and serves herself. The two of us sit on the stools at the counter while Dad stands; four empty chairs at the table are better than one.

"Want some more?" Mom asks.

"I'm actually not all that hungry," I say, and when the immediate concern springs to their faces, I add, "I'll be fine. It's been a long day after two days of doing nothing in the hospital."

"Are you sure?" Mom says, setting her fork down. "I can—"

"Julie," Dad interrupts. "It's fine." He shoves a bite into his mouth.

"When will people be allowed back at Shady Oaks?" I ask, pulling their attention off each other.

Dad finishes chewing. "Later today, I expect. Even though the police said they can't formally invite the public onto the grounds for liability reasons, they also aren't turning anyone away."

"I want to help." Visiting the area might trigger a memory, or there might be someone volunteering who was on the trip, someone I can talk to.

"Detective Howard said we should keep ourselves available to answer any questions they might have," Mom says, absently checking her phone again. "At least for now."

"I think joining the search is a great idea," Dad says. "Why don't we drive out after lunch?"

Mom stabs at the casserole. "You just got home from there."

Dad sets down his fork. "If you'd like to stay here and clean, you're more than welcome to. The rest of us can go out and do what needs to be done."

"I'm sorry, is staying at our daughter's bedside in the *hospital* after the most traumatic experience of her life not *doing what needs to be done*?" The tears spring to her eyes again, but this time she makes no attempt to hide them.

"There's only so much we can do from home."

"And there's only so much we can do out there. The doctor says she needs to rest, and it wouldn't hurt you either."

"I'm fine," he growls.

"You haven't spent more than fifteen minutes at home since we got that phone call. You can't keep avoiding the house—avoiding us."

"I'm not!"

I pretend they aren't fighting. I pretend all the way out of the kitchen. Pretend I'm tired. Pretend I'm full. Pretend I can't hear their harsh words chasing me up the stairs, that it doesn't bother me, that I understand they're not really mad at each other and are only mad at the situation.

I flop onto my perfectly made bed, with my back against the perfectly fluffy pillows, feeling like a perfect stranger in my own room. In my own house. In my own life.

Their muffled voices penetrate the closed door.

The sunset casts an orange light through the window at my back and highlights the calendar on the wall. Maddy drew green stars all over the last week. She was so excited. More than I was.

I cross the room and flip the calendar to June. It says "PROM!" in big letters over the first Saturday and "GRADUATION" in bigger letters later in the month. Those milestones don't matter now, not until we find Maddy.

I hate it. I hate that she's not here when I am. I hate that Dr. Thelsman accurately predicted my pattern of headaches and that they creep in when the police ask questions or Mom needs me to remember most. I hate acting strong, like my heart isn't smashed under a concrete brick of regret. I hate this clean room and the made bed and the precise pile of books.

So I knock the books over, yank off the bedspread and bunch up the sheets, throw down the pillows and sit in the mess, collapse on the floor, not bothering to push the hair out of my face.

The destruction doesn't make me feel any better. It only makes me tired. Very tired. I try to remember what happened to us that night, to find some reasonable explanation for why we were outside, if there was anything I could've done to stop it . . . but the ache in my head argues against every attempt.

Something pokes my foot, a book I knocked over. A notebook. Maddy's notebook.

She's always buying notebooks. This one is a Molskine, with an elastic strap that secures the cover. She keeps it next to her bed, on the nightstand.

I open it to a random page and find a poem. Maddy always says poetry is her way of sorting through whatever's wrong inside, that she can find a few words to say the parts she wants and leave enough white space on the page to hide the parts she doesn't.

I select a pen—Maddy's favorite, with green gel ink—and flip a few pages until I come to a blank one. Clean lines cross the page. Fresh, white space. No expectations. Writing might help, writing everything I can think of concerning the trip. I put the pen to the page.

No words come.

No ideas, theories, or memories.

I scribble circles, darker and harder until there's barely any white on the page, and the pen tears through it.

I drop the pen and close the notebook, but then I spot a picture on the floor. It's me and Nicole, wearing our bikinis while the sun sets in the background. We each have one arm wrapped around the other and one arm raised in the air. It might be from last summer, at her lake house.

Goose bumps prick across my arm like ice.

I remember something. I remember being in the lake. On the trip. With Maddy. It was dark. Night. I was pulling her through the water. She was heavy. So heavy. I made it to a leafy sandbar. I tried to check if she was breathing, but it was so dark. And I was shaking. I remember that. Shaking.

I rush to the door and dash down the stairs. "Mom!"

"What? Are you okay?" I stumble into her. She pushes the hair away from my face. "You're sweating."

"I—I remember," I say. Dad's beside her now. "I saw her."

"You did? You're sure? What do you remember?" Her

questions fall on me like the rain that night. It was raining. It was raining when we were in the lake.

"We were in the water—" I stop when the color drains from her face, and I'm not sure how to tell her the rest. "We have to call the police right now!"

Dad moves to the kitchen and rifles through a drawer, finds a business card, and pulls out his phone from his pocket, hands trembling slightly.

I can't stop picturing it. My sister, faceup on the ground. Her wet, dark hair half covering her cheeks. Her closed eyes not even fluttering. The sand and mud smeared across her clothes.

It's the first memory I've had since waking in the hospital. I'm trying to hold on to it, to memorize it all to tell the police.

But every detail—the cold water, the weight of her body, the sound of her arm flopping against the wet sand—makes me want to forget.

CHAPTER 6

Maddy: April 22

I want to remember every detail of this place.

With bags slung over our backs, we enter through the main doors, and while the exterior of Shady Oaks Lodge looks old, it's clear the interior has been renovated. The floors, walls, and ceiling are all made of wood and polished with a golden oak stain so every surface appears to have been dipped in honey. Intricately carved archways mimic the climbing ivy from outside.

On the right is a large, open room with square tables, each having three slim chairs with red, yellow, or orange cushions, giving the room an autumn vibe. Clusters of electric wrought iron chandeliers hang from the ceiling, but most of the light enters from the large windows along the back wall. Outside the floor-to-ceiling glass, the sun illuminates the green grass climbing the mountains and trees lining the way.

"It's like a room from Rivendell," I say breathlessly.

"River what?" Nicole asks, giving me a weird look next to

Grace. From everything I know about Grace's friend, nothing suggests she's a *Lord of the Rings* fan. Instead of reading, she spends her study hall searching makeup tutorials for the right shades to highlight her icy blue eyes. Her hair and teeth are both straight and shiny. If she was eight inches taller, she could've been cast as an elf in one of the movies based on Tolkien's books, but it's not worth explaining the reference.

"Never mind," I mumble. I hate that I care what Nicole thinks of me.

"Assigned seats?" Grace groans. Each chair has a folder, and she's already scanning the nearest tables for our names. I should complain along with her, like everyone does the first day of school when the teachers claim it's the only way they'll learn our names. Secretly, I appreciate assigned seats. Zero pressure to read the room and find a seat next to someone who won't make fun of me while I constantly worry if they're disappointed I sat next to them instead of someone else.

But I'm not about to say any of that out loud.

We dump our bags along the wall like the others.

"Grace, over here!" Alyssa Griffin calls, waving the folder from an empty seat and practically jumping up and down. Grace skips over to hug her, and I lift my chin like I'm not painfully aware of no one calling my name.

When I find my folder, no one else has arrived at the table yet. The tabletops are slices of massive tree trunks, coated in a clear resin so the rings shine. In addition to a folder, each seat also has a marble composition notebook and a pencil. In the center of the table is a half sheet of paper instructing everyone at the table to play Two Truths and a Lie. The paper has step-by-step instructions, though I can't imagine anyone having difficulty deciphering the rules after reading the name.

I read the other folders: Ryan Jacobs and Adrian Clement. Grrrreat. Two guys, neither of whom I know very well. Not exactly the seating arrangement I would have chosen, but if I don't want someone to be disappointed sitting next to me, I can't complain about them. So when Ryan Jacobs sits down, I smile.

Rather than acknowledging my presence, however, he makes eye contact with a friend across the room, mouths something, flips him off, and laughs. All four years, he's been considered one of the heartthrobs of our class, but I honestly don't understand it. Arrogance is powerful enough to make even the cutest dimple look repulsive.

I'm picking at a sliver on the edge of the table when Adrian approaches. His hair is floofy—curly enough and long enough to stick out in random directions, so it's impossible to tell whether he strives for the messy style or simply slept on it wrong. His sweatshirt features a picture of a fishing rod and the words REEL COOL GRANDPA.

"Hey, hey, my groupies!" Adrian extends a hand to both me and Ryan, waiting for us to slap it. Ryan does almost immediately, even though I've never witnessed them speak. I miss his palm, so it's awkward and clumsy.

"All right," Adrian says now, taking a chair, swinging it around backward, and straddling it so his arms cross over the back. "Who wants to go first?" He skims the rules for Two Truths and a Lie.

"Melody can," Ryan says nodding in my direction.

"I still need to think of mine," I say.

"Wait," Adrian says. "Her name's Maddy. She sat behind you for the whole first semester in math. How do you not know her name?"

Ryan and I both freeze, Ryan probably because he's not used to being called out on a minor infraction. Or any infraction.

I, on the other hand, am stunned to discover that Adrian knows not only my name but also where I sat last semester in math. He's always struck me as being too chaotic to remember details like that. I don't think I would remember that Ryan sat in front of me if it wasn't for the fact that I had to tap him on the shoulder every other day when he'd forget to pass the papers back.

Ryan has the decency to look down at his shoes and mumbles something that sounds like "Knew it started with an *M*."

"It's fine," I say quickly, waving off Adrian's concern. I'm more worried about what I'll say when it's my turn. Choosing the lie is easy. It's the truths that are hard. Breaking my arm when I was six makes me sound boring. I'm not about to admit I've never been kissed. Mrs. Sanderson has no idea how much stress she's induced by giving me a few brief minutes to whittle down the truths about myself I'm willing to share with these almost-strangers.

"Fine, I'll go," Ryan says, evidently recovered from his brush with embarrassment, and Adrian waves him on. "I have two sisters. My eyes are brown. And, umm, I'm going to play for the Patriots next year."

Adrian and I make eye contact. I probably shouldn't be overthinking it if this is the bar we're setting.

"The Patriots one," I say.

He snaps and finger-guns me.

"Okay. My turn." Adrian rubs his hands together impressively fast and abruptly stops. "I'm a closet beatboxer. I won a twenty-thousand-dollar scholarship from Google. I have two tattoos."

Ryan studies him up and down, and I'm surprised he's seriously deliberating. "I bet you could throw a beat, but I don't see any tattoos."

Adrian raises his eyebrows and turns down the corners of his mouth, as if considering Ryan's assessment. He hasn't changed much since ninth grade. I have a distinct memory of Adrian from back then. I was so terrified about doing a presentation in Mr. Triker's history class that I ran into the hall hyperventilating. Adrian chased after me and told me that instead of picturing the audience in their underwear, I should picture our hairy, middle-aged teacher in a bright orange Speedo and matching swim cap. The combination of his deadpan expression and the image he'd created in my mind made me burst out laughing, and I forgot about my nerves.

Adrian might still be the clown from freshman year, but he has changed physically. He used to be scrawny, *really* scrawny, but by now he's bulked up. His arms are thicker, and his shoulders too. As far as I know, he doesn't play any sports at FLA, but maybe he has a job that requires some manual labor.

"The tattoos might be hidden under his clothes," I suggest.

"Stop looking at me that way!" Adrian moves his hands so one covers his chest and the other his groin.

I ignore him, stifling my blush. "I think the scholarship thing is a lie."

Adrian glances back and forth between us. "Final answers?" He takes a deep breath and beatboxes a few rounds before saying, "I do have two tattoos. No, you can't see them, and while I did win a scholarship, it wasn't for twenty grand."

"Was it for a full ride?" Ryan asks. "I'm playing next year at a D2 school. I can't imagine having to cover the cost myself and graduating with all that debt."

I squirm at the reminder of my own unanswered college questions and pick at a spot on the table. I stop when I notice Adrian watching me.

"Nah, nothing like that," he tells Ryan. "It's okay though. Student loans aren't the end of the world. I'll be okay." He faces me. "So, let's hear it. Two truths and a lie."

I was hoping they might've forgotten I didn't go. My fingers fidget with the hem of my shirt, and I move them under my legs to stop. "Okay, I know CPR. I'm double-jointed. And I'm a twin."

Ryan snorts through his nose. "Well, we can see you're a twin." He points to the other side of the room. Grace says something to her group, brushing off her shoulder dramatically, and the other two laugh. "I bet CPR."

Adrian purses his lips, making a show of considering. I'm not used to someone watching me for this long. Finally, he says, "Agree. CPR."

"I had to get CPR certified to babysit. And . . ." I lock my hands together and twist my arms out.

"Whoa!" Adrian says, scooting back in his seat while Ryan shields his eyes and cries, "That is nasty!"

I drop my arms as they recover.

"Wait," Ryan says. "You played wrong. You have three truths."

"No, I don't have a twin. Grace is ten months older than me."

Ryan looks more confused than he did last week in English class when Mrs. Haines assigned a poem from Lord Tennyson. I explain further. "She was born in early August, but my parents got pregnant again right away, and I was born the next June."

Ryan's eyes flick between me and Grace three more times.

"You were so smart, they didn't want to keep you back a year, huh?" Adrian jokes.

"Something like that," I say. "Day care was ridiculously expensive. Keeping me back from kindergarten would've meant thousands of dollars for the year."

"Wait," Ryan says. "But you look almost *exactly* the same."

"Just happened that way."

"I don't know," Adrian says carefully. His dark eyes lock on my face and won't let go. "Not exactly the same."

I find myself smiling, too—and not because of his wild hair or ridiculous shirt.

"All right, Hawks!" Mrs. Sanderson shouts from the front of the room, not giving me a chance to decipher if this is what flirting looks like. "Now that you know a little about each other, it's time to discover more about yourselves."

Everyone decorates their own notebook. I write my name on the front cover with a Sharpie and fill the inside with a sea of doodles and designs without any particular pattern. Mrs. Sanderson tells us the goal of this first day is to open up to each other, but in order to do that, we must first learn about ourselves.

Mr. Gutter distributes various personality quizzes that we tape in our notebooks. An hour later, I've discovered I'm a 9 on the enneagram, an INFP on the Myers-Briggs, and a blue on the color test. All of it tells me I put others before myself and care for them a lot, sometimes at my own expense.

"Now for your roommate assignments," Mrs. Sanderson calls.

Oh no. Roommates. I don't want to ruin anyone's trip by not being their top pick, but I'm grateful Sanderson made the matches. At least if they're assigned, I don't have to worry about being the last one chosen. In seventh grade we requested roommates for hotel rooms for the Washington, DC, trip. No one wrote my name on their list. Ever since, whenever teachers announce we get to pick our own partners, my confidence crumbles. I hate the risk of rejection.

Grace and I have been rooming together at home for four years, and—thanks to my missed scholarship—we'll probably do the same at Five Lakes Community College. I doubt Mrs. Sanderson would place us together.

I survey the room for other possibilities. Tori Syblonski gazes out the window, twirling her bushy hair around her finger and not listening to Mrs. Sanderson making what sounds like the most important announcement of the week. The bus ride might've been a tad uncomfortable, but Tori would be okay.

There's a chance I'll get paired with Alyssa Griffin. She's a cheerleader, but she's never been one for cliques. Forest Lane Academy is not known for its diversity, so she's the only Japanese student in our grade. She moves from lunch table to lunch table every day, seamlessly breaking into each bubble without popping it or making the other tables jealous. We haven't had a class together since sophomore year, but if anyone would be willing to get to know the real me, I bet it'd be her.

"Adrian Clement and Clyde Gable, room 103."

"Yeah, Clyde!" Adrian stretches for a high five from Clyde, but can't reach that far. He throws a quick glance at Mrs. Sanderson before somersaulting once across the floor and landing right in front of Clyde, holding up his hand for a closer high five. Clyde obliges.

"I'd like to remind everyone," Mrs. Sanderson says with a pointed glare at Adrian, "not to move until *after* I've called each person by name."

Adrian waves apologetically before army-crawling back to his spot. If Ryan Jacobs tried that, it'd be obnoxious. Something about Adrian makes everyone laugh, including the staff. Like Alyssa, he's not exclusive to any group.

Once back in his seat, Adrian shakes out his hair, increasing the floof factor.

Mrs. Sanderson calls a few more names before saying, "Grace Stoll and Tori Syblonski, room 114."

Tori's head jerks up at the sound of her name; Grace gives her a big smile and a bigger wave.

"Maddy Stoll and . . ." She checks her list. "Jade Coleman, room 118."

I find Jade approximately four people to my left. Her bright red, box-dyed bangs run straight across her forehead. The red, which covers the top layer of hair, is a sharp contrast to the dark brown underneath. She's one of the few girls not in jeans. Instead, she's wearing a black swing skirt with suspenders, lacy floral tights, and combat boots. The two buns on the crown of her head instantly remind me of a teddy bear. Her confidence and self-assurance give her this special glow I could only dream of. Yeah, Jade might be okay.

Mrs. Sanderson rattles off the rest of the names, and there's a chaotic rush to grab bags from the mountain piled against the wall. I hang back while Ryan Jacobs races out the door first, with his bag over his shoulder. Mr. Gutter calls for everyone to walk, not run, but his attempts are futile.

With each step up the staircase, I prepare another question I can ask Jade to make small talk, to show her I'm interested, to make her like me. It will be fine. It definitely will be. I need to stop worrying. *Stop.* Stopstopstop.

When I get to the room, Jade's already claimed the bottom bunk. There's barely enough room to walk past and reach the dresser under the window. A mirror on the wall reflects the gray clouds from outside now covering the sun.

Jade stops digging through her bag when I walk in, her expression unsure. Her impeccable eyeliner skills and perfectly plucked brows highlight incredibly dark brown eyes. "Mallory, right?"

"Maddy," I correct. People always forget the names of students who don't talk in class.

"Right, sorry. Bad with names."

"It's fine. At least you didn't call me Grace," I joke.

She doesn't laugh and returns to arranging her pillow.

Ouch.

It's okay. Some people need more time to warm up.

"Wow, they really don't want us spending a lot of time in our rooms, do they?" I ask, squeezing past her to reach the dresser.

"Hope the dorms next year are bigger."

A response! I did it! This isn't so bad.

"Have you decided on a college?" I ask, pulling the question from my mental stack.

"Yeah, and I'm majoring in fashion and design."

"Oh, that's—" I turn around but stop short when I see Jade scrolling on her phone. "How did you get that past Mrs. Sanderson?"

She looks at me as if I asked how she got a candy bar out of a vending machine. "I left it in my pocket. Not like I get any service up here anyway. You're not going to tattle on me, are you?"

She stares at me longer than necessary when I shake my head and then returns to scrolling on her phone.

"So, fashion," I say, attempting to prove I'm not interested in snitching on her. But I have no ready-to-use questions to keep the conversation going. "Does that mean you'll study clothes?"

"It's more complicated than it sounds, I promise."

I open the second drawer and unload my bag into it. "I'm going to the community college with my sister. I'll save some money, and I won't have to deal with the drama of a stranger for a roommate, you know?"

But she doesn't know, or I assume not, because by the time I spin to listen for a response, Jade is gone.

"Good talk. Glad I got to know you better," I mutter to nobody but the mirror. I might as well have stayed silent.

People will love me for who I am
People will love me for who I am
People will love me for who I am
People will love me for who I am
People will love me for who I am
People will love me for who I am
People will love me for who I am
People will love me for who I am
People will love me for who I am
People will love me for who I am
People will love me for who I am
People will love me for who I am
People will love me for who I am
People will love me for who I am
People will love me for who I am
People will love me for who I am
People will love me for who I am
People will love me for who I am
People will love me for who I am

No one could love me like this.

CHAPTER 7

Grace: April 28

I want to see Maddy pretending to sleep on the couch so she doesn't have to let Fizzy out, and to listen to her laugh while she tries to catch popcorn in her mouth. Instead, the images of Maddy floating in the water ebb and flow like waves. I see her quiet face in the rain. I feel her cold hand in mine.

I want it to stop. *Please.* I don't want to remember her like that.

But I have to hold on. I have to tell the police everything I know.

Mom sits next to me while Detective Howard reviews something on his laptop. He says the conversation is being recorded, but there's no box with a blinking light in the middle of the table, so I don't know how.

"The divers have already searched the lake," the detective says.

"I know," I say, "but she's not in the water. I pulled her to a . . . a little sandbar thing in the middle."

Detective Howard takes notes. "A sandbar?"

"Sort of." I pick apart the details from hazy images in my

head and fidget with my fingers. While the memory of her face haunts me, the details remain difficult to grasp. "It wasn't all sand. More like weeds and plants. But I know I brought her there. You have to go find her."

"Your roommate from the trip said she woke up and you weren't in the room, that you didn't appear to have been there all night. Do you know where or with whom you might have spent the night?"

"Just exactly what are you implying, Detective?" Mom jumps in.

Detective Howard doesn't answer, but keeps his gaze trained on me.

"I—I don't know."

"Do you remember anything else about where this might be on the lake? Any other landmarks or the position of the sun, or—"

"It was dark. I already told you that."

"Is there anything else you can remember? Anything you did the night before?"

"No, I—" I pause, trying and failing again to sift through the fog for another memory. The effort ignites a flash of sharp pain. I rub my temples, wishing it away. If I hadn't forgotten Dr. Thelsman's meds at home, I might be able to remember. But this hurts. I run my hands through my hair. It will be worth it if we find Maddy. I can do this for her. I can overcome the pain. I—

"I only remember splashing through the water with Maddy under my arm and dragging her out of the lake."

Mom twists in her chair. "What about any of the lake houses? Can you remember any of those?"

"No." I wish I had something more to offer, a reason to hope. But this is what I remember, and it should be enough. It has to be. "I'm sorry."

"Close your eyes and take your time," she says, but it sounds like, *Try a little harder.*

I follow her advice, but the ache in my head screams against the attempt. I exhale a low, slow breath between clenched teeth. I'm the one person capable of finding Maddy, and yet I'm entirely useless. I direct my attention to a spot on the table, away from Mom. "I have been trying to remember."

"Maybe," the detective says leaning back, "we can get a couple cans of soda." He smiles, lightening the mood. "Or pop. Sorry, I'm not from the Midwest." The door opens and another officer in uniform steps in. "Mrs. Stoll, will you please accompany Officer Jones to the vending machine and select something you and your daughter would like? It's our treat."

Mom hesitates.

I rub my temples. "A root beer would be great."

"I'll be right back." She glances at me once more before stepping through the door. Detective Howard waits until it closes.

"I know how mothers can be," he says dryly. I don't respond, but I must admit the energy in the room has shifted by simply removing one person.

"What happened after you brought her to the sandbar?" Detective Howard asks.

"I tried to get to shore myself. But I don't remember what happened. I must have blacked out and collapsed on the road before I could get help."

"Because of the head injury?" He gestures vaguely to my head.

"That's what the doctor tells me."

"But you don't think anyone on the trip would want to hurt you?"

"I already said no." But that was before I read that blog post about Mr. Gutter.

"So how do you think you got that blow? Or that bruise?"

"I . . . I don't know." But that's not entirely true. Even if I don't know for sure, I can't deny the nagging suspicion, the seed of fear, that Detective Howard is right: maybe someone on the trip did want to hurt us.

As scary as it is to think, it's even more frightening to admit out loud. There has to be another explanation. *Please,* let there be another explanation.

"Maybe I fell or something," I mumble. As long as Detective Howard can doubt that someone did this to me—to her, to us—then maybe I can keep denying it too.

Detective Howard tilts his head and checks his computer. "When I spoke with the teachers on the trip, they said leaving the lodge was expressly forbidden."

It's not a question, so I don't respond. I'm sure leaving was against the rules, but I don't remember hearing that. I also don't remember leaving.

"Do you know why you and your sister were in French Lake, a mile and a half away from the lodge in the middle of the night?"

"No. I told you I can't remember anything else." I don't like the suspicion looming in his eyes.

"Sometimes teenagers are afraid of getting in trouble, so their memory gets a little . . . foggy. But if there was any drinking or drugs involved, it's not worth hiding with your sister missing."

"No. We wouldn't do that." I don't think.

"We found two broken vodka bottles on the grounds outside the lodge."

I shrug. "I don't know anything about that."

"What can you tell me about your old school? The winter dance?"

I don't move.

I don't blink.

I don't breathe.

Detective Howard leans in at my silence.

"Nothing," I say. "That was four years ago."

"You don't think it might be relevant?"

"Do you?"

He folds his hands in front of him and studies my face. I wish I knew what he could see. "What else do you know? How did you get to the lake? Why were you there in the rain?"

"I wouldn't hide something if I thought it would help Maddy." He stops typing. "Except . . ."

I don't know why I haven't already told him the next part. Maybe because I can't trust it's real.

Detective Howard cocks his head and narrows his eyes, like he's curious or attempting to solve a puzzle, but doesn't speak. Real or not, I have to tell him everything if I want to find my sister.

"I've had flashes a few times since I woke up. I keep running over them in my head. A Sharpie in my hand. Maddy's shoes running down a hall next to me. A shout in the darkness."

The memories don't mean anything. They're glimmers, flashes. Nothing that will help. Still, they torment me. *Sharpie. Shoes. Shout. Sharpie. Shoes. Shout.*

It's as if my brain wants to quiet me: *Sh, sh, sh.*

"Maddy's shoes, you said? Are you sure?"

"Yes. Maddy always wears Chucks, and they sound different from my flip-flops."

Detective Howard pushes his seat back and checks my feet under the table. "Your flip-flops," he says, making a note.

I cross my feet at the ankles and pull them under my chair. "Are you going to find my sister?"

He stops typing, and I don't know if I want him to tell me the truth or if I want him to lie. I only want to stop feeling useless.

"Yes," he says. "We're checking phone data, reading notebooks, and reinterviewing kids from the trip. We'll find her." The door opens again, and Mom returns with two cans in her hands. "I think we're done here," Detective Howard says, getting to his feet. "I'll be sure to keep you updated with any new information. Mrs. Stoll," he says, more quietly. "A word?"

Wisps of conversation follow me into the hall. ". . . concerns . . . Maddy . . . monitor . . . Grace . . ." A headache sears so sharp and so sudden I suck in my breath and close my eyes as tight as I can. I concentrate on my breathing, but my heart keeps begging me to see more, to explore those moments I remember and notice what else surrounds me. Detective Howard's questions ring in my ears.

How do you think you got that blow? Or that bruise? How did you get to the lake? Why were you there in the rain?

But I listen to my doubts—whispering that knowing might be worse than not knowing—and I walk as far away from the pain as I can.

Outside the station, the warm spring air hits me, and I take deep, gulping breaths, willing the pain in my head to subside, fighting to ignore the suspicion rising in my chest . . . the one that raises the hair on the back of my neck despite the sun on my face. The one that says we weren't just running in that flash of memory. We were being chased.

Maybe . . . maybe it really was someone from the trip. And if my sister gave a shout, then maybe we weren't fast enough to—

Off to my right, several car doors slam, and two men in business suits approach the front doors with a girl. A petite girl with long blond hair.

"Nicole!" I call.

Her eyes clear, as if from a haze, when recognition slides over her face. She rushes to me in a few quick steps, and then her face falls with the same concern that I apparently need to grow accustomed to. "Are you okay? I heard you were in the hospital, and—"

"Yes." I duck my head as if I could hide the marks on my face. "The doctors cleared me." There's a moment where I know we would have normally hugged, but Nicole doesn't move forward. My declaration of health must not be enough to convince her that physical touch won't break a rib or add a bruise.

Nicole's hair is still perfectly styled. Her outfit is as trendy as ever. But her eyes . . . no amount of makeup can hide the puffy, dark circles that come with stress and worry under her eyes.

Maddy's disappearance is affecting everyone in the community.

"I would have called, but"—she throws a quick scowl behind her at the men approaching—"my dad has my phone on lockdown. No social media. Only communication with family."

So even if I'd gotten into my accounts this morning, she wouldn't have gotten any messages.

Both men come to a halt behind Nicole. If I imagine a polo instead of the suit and a blotchy red face yelling at a ref instead of the composed expression here, I can recognize the man on the right as Nicole's dad from volleyball games when she was still on the JV team freshman year.

"No, it's okay, the police still have my phone from the trip, and—" Suddenly it occurs to me that the police station is not where I would expect to run into Nicole. "What're you doing here?"

"They called me in to—"

The other man, the one I don't recognize, steps forward, placing a gentle hand on Nicole's elbow, and hunches to address her more privately. "Remember what we talked about. Do not offer any information unless necessary. Do not discuss anything related to the events or your involvement without clearing it with me first."

"Right, sorry," she says.

Deciding I'm finally worthy of acknowledgment, the man puts out his hand. "I'm Marc Reyes-Castillo, Ms. Harris's attorney."

As if on autopilot, my hand is shaking his, and I'm slowly

processing the information dropping in crumbs before me. Nicole is being questioned by the police, and it's serious enough that she needs a lawyer.

"I'll call you as soon as I can," she promises over her shoulder as her dad guides her to follow their attorney into the building with a hand on the small of her back.

My lungs clench, like I've missed the last step going down the stairs. Only once they disappear inside, after the door clunks back into its frame, do I realize how much comfort seeing my best friend should have brought me. I should have fallen into her arms and confessed all the thoughts and fears and horrors crashing together in my mind. I should have been filled with relief at the sound of her voice alone.

But none of that happened. I'm as hollow as I've been since Maddy disappeared, and left wondering if it's true that only guilty people need a lawyer.

CHAPTER 8

Maddy: April 22

Once all the seniors have finished lunch, we're led outside the lodge, where roughly fifty yards of grass stretches in every direction before the tree line. The west side stretches to a wall of mountains and the east slides down to the main road and town. It's not visible from here, but I know somewhere in that direction lies the lake. Grace and I used to go to fishing at a lake as kids during summer camp. Grace never enjoyed touching the worms. Or the hooks. Or the fish. Yet, she always caught more than me.

The thirty of us follow Mrs. Sanderson, while Mr. Gutter brings up the rear.

"This hike is supposed to happen Thursday," Mrs. Sanderson calls back to us, "but with some rain now in the forecast, this is our best chance. Last year, the trails were completely washed out by the rains, and we couldn't go at all. The year before that, there was a tornado warning in the area, and we spent the evening in the lodge's basement, so you'll be the first April trip to go in a few years. Spring in the Midwest is so unpredictable, am I right?" She laughs at herself and charges ahead between the trees.

Jade falls into step near the front of the group, and I find myself next to Grace.

"Weren't you supposed to bring hiking shoes?" I ask her.

She points to my Chucks. "Like those count?"

"More than your flip-flops."

Adrian spins around. "You'll need to watch out for poison ivy with those," he says. Grace hops closer to the middle of the trail until he laughs.

"Stop messing with me," she says, playfully smacking his arm like it's no big deal, like she effortlessly breaks through social barriers all the time. I've never been able to grasp how to do that.

"I'm serious," Adrian says again, but his grin suggests he's lying.

"Where?" Grace scrutinizes the vegetation along the edge of the path like she's been asked to name a criminal in a lineup.

"You two don't camp much, do you?" he asks.

"I take it you do?"

"There are four kids in my family. Camping is the Dollar General version of vacation." He grabs a stick from the ground and walks with it like Gandalf. "I live for this."

I haven't been on a hike since third grade. I remember being hot, sticky, and tired. Not at all like this. The air stays cool and breezy in the shade. Even following the path of my classmates,

I need to decide where to put my feet on the trail, over a branch or on a rock. I need to pay attention so much more than when I'm walking on a sidewalk or in the mall. My brain's forced to focus on the trail and not my worries. I wish we *had* camped more as kids.

Perhaps the air is actually thinner up here and I'm deprived of oxygen, but something about it invigorates me, like I could climb for miles and never reach the top and it would be okay. I inhale that sense of assurance and hold it in my lungs.

"You're rooming with Jade, right?" Grace says as I exhale my doubts about this week. "How's that going?"

"She seems . . . nice. How's Tori?" I whisper.

"She's so interesting. Did you know her dad used to be a movie director in Hollywood?"

I look at her like, well, like she said Tori's dad used to be a movie director in Hollywood. One hour on a bus ride and the most interesting story I drew from her was a detailed account of Mr. Mittens jumping into her bedroom window blinds.

"She lived in California before he retired from show business after her grandparents got sick. That's why she moved here this year."

"Oh," I say. "That would suck as a senior." Switching to an out-of-district school at the start of freshman year was bad enough. "Glad you two hit it off, though." As if there was ever any doubt Grace would get along with someone.

The climb gets steeper, and the chatter fades as breaths come harder. Nicole and a few others fall back next to Grace and take over the conversation. The ground levels and below us opens the sweeping expanse of green. I've never seen so many trees in my life. They extend all the way to the horizon. This is one small piece of the world, and suddenly I want to experience it all.

"Look, you can see the lake from here!" Nicole slides her designer sunglasses on top of her head, pushing back her silky blond hair, and stands on her tiptoes. "I bet if I had binoculars, I could see our lake house. I wonder if the contractors finished our new patio. We had it redone to repair the flood damage from last year."

"Are we going swimming?" Caleb Simonson asks, and drapes his arm around Nicole's shoulder, but she ignores him, apparently finding her second house on the lake more interesting than her boyfriend.

Mr. Gutter points at the clouds. "Even if the rain held off that long, do you honestly believe Mrs. Sanderson and I want to supervise you all in the water?"

"I hope we still get to visit the caves," Nicole says, dropping her voice, I assume so Mr. Gutter either won't butt in or won't know how much she's heard regarding the secret Sabbatical events. "Shelley Graber said there's a tradition of writing your name on the cave wall next to your friends'." She pulls out her disposable camera and snaps a picture of the view. "I wish I knew if it turned out good," she says, pouting.

Mrs. Sanderson appears next to her. "No picture will ever replace the image before you at this moment. Take in as much as you can."

I capture my own panorama in my mind, breathing in every bit of this moment. I know I've read poems emphasizing the beauty of nature, Whitman or Frost or Silko, but I can't remember a single one of them now. Sometimes words truly fall short, and not a single one is capable of capturing this. It's utterly incredible.

Mrs. Sanderson moves on to make sure Clyde brought his inhaler, and I dodge more stories about Nicole's lake house by sneaking over to Grace, who's talking to Tori.

"That's where I'm going next year," Grace says, her voice reaching a higher octave in excitement. "I can't believe your dad graduated from there, too."

"Yes," Tori says. She tugs at the sleeve of her sweatshirt, which features a cat's face on the front. "Then he got his job in California."

"Wait," I say, coming up next to them. "Your dad graduated from Five Lakes Community College?"

"No." Tori looks confused. "He graduated from Trinity University."

"But Grace is going to Five Lakes with me."

Grace inspects the ground, digging her toe in the dirt.

"Uh." Tori looks back and forth between us.

"Wait," I say. "You're going to Trinity University?" Grace looks remarkably like she did the time I caught her borrowing my new swimsuit without asking. "You're—you're not living at home next year? How?"

I knew she applied and was accepted, but it wasn't feasible without a scholarship.

"Oh," Tori says, her face falling. "I think I'll go, uh, ask Mr. Gutter a question about history." She disappears, but Grace doesn't seem to notice.

"I decided to play for them," she confesses, the words all tumbling out in a rush. "The coach called me yesterday. I guess a few of the other girls who had signed got in some trouble for a bad viral post or something, so he returned to the recruitment pool." She locks her knees and squares her shoulders. "I'm going to sign a letter of intent next week."

"I thought you weren't really interested in living away from home, the three-hour drive and all."

She shrugs. "I never thought of Trin U as my dream school or anything, but if they're going to pay me to go there, I might as well."

"That's—that's great! I'm so excited for you!" I lean in for a hug to hide the hurt on my face. Now she has a way to pay for college. She has everything.

"The scholarship won't cover all of it," she says with relief, "but the meals and books will be about the same as tuition at Five Lakes anyway."

"So, then it all makes sense. It makes perfect sense," I say smiling too wide. I'm happy for her. Truly. She deserves this.

Even if she is getting everything I've always wanted.

College was going to be my chance to get away, to make my parents proud of *me*, to be outside of my sister's shadow. Now Grace is already three paces ahead. Pursued by a coach. Easing the financial burden. Enrolling in the prestigious school, while I'm left behind scrambling to make the best of my plan B.

No, it's selfish for me to think of myself. This is Grace's moment. I don't want to spoil it for her. Her happiness should be enough for me. I don't need my own.

"I already checked," she says, grabbing my hands and swinging my arms. "They're known for a great writing program, so once you hear back from the poetry foundation, we'll sign up and room together! I wanted to wait until you heard back from the scholarship committee before surprising you. Next week you'll know for sure, right?"

"Yeah, um, next week sometime."

"You're sure you're okay?"

"Yes." My cheeks hurt from smiling. "Of course."

"Maddy?" She knows me too well. "You sure you're okay?"

"Grace. Yes. Congratulations. You've earned this."

She hugs me again, but before I even register her arms embracing me, Caleb and Nicole pull her over for a picture. Her hard work in volleyball paid off, and my writing didn't. It's not her fault. I thought I tried my hardest, too, but it wasn't enough. *I* wasn't enough.

There's no point dwelling on it.

A cloud covers the sun. The temperature instantly drops, and a breeze whips my ponytail across my face. I'm standing all alone. And I'm going to stay alone next year unless I do something different, become someone different. Forest Lane Academy might've created Senior Sabbatical so we could get to know ourselves, but I need to reinvent myself instead. It's time to take risks.

Starting now.

It's time to become the person others want to see.

It's time to admit the truth I've been trying to deny.

It's time to change from the me I thought I was.

Before my time in the here and now runs out.

Tick tock tick tock Tick tock

tick Tick tock Tick

CHAPTER 9

Grace: April 28

The police released our bags from the trip, apparently finding nothing useful in my sweatpants and T-shirts, but Detective Howard's keeping my phone a few more days. Or at least I hope it won't be longer than that. I tried to come home and sleep, but Detective Howard's questions and images of Maddy keep snaking through my thoughts.

How do you think you got that blow? Or that bruise? How did you get to the lake? Why were you there in the rain?

No matter which way I turn the questions over or try to dodge them, I keep arriving at the only conclusion that makes sense: Someone must have taken us out there.

And we only would have gone with someone we trusted.

I don't want more missing memories. I don't want wild theories about Mr. Gutter. I want the truth. And I want a safe place. Someone to talk to who won't look at me with accusations or pity or worry. Nicole should be that person, but her lawyer would never let that happen. Maybe someone else, though . . .

This time when I type a teacher's name in the search bar, no shady posts come up for Mrs. Sanderson. Only the email address I need.

After three different drafts explaining everything I remember and everything I don't, I delete it all, settling on the one question I need answered now: *Can you tell me what happened on Senior Sabbatical?*

Send.

"How're you holding up?" Dad walks into the living room, pacing like Fizzy does when there's a storm and she can't go outside. He wanted to go back to French Lake with the police, but Detective Howard told him it was best to go home while they searched for the sandbar.

"Oh, um, yeah. I guess I was more tired than I thought," I say, sitting up and stretching as if I'd been napping again instead of obsessing.

"Dr. Thelsman said that's to be expected." He bites his fingernails and checks his phone again. I imagine Mom doing the same in the kitchen. The desperation for updates presses in from the walls around us.

Dad's still watching me.

"Did you . . . need something?"

"I know it wasn't easy for you at the police station." His whole body relaxes, more than I've seen since I woke up at the hospital. I don't know why, but I hunt for somewhere to look that isn't him. "I'm very proud of you for everything."

His face is so serious. Dad's told me he's proud of me plenty of times. After volleyball games. After a good report card. But never because I made a meaningful contribution to a police case for my missing sister. His voice doesn't have the same note of happiness you'd expect when a parent is proud. It's hollow now, empty, like our lives since Maddy disappeared.

"Your mother and I agree it might be a good idea to visit Dr. Cramer for a bit."

"The therapist?" I ask, remembering the name from years ago. I went to her before we enrolled in Forest Lane, when my life was still a living hell at the end of eighth grade.

"Yeah, to help you remember."

I wonder if that's the only reason, or if he can see the trauma seeping into my bones like I can see it leeching on to him.

"Good," I say. Dr. Thelsman. Dr. Cramer. One for my body and now one for my mind. I'd visit twenty-seven more if it would help find Maddy.

"This has been hard on all of us," he says, and the awkwardness grows. If he cries, I won't be able to take it. I've never seen my dad cry. Even at the hospital, he left the room. I suspected he might've been getting emotional, but I never had to watch it. Maybe that's why he's avoiding the house. Maybe he thinks he has to be strong for us and only lets it out when he's alone.

Every time he looks at me, I know he's searching for answers. Answers I don't have for questions I keep asking, too.

What happened at the lake? Why were we out in the rain?

Sh, sh, sh.

The doorbell rings. Fizzy crashes through the living room, barking ferociously when we all know she only wants to smell someone new.

Dad opens the door to our elderly neighbor Mrs. Finch. She

hands him a fresh casserole. "I brought you all some dinner," she says, peering around my dad to get a better look at me. "I wanted to stop over and see how you're all doing."

"Thank you," Dad says. "We're doing the best we can." He struggles to hold Fizzy back from jumping up on Mrs. Finch, who throws the dog a quick scowl before leaning around Dad again.

I abandon the couch to dig my old sneakers out of the hall closet.

"Going somewhere?" Dad asks.

"I thought some fresh air might clear my head."

"That's a good idea." He shifts his weight and says something to Mrs. Finch, but I lose his words as another headache slices through my thoughts. I wince and push my palm to my forehead.

"Are you okay, dear?" Mrs. Finch asks, and Fizzy strains against her collar to reach the nosy neighbor.

"Yeah," I say, massaging my temple as the pain subsides. I finish tying my laces and stand. "I'm fine."

I grab a leash for Fizzy and pull her past Mrs. Finch, who flattens herself against the wall but hasn't taken the hint to leave. I shut the front door and walk away from Dad, Mrs. Finch, and anyone else who wants to ask me questions. I walk past the rest of the two-story houses, into the older part of the neighborhood with the cracked sidewalks and dated siding.

I can't remember anything else, but I remember Maddy on that sandbar in the middle of French Lake. That has to help with the search. Whatever cosmic fate or God exists clearly wants me to keep this one vivid image: me, dragging Maddy from the water.

There must be a reason.

I pull out my phone to check for an email from Mrs. Sanderson, but my inbox is still empty. Teachers don't always check their email during the weekend, so I shouldn't be surprised. When she reads it, I know she'll want to help. Fizzy tugs hard on the leash. I expect to spot another dog or a squirrel, but the reality surprises me more.

Adrian Clement. I recognize him from school. While I wouldn't exactly call us friends, he's friendly with everyone. He'd talk to a tree stump if it'd laugh at his jokes.

But more importantly, he was registered for Senior Sabbatical. He was there.

"Adrian?"

With dirt streaked down his arm and a bit flecked across his face, Adrian drops a bag of mulch and squints in my direction. He removes his hat and shakes out his hair. It's short on the sides, as if it's been recently cut, and only a few inches long on top. It's the tidiest I've ever seen his wild hair. He returns the cap to his head and squeezes the bill, walking over to me with a hesitant wave, almost as if he knew this moment, this meeting, would come eventually.

He's probably trying to figure out what to say to the girl with the missing sister. I can't blame him. I wouldn't know what to say either. But at least he's coming over instead of "giving me space," like I can only assume my absent friends are doing.

He bends to satisfy Fizzy's intense and sudden desire to be

petted by him. Maybe he genuinely loves dogs and I'm being paranoid, but he doesn't meet my eyes.

"Hey, girl," he says to the dog, letting her jump up and lick his face.

Well, Fizzy certainly seems to trust him.

"I didn't know you lived around here," I say. That's the thing about a private school. People live all over.

"I don't," he says slowly. He's not avoiding me now, but he's hiding something. An expectation, maybe. Of what? "This is my grandma's house."

"You were on Senior Sabbatical, right?"

He adjusts his hat, squeezing the bill again. "Um, yeah?"

"I'm having memory troubles from last week," I confess. "I can't remember much."

"So, you . . . you don't remember anything that happened?"

"Not really." I expect to be embarrassed, but it's a fact I've come to accept.

The breeze shifts.

"Oh, sorry to hear that." His face relaxes as a miniature Adrian comes from the side of the house. He, too, has a hat covering wavy brown hair. He's scrawnier and shorter, but his face is nearly identical. Adrian's voice lightens as he drops a hand over the younger boy's shoulder, probably thankful for a distraction from this awkward meeting. "But, yeah, I was there."

"Do I have to do this all by myself?" the kid whines.

"My brother Kyle and I are doing some landscaping for my grandma."

"That's nice of you," I say. "I bet she really appreciates it."

Kyle rolls his eyes. "It's like getting paid for a workout," he says, and I can tell he's trying to flex his arms without making it obvious that he's flexing his arms.

"Don't worry, Stoll. I'll make sure he works on that personality first," Adrian teases.

"Stoll?" The younger boy's eyes go wide with recognition. "Does that mean you're the one who—"

"Hey," Adrian interrupts. "Why don't you grab that bag of mulch and bring it up to the side of the house?"

"But—"

"It will give you a chance to show off those muscles."

Kyle grumbles under his breath but drags the bag from the curb. I scratch the back of my neck, careful to avoid my stitches. I've been in the paper before, but that was for volleyball, with my team. Now kids on the street know me for the worst day of my life. It's bizarre.

"Sorry about him," Adrian says. He calls over his shoulder, "He should be more concerned about his manners than his muscles." Kyle makes an obscene gesture in response, but Adrian only shakes his head and asks me, "How are you since . . . everything?"

"You mean since my sister went missing or since I woke up in the hospital with seven stitches on the back of my head?"

"Sorry, that was a stupid question."

Fizzy sniffs the ground at both our feet. "I . . . I wish I knew what happened on the trip so I could help her." Adrian doesn't need me to say her name. From the downward tug of his lips, he knows. Everyone does. "It's like sitting through a movie and noticing you've skipped a part, but the streaming gets interrupted every time you try to go back and watch it."

Adrian bites his cheek, as if he's considering the analogy. "Have you tried reading your notebook? That might help."

"The detective mentioned they're searching through notebooks."

"Yeah, everyone got one the first day to write in during different activities. Reading your own thoughts might help fill in some holes."

"Did my sister write in hers?"

"We all did. Well, everyone else wrote in them. I mostly doodled. But it was still constructive. I promise"

"Do you remember seeing me or my sister that day?"

"No one remembers seeing either of you since Thursday night, not even your roommates."

Roommates. Right. Detective Howard said at the hospital that we were reported missing by them . . . and someone else.

"The police told me Ryan Jacobs was with Tori and Jade when they told the teachers we were gone." I wonder if that's why Nicole was at the station earlier. Maybe the police are questioning all of them.

"Huh, that's weird." Adrian twists the bill of his cap again.

"What?"

"Nothing, but, well, before we knew what was going on, Mrs. Sanderson and Mr. Gutter gathered everyone in the main room. Only, Ryan was a few minutes late. He was the last one to walk in."

"Where was he?"

"I don't know," Adrian says. "But I can ask around, see what I can find out. Here." He wipes his hands on his shirt and pulls out his phone. "Give me your number, and I'll let you know if I hear anything."

"Oh, uh . . ." I twist Fizzy's leash in my hand. Adrian and I barely know each other.

He must read the thoughts on my face. "I promise I'm not trying to be weird or ask you out or anything. I'm actually in a very healthy relationship with my rake right now." He points to the ground behind us. "She eats up all my free time and is known to be the jealous type."

I smile, and it feels good. I think I might have forgotten how to smile until this moment.

"No, it's not that. It's . . . well, I'm trying to be really careful who I share information about the case with so it doesn't end up online."

"Oh." Adrian stands up straighter and clenches his fists. "You mean like 'The Stoll Sisters Secrets and Theories'?" He shakes his head. "I don't know who's behind it, but they've been posting a new theory every hour. I can't believe they went after Mr. Gutter like that. People keep feeding into it. I finally deleted all my social media to get away from it."

"Yeah, I haven't checked any." My parents shut down their accounts, too, after seeing comments suggesting something fishy was going on, since my mom wasn't at the lodge to help search with my dad. When someone else tried to defend her by explaining she was taking care of her other daughter, a third commenter hinted my dad might be a suspect for trying to stay close to the investigation and he must not be a good father if he wasn't at the hospital with me. The gossip is rampant. "Everyone wants to stake a claim in their own theory. People need to learn that everyone deals with grief differently and leave us alone. Especially that blog. I only saw the one post, and that was enough."

"Definitely. You all deserve more than that." He waves his phone at me with a sympathetic smile. "But I promise: updates only." He waits.

Fizzy wags her tail at him and whines until he pets her again. I guess if she can trust him . . .

"All right," I say, and give him the number for this phone.

He enters it in his with a promise to send me any new information, and I pull Fizzy's leash, heading for home. Adrian seemed just as surprised as I was about the accusation against Mr. Gutter. I try to convince myself we were safe with our teacher, that no one we know would have hurt us, that Ryan Jacobs being late to the meeting means nothing.

I'm letting paranoia get the best of me. Everything's going to be fine. Maddy will be home soon. The hospital will fix any injuries just like they fixed mine. Maddy will be fine. By the time I turn onto my street, I've almost convinced myself it's true.

Until I see the police car parked in our driveway.

CHAPTER 10

Maddy: April 22

I need to get out of my head.

We're all sitting around the fire. Even though my hair and clothes will reek from the smoke, the flames are hypnotizing, and it's easy to lose myself in my doubts. Ever since Grace told me she won't be going to Five Lakes Community College, I've been second-guessing if I should go to college at all. If I couldn't win the Dorene Williams scholarship, I probably shouldn't pursue writing as a degree, anyway. And if I'm not sure, I shouldn't be wasting money—even if tuition is cheaper there—while I figure it out.

Instead of questioning my future, I focus on the present. The bonfire behind the lodge is massive. Mr. Gutter said this event was supposed to be held tomorrow, but we had to reschedule it, like the hike, to this first night because of the forecast. It's still cloudy, but the faint glimmer in the sky tells me the moon is full, even if its outline hides in the haze of clouds.

If I was more secure, I'd assume Jade was too caught up in the fun to look at me, but I can't shake the feeling she's avoiding me. I'm probably overthinking, like always. Clusters of people are grouped all around the fire. I could walk up to any one of them and join a conversation. That's how other people do it, right? They simply . . . go? And talk?

Tori sits off to the side by herself. She's even quieter than I am. I bet she'd like someone to start a conversation.

I take three steps toward her before Grace calls, "Tori, come tell that story you told me earlier." She's sitting on a bench with Caleb, Nicole, and some others.

Tori joins them, and I stop in my tracks like this is where I was headed anyway, to this random patch of grass, awkwardly standing by myself.

I keep shrinking into the shadows. I've practiced making sure no one notices the pain I carry. Not Mom and Dad, not Grace, not Erica. Not my teachers. While I so desperately want someone to *see* me, to love me in spite of my insecurities, I don't want to show it. I don't want to be desperate.

But I am.

I'm desperate for someone to know me well enough to sense that I'm lonely even if I don't say it. I'm desperate to be acknowledged when I walk into a classroom. I'm desperate for the Senior Sabbatical leader to match me with a roommate who will rip me from the shell I can't claw my way out of. I *am* desperate.

And I hate it, because desperation repels people. It's like bad breath. You know you have it and hope no one else notices, but they do. They're too polite to say it, so they act nice, but they end the conversation quickly and keep you at a distance forever after.

But so what if they called Tori's name instead of mine? I said I was going to be a new person on this trip, and I will be. The old me wouldn't have even tried, so the new me can't retreat so easily.

Before I can doubt myself again, I march up to the group as Tori finishes a long story featuring a celebrity.

". . . and since he worked with my dad on his last project, he agreed to stop by my birthday party."

"I think I would literally die," Nicole, sitting in Caleb's lap, says. "I can't believe you actually met him."

The conversation flows without one-word responses from Tori or stories starring her domestic felines. Maybe Tori simply needed the right people to talk to. Maybe I do too.

"I love that it's so normal for you," Grace says. "You tell it like it's no big deal. Not everyone could be that down-to-earth about it."

Tori's cheeks glow. She fits naturally with them, like they've all been friends for years. She makes it look easy enough to believe I can have that too.

"Did you—" I begin, but Nicole interrupts to ask what car the guest of honor arrived in, and my words die a quiet death.

"Can you take a picture for us?" Grace asks me.

"Yeah, sure." I accept the camera from her. She, Nicole, Tori, and a few other girls scoot together, arms embracing each other.

"Don't forget to turn on the flash."

"There's enough light from the fire."

"Fine, but if it doesn't turn out, don't blame me."

That's Grace. She can't stand being blamed for something she didn't do. She plays her heart out in every volleyball game, but it's less so her team wins and more so no one points a finger at her if they lose.

"On the count of three," I say. As soon as the flash ends, they fall back into conversation. Grace reaches for the camera.

"Thanks," she says and bounces back to her seat.

There's no room on the bench for me, just like there was no space in the conversation for my voice.

I walk to the other side of the fire, where Mr. Gutter distributes sticks to roast marshmallows. I shove my marshmallow on the stick and lower it to the flames, surprising myself with how much I miss Erica. At least I wouldn't be sitting here alone. She thinks of me. Eventually. Or at least she did until Zoey jumped into the picture. I never had reason to hope for more, because Erica's almost always had a boyfriend. I never cared if she was busy hanging out or talking to one of them. I don't need her to put me first all the time. I'm used to being second. I'm probably setting myself up for disappointment by dreaming of anything more.

I rotate my marshmallow in the flames like the memories spin in my mind. I had a crush in junior high, but the rejection was so harsh, I've never tried putting myself out there again. Any guy I like needs telepathic powers to interpret my awkward silences and stiff smiles as a sign of interest.

I'm tired of waiting for someone to notice me. I'm tired of being afraid of rejection. If those girls only want a quiet photographer, there are other people I can hang around.

Adrian circles the edge of the fire.

"There's a spot over here," I say, shifting to the left.

"You're destroying a perfectly good marshmallow," Adrian says, bringing his own roaster and two marshmallows next to me.

I lift the flaming end of my stick and blow it out, until all that remains is a crunchy, black glob at the end. "Eh, looks fine to me."

"Here," he says, juggling his roasting rod so he can prepare a graham cracker and chocolate for me. It's sweet. If he were doing it for anyone else, I might consider him flirting, except this is me—I couldn't attract a magnet if I was a refrigerator.

Although, that was the old me, before Sabbatical. I don't need to get my hopes up, but I don't need to panic either. Deep breath.

"You must be one of those high-maintenance-s'more people," I say before taking a bite.

"If by high-maintenance, you mean expertly skilled at getting the exact golden shade of a cornfield in October at sunset, then yes, I daresay I am." He shifts to the right, balancing the stick near some coals at the bottom, rotating it ever so slowly. The fire pops. A twig snaps. A silence settles in, one I'm painfully aware of as every second ticks by.

Say something.

Anything.

Don't be weird.

"I have a theory about your kind," I say.

"All right. Lay it on me."

"You've never actually had a burnt-marshmallow s'more. You're convinced it would be bad based on presentation."

"I will neither confirm nor deny this. Burnt s'mores are for people unskilled in the art of roasting."

I finish chewing, my heart rate slowing. Adrian kind of makes this talking thing easy. "If you tried it, you'd know that the chocolate and the graham cracker basically erase the blackened flavor, and the inside of the marshmallow still tastes exactly the same."

"I don't trust you. You're lying."

Before I can doubt myself, I jolt his beautifully browned marshmallows near the flames where they promptly catch fire. He yanks them up and blows them out. Rather than saying anything, he pouts like a grumpy fish. An adorable, grumpy fish.

"I guess you'll have to test them now." I shrug innocently and offer two sets of prepared crackers and chocolate. Is this flirting? Am I doing it right?

"A burnt s'more has to be better than no s'more, right?" He eyes his blackened snack suspiciously before biting into it. His nose scrunches up instantly. "I was wrong. Totally wrong. No s'more is better. That disgusting charred taste cancels every other flavor."

"Yeah, no, it totally does. But now I have two more s'mores." I take a bite from the other and offer my hand to accept the rest of his.

"Well played, Stoll. Well played."

While he reaches for fresh marshmallows, Mrs. Sanderson climbs atop a large stump and calls for our attention. Less than a day here and everyone's already learned to quiet down immediately.

"As our first night draws to a close, we want you to take

a moment to reflect on your past and dream of your future. Mr. Gutter is passing out a small rock, some paper, and a marker to each of you. Before we head back inside for the night, I want you to write your single greatest regret on the piece of paper and your deepest heart's desire on the rock." She pauses, allowing the crackling of fire to permeate the hush. "These will be private. We're not going to ask you to share, so please be honest. When you're finished, place both, one atop the other, up here." She indicates the stump beneath her feet, wide enough for me to lie across.

Some people turn over the rocks and papers thoughtfully. A few uncap their markers and set to work instantly. Others make their way to the stump next to Mrs. Sanderson.

My regret and my desire.

The rock and paper sit in each hand, and somehow the paper feels heavier. I set it aside for now and find the smoothest side of the rock. My desire.

I want a scholarship to enroll in the college of my choice. I want to be accepted into a great writing program. I want to grow up, get married, and have children someday. But those are all things I want to do. Not things I want to *be*.

I want to be the girl I pretended to be a few moments ago: confident, charming, comfortable. I want to be someone else. Someone who isn't overlooked for an award. Someone who doesn't stay behind while her sister ventures off to a better college. Someone who *can't* be ignored or forgotten.

I uncap the Sharpie and write the word pounding on my heart: *Wanted*.

My throat closes imagining what it would be like to truly experience that. To *know* beyond a doubt that I am wanted. By my parents. By a boy. By friends. That someone would want *me,* deeply.

But then there's the tiny scrap of paper resting in my fingers. I've filled pages and pages of notebooks with words, and all I need to fill this piece of paper is one. One word to represent my greatest regret. Some options swim on the surface of my memories: Not going on the first Sabbatical with Erica, and letting Zoey replace me. Not visiting Grandma Patty one more time before she died. And I do regret that those things happened, but I couldn't have necessarily changed the outcome.

Instead, I know the regret I need to write down. It sits in the bottom of my stomach, churning a tide of nausea if I dwell on it too much, so I usually don't. But here in the dark, with only the soft glow from the campfire over my shoulder, I'm strong enough to face it.

Mateo.

One word, a name, written in black on the white paper. A stain on who I am, who I want to be.

I place the paper under the stone on the stump so only the white corners poke out from underneath. The stump fills with papers touching, overlapping, and linking together. None of our regrets are visible, but they're there, hidden under our desires. The firelight flickers over words scrawled unsteadily on bumpy stones: *love, identity, known, future, forgiveness, hope.*

I connect with each one. They are all pieces of the puzzle I want. There's a chance I'm not as alone as I imagined.

Once everyone's papers and rocks are placed, Mrs. Sanderson speaks again. "On the first day of Sabbatical, we open up. We allow others to know who we are. On the second day, we'll concentrate on remembering where we've come from, what's shaped us. We'll acknowledge our past. Our desires often feel like rocks weighing us down, burdens we carry that grow heavier over time. We're so busy striving to cover our regrets, we might forget to lift our rocks."

She takes a stick out of the fire, its end burning in a small flame. "Sometimes you need a spark to release you from your past and help you focus on what you want most. You're worth it."

Everyone's quiet. The fire pops. Mrs. Sanderson lowers her stick and touches one paper. It catches, the flames consuming the edges and eating into the white until it blows away in the black night. The fire spreads, licking each corner of everyone's regrets, burning out fast enough to not ignite the stump.

In a few minutes, the fire has danced from one end of the stump to the other, leaving only our desires behind.

Wanted.

When you're a kid,
you get skinned knees
and loose teeth. You
ride bikes and do cannon
balls off the diving
board. Cherry popsicles
drip down your chin. Santa
is real and so is the
boogeyman.

What's the worst than can happen?

When you grow up,
decisions weigh and hearts
break. You scream
at concerts and cry
in the shower. You learn
to drive and how to love.
You know that in the end,
everyone has to die.

But that might not be the worst that can happen.

CHAPTER 11

Grace: April 28

Fizzy and I race past the police car, push open the front door, and rush into the house, both out of breath.

"Mom?" I drop Fizzy's leash.

Dad steps out, his face pale and drawn, eyes distant and empty. Mom cries at the kitchen table, face in her trembling hands.

Detective Howard stands in the kitchen with Officer Jones, hands bent out stiffly from their waists to accommodate their heavy belts. They feel too big for the space next to the stool where Maddy does homework, like they might bump their heads on the light fixture.

"You found her?" I ask.

Detective Howard nods twice before destroying my world forever.

"I'm sorry."

I hear it in his voice, see it in Mom's shaking shoulders, feel it in Dad's absence at my side.

Maddy is dead.

My knees buckle, and Detective Howard springs forward, guiding me into a chair next to my mother. He says something to the other officer about finding me a drink of water, but it won't help. Remembering how I left her, where I left her, didn't help. Nothing will help.

Maddy is dead.

A piece of me knew this was a possibility. Of course it was. But it was the possibility I tried to ignore, to pretend I could prevent or change. Even knowing it's true doesn't make it feel like a reality.

Maddy is dead?

Detective Howard's voice remains soft and low. "Has anyone contacted you since you've been out of the hospital?" He leans in, earnestly. "Anyone unusual? Anyone you didn't have a strong relationship with in the past?"

His tone sends a chill down my arms. "What do you mean? They can't. You took my phone."

"Any contact at all?"

"She answered all your questions," Mom says, "and you still couldn't help." Her eyes are as red as the tip of her nose, her hair tangled on one side.

Detective Howard catches his partner's eye for the briefest moment before Officer Jones responds and sets the glass of water in front of me. "During an open investigation like this one, we need to explore every possibility."

"I know this is difficult for you," Detective Howard adds, "and it will take a few days before the full autopsy comes back, but protocol dictates we treat this as a homicide until further notice."

"Homicide?" I echo, my throat dry and the water still untouched in the glass before me. I wanted to believe we would find her, that Maddy would be okay. I hoped remembering where I left her would be enough. The pain of the stitches on my head suddenly feels sharper.

Someone tried to kill us.

And Maddy didn't survive.

Dad's hands pull on his cheeks, like he can tear the anguish away.

"The initial examination shows she experienced some severe bruising, particularly around her chest and upper limbs." Detective Howard's voice is calm, quiet, trained. He turns to me. "Do you remember doing anything on Sabbatical that might've caused those injuries before Thursday night?"

A flash of Maddy's wrist wrapped in my grasp appears.

"I still can't remember," I whisper.

Just like I can't remember anything else.

Except her shoes. A Sharpie. A shout.

Sh, sh, sh.

"We found blood on her clothes," Officer Jones says. "We're having it tested and compared to the blood we found on your clothing, but her injuries don't match your head wound."

Mom collapses with her head in her arms on the table. Dad rubs her shoulder, his face crumbling like old concrete. All their bickering, the arguments, have fallen away.

"What about from before the trip? Do you remember anything

unusual happening before you left?" Officer Jones asks. "Anything at all?"

I shake my head.

"The doctor said it might take months for her memories to come back," Dad says.

If they come back at all.

I don't know if he never heard that part of Dr. Thelsman's diagnosis, if he's forgotten it, or if he believes ignoring it can make it disappear.

"We understand," Officer Jones says.

"We don't know how you and your sister got so far away from the lodge," Detective Howard says. "We're exploring every option—"

"Is that why Nicole Harris was at the station?" I interrupt. "Are you talking to Mr. Gutter again? What about Ryan Jacobs. He was—"

I'm about to say he was late to the meeting, but then I'd have to explain I don't actually remember that detail, and Detective Howard is already looking at me with concern since my questions stopped as abruptly as they started.

He waits, maybe to see if I'll finish that thought. Eventually he says, "We're doing everything we can. If you remember something, or if someone out of the ordinary tries to contact you, call us." He offers a business card with the police department logo.

"We already have one," Mom says with a hollow voice.

I take it anyway. Anyone contacting me right now would be out of the ordinary. All my friends must be too scared to say the wrong thing or, like Nicole, have scared parents and controlling lawyers. It's the only explanation for their distance.

"Is there anyone you want me to call before I leave? Family? A church leader?"

"I think we'd all like to be alone," Dad says, gesturing weakly to the front door. The officers show themselves out. Fizzy doesn't follow. She drops her head on my knee and whines. Mom sobs into her hands at the table.

Maddy is gone.

She's not upstairs, lying in bed and watching videos on her phone. She won't send me selfies of food stuck in her teeth. She'll never braid my hair after I get out of the shower.

Because she's gone.

Dead.

I heard once that you're supposed to use direct phrases like that. No euphemisms like "kicked the bucket" or "moved on." Instead, you should use simple language, easy to understand.

But no matter how many times I tell myself the truth, I still can't fathom it. Black spots dance in front of my eyes.

Someone out there attacked us.

I stand up, my head light.

Someone gave me these stitches.

I stumble.

Someone killed Maddy.

Mom cries out her name as I slip to the ground.

April 29

Dad helped me to bed last night. My head hurts. I haven't eaten. Everything hurts, and none of it matters because Maddy is dead.

April 30

I'm still alive.

Why not her?

May 1

When the morning light streaks through my window, a dream startles me awake. I reach for my phone to check the time. But it isn't there. The nightstand where I put it isn't there either. Because I'm not in my own bed.

I fell asleep in Maddy's bed last night. The edges of pain still linger from my headache. I took some of the medication Dr. Thelsman prescribed. I can't remember climbing in and tucking myself under her covers. I was so desperate for relief, for the pain to leave and sleep to arrive.

I'm vaguely aware of some people at the door, family friends or my parents' coworkers, maybe. The pounding at the back of my skull makes it hard to identify the voices from downstairs.

I pick up some clothes off the floor of our bedroom.

Except that it's not *our* bedroom anymore. It's only mine, and remembering that makes it lonelier than ever.

Black stars dance before my eyes. I brace myself against the bed, and an image flashes before me. *My fingers. Wrapped around Maddy's wrist. Cold. A shout—her voice—in the darkness.*

No—stop. I was dreaming before, but now I'm awake. I'm awake and I'm in my room. I'm not on the lake.

I steady my trembling hands. I can't live like this.

My cuts and scrapes are healing, but knowing she's dead tears open my heart. That wound won't heal until I know who did this to her. To us.

Mrs. Sanderson still hasn't replied to my email. As I predicted, no one else has reached out. There's no manual for helping a friend through grief, and some people want space. Still, they could at least ask, stop by to see how I'm doing. Something. Instead, my "friends" have shown their true colors when I need them the most. There are only two notifications on my phone, both from Adrian.

The first is from two days ago: *I'm sorry to hear about your sister. I'm here if you want to talk.*

The second is from late last night. *Not sure if you still want it, but I got Ryan Jacobs's number. 555-2184.*

I don't even know what to say to the first message. My sister is dead. I'm an only child. My family is broken. None of that comes close to explaining the empty ache inside of me.

But the second message . . . that's something I can grab hold of and use to push myself forward. Detective Howard wants me to let him know if anyone out of the ordinary contacts me, but Adrian's the only one with my number. I can't wait around any longer.

I send off a quick note of thanks to Adrian, and then type Ryan's number into my phone with the message, *This is Grace Stoll. I need to talk to you about Sabbatical.*

It's not much, but it's a start. He was there when we were first reported missing, and I want to know why he was late showing up to the meeting, like Adrian said. That can't be a coincidence. Maybe he can tell me something about Mr. Gutter, or Nicole, or . . . or maybe he'll reveal something about himself.

I plod halfway down the stairs before Fizzy greets me. I scratch her behind the ears, and she licks my leg. At least something is still the same.

Whoever was at the door has left. Dad's on the phone in the living room. Mom's back to cleaning the already-pristine kitchen. She stops scrubbing when I enter the room. When she speaks, her voice is tired, resigned. "Are you ready to eat?"

I shrug, grabbing a box of honey cereal from the pantry and a bowl out of the cabinet.

She nods at the cereal. "I couldn't remember if you liked those or—"

She stops short, and I stop pouring. We haven't said her name out loud since the hospital. It's too hard.

Mom clears her throat. "Well, Dr. Thelsman said you should be getting plenty of sleep. You have an early appointment with Dr. Cramer today, and later this week, we'll go into school to figure out plans for the end of the year."

I put the milk in the fridge without commenting. I don't know how school could expect me to take final exams when the only thing I'm capable of concentrating on is who killed my sister and why they tried to kill me.

My parents haven't discussed it with me. I don't expect them to. Mom once found a lump on her breast and went in for a biopsy, but she didn't tell us until we came home from school and found her sitting on the couch with a bag of frozen peas on her chest. In fifth grade, Dad was laid off, but they told us work gave him extra vacation days, so we wouldn't worry. My family doesn't discuss important issues like health or money or my sister's murder.

It's easier to pay someone else to do it, so after breakfast, Mom drives me to the counseling center and fills out paperwork in the lobby while I sit across from Dr. Cramer. The office's AC blasts a few degrees too cold and a box of tissues sits on the low table in front of me. Today's the first day in three that a headache hasn't confined me to my bed. I could barely stand up, let alone get my memory back. I want Dr. Cramer to help. I wish I knew how she could.

Dr. Cramer examines me with a patient smile. Her face doesn't appear any older, but she's letting a streak of gray hair against her deep brown skin announce she's been at this for a long time. I haven't been in her office since eighth grade. I expected her to be dressed in something formal like a suit, but instead she's in jeans and a bright, fitted blouse.

Windows on two walls fill the office with lots of natural sunlight, which flows over the muted tones of the room. Her degree from Howard University hangs on the wall. I sit on a gray couch next to a swirl-patterned pillow. She presumably remodeled in the last four years, because I don't recognize any of the decor.

"I want to remind you," she says, "everything you discuss with me will be confidential, unless you're thinking about harming yourself or others, or if someone is harming you. In those cases, I will need to let your parents or the authorities know to keep you safe."

She probably recites those same words to all her clients, but she still manages to make them sound sincere.

I shift on the seat.

"I'm patient, so it's okay if you want to sit for a while, too."

"What did my mom tell you?"

"I prefer to hear about my clients from their own perspectives. What would you like to tell me?"

"My sister died."

She doesn't flinch. I take that as confirmation that she already knew. She waits.

A minute passes.

She prompts, "Tell me about your sister."

"You met her," I say, referring to the times Maddy waited in the lobby while I had my sessions in junior high. She cocks her head at me, and I repeat her words from earlier with a sigh. "But you want to learn about her from me."

"I knew you were a quick learner."

I ignore the compliment, or joke, or whatever she intended it to be. "Maddy was always quiet."

Dr. Cramer sits up straighter, a crease between her eyes that I take as a sign she's listening intently. "Grace?"

"What?"

"Did you—?" The crease in Dr. Cramer's forehead deepens, but she must decide against whatever she's about to say. "Sorry, continue. Your sister?"

"I always told her she was smart. She was so passionate about her writing and good at it too. But that's when she was by herself. Around other people . . . she kept waiting for things to happen to her instead of making them happen for herself. Waiting for people to talk to her. Waiting to be included."

She pauses, like she's deciding where to direct the conversation. "Did that bother you?"

There's no clock in here, but I know each session lasts almost an hour, whether I use it well or not.

"She made it harder than it needed to be," I say. "She never went up to people and started talking." There's more irritation in my voice than I expect. I don't enjoy talking about Maddy this way. I don't know why I am. "The police believe she was murdered." If Dr. Cramer notices I'm changing the subject, she doesn't call me on it.

"And what do you believe?" she asks.

"If it was murder, someone should've seen something, seen us leaving the lodge. Something. We wouldn't have left alone."

"Why not?"

"Because my friends were on the trip, and I never spent time with Maddy when my friends were around." The words taste disgusting. But they're true, and I hate them. I have no excuses here.

That's the kind of sister I was. And it's the end of that discussion. "I can't remember any of it, though."

"Do you want to?"

"Want to what?"

"Remember."

"What do you mean? Of course I want to remember. I've been trying to remember since I woke up in the hospital."

"Why?"

"Because then we'd know what happened to her. To us. We'd have answers."

Dr. Cramer leans forward slowly. "What will happen if you don't remember?"

I can't look at her. If I do, she might learn the truth. I don't know what the truth is, but I don't want her knowing it before I discover it myself.

"I'll be stuck in pain like this. Forever."

Dr. Cramer sits patiently, apparently undisturbed. She crosses her legs and adjusts her notebook. "When you consider the reality of never remembering, how do you feel?"

"Afraid." The word slips out before I realize it's been hiding within me. But it's true. I'm afraid of never having an answer, of being the reason my parents don't have closure, of wondering if I could've done more to save her.

"Anything else?" Dr. Cramer asks.

My mouth goes dry, because I do know how else it makes me feel, and as much as I want to deny this feeling exists, I want to be honest about it so much it hurts.

So I am.

"Relieved," I choke out. "Because wondering if I couldn't save her is better than knowing I could have."

Forty minutes later, my time with Dr. Cramer is up. She promises to keep our confidentiality, but she's going to talk with my mom for a bit. When Dr. Cramer says the session was "productive," I'm not sure if she means for me or for her. She follows me down the hall to the lobby.

"You can wait here," she says to me, and then faces my mom, who sits on the love seat in the waiting room. "Mrs. Stoll, if you'll follow me for a few minutes."

Mom tucks her phone into her purse and offers me a reassuring smile before she goes. I take her spot, slouching in the seat. I pull up my email, expecting the usual and getting a surprise instead. There's an unread message from Mrs. Sanderson. A response to my request for information about the trip.

I'm so sorry. I wish I could help you more. The school's legal team has advised all staff members to not discuss the events of Senior Sabbatical without a lawyer present. All communications are subject to monitoring and could be subpoenaed in a court of law.

Every hope keeping me upright crumbles. Of course the school would be worried about a lawsuit. Schools are always worried about lawsuits. Isn't that why we need to get permission slips signed to learn about sex in health class? The media attention surrounding our accident probably dumped a hurricane on them. They'll likely never be able to host another overnight trip again.

And all those fears add up to the same result: Anyone who could've given me some answers is bound not to talk. This shouldn't be so difficult. I should be more useful. Maddy deserves better.

I pull out Detective Howard's business card. I can call him to ask if he found any leads or if there's anything I can do to help. Something to not be so useless.

My phone flashes a message from Ryan Jacobs. *Stay away from me, psycho.*

What the—? I fire off a series of texts, each more desperate than the last, but there's no response. Nothing. Blocked, probably.

I only wanted to ask him a few questions, and that's how he's going to react? Shut me down and call me names? Why? I just lost my sister, and he can't even talk to me about it? First Sanderson and now him? I slam my phone against my knee to keep myself from screaming.

If anything, this just makes him look guilty. Who treats another person like that? Especially since Maddy died?

"Arghhh!" I squeeze my fists and pound the arms of the chair, and then promptly massage my hands with regret.

That's when I notice the girl sitting across the waiting room. She's angled away, shoulders hunched and curling in on herself. Her greasy, stringy hair covers her face, but it's a rusty red, obviously colored, and falls right below her shoulders. She's wearing a Forest Lane Academy cross-country shirt and sweats.

"Jade?" I say, and her head jerks up. Adrian said Jade was on Sabbatical too. My sister's roommate.

She tucks her hair behind her ear, eyes flicking to the receptionist, then the entrance. Anywhere but me.

I haven't had many classes with her, but I've never known her to be shy.

"On Sabbatical," I say, moving to the seat next to her and shoving Detective Howard's card back into my pocket. Jade sits up like I'm approaching her with a snake instead of a question. Her eyes have dark circles under them. "Can you tell me what happened?"

"What do you mean? You were there . . ." She trails off, shifting in her seat and darting her eyes around the room, as if hoping someone will interrupt us.

"Yes, but did you hear anything that night? The night we—"

"I don't know anything. I woke up. Tori woke up. You were both gone. We told the teachers. That's it."

"What about Ryan Jacobs?"

Jade glances again at the receptionist, but he's engrossed in his monitor. "What about him? Tori and I saw him in the hall. He said he was coming from Clyde's room. There's nothing to tell."

"But you must have noticed something if you shared a room with—"

"Look, I already told the police everything I know!"

A man enters the lobby and scans the room before settling on Jade. "Ready to come on back?"

She stands to follow him.

"But isn't there—?" I call after her.

She whips around and hisses, "I said I don't know anything. Stay away from me."

She disappears into the hallway, and I realize she held no anger in her voice.

Only fear.

CHAPTER 12

Maddy: April 23

No fear.

Not today.

Roommates get close on Sabbatical. Erica and Zoey proved it. Obviously, Grace and Tori prove it. After the campfire last night, I'm ready to make my desire a reality.

"Morning," I tell Jade as I sit up in bed and stretch. She's standing in front of the mirror applying eyeliner.

She makes a noncommittal noise and moves on to mascara.

Right. I shouldn't expect this to be easy.

Food is a good conversation starter. "I wonder what we're having for breakfast."

She ignores me.

I swing my legs off the bed. I have as much impact on this roommate relationship as she does. It's time for the direct approach.

"Have I done something to upset you?"

She spins around. "What?"

"Did I leave my socks on the floor? Or accidentally use your toothpaste? Or break some other unspoken roommate code?"

"No?" She says it slowly, like she's confused why I'm talking.

"Then why haven't you wanted to hang out with me? On the hike, at meals, at the fire, you always seem to be as far from me as possible."

Jade lowers her mascara brush and blinks. "I—I figured you wouldn't want to be friends with me."

"Why?"

She hesitates and unzips one of her makeup bags.

Trust me. I focus on the words, sending a telepathic message across the small space between us. *Trust me, and we can start over.*

She sighs, and I can see the wall she's built around her cracking. "Remember how Grace and I used to be friends before I moved in with my dad, and we drifted apart?"

I have a hazy memory of them eating lunch together at the start of freshman year, but decide against admitting she doesn't stand out as one of Grace's many friends.

"Well, I figured you might be like her."

There could be an insult hiding in that confession, but it worked. She's being honest. The magic of Sabbatical is working! "I'm not," I say. "I'm actually nothing like her."

"Yeah, sure." She zips her bag.

"It's true. Grace is a straight-A student. She's a volleyball champion. She got a scholarship to a dream school. She's the shining star of our family. That will probably be engraved on her tombstone." I laugh. "Mine will say"—I move my hand across the air, miming reading the text—" 'Here lies Maddy: She existed.' "

Jade laughs. "Come on, that's not true. I'm sure there's something you're known for."

"If I'm known as anything other than the Quiet Stoll Sister, please enlighten me."

Jade doesn't contradict me, which might have hurt if it wasn't a truth I'd accepted long ago. Instead, she says, "Grace might seem perfect, but she can't be. There must be something to stain that reputation of hers."

"Not only does she floss, but she throws it away and wipes the counter clean when she's done."

"That would be annoying to live with."

I've never heard anyone revel in teasing Grace's perfection before. I bounce off the bed and dig through my drawer for clothes. The sky isn't so dark any more. "What about you? Do you have siblings?"

"An older brother. But my mom got custody of him in the divorce, and I had to go with my dad, so we didn't live together the last two years. He graduated and moved out before I moved back with my mom."

"Oh. Are you close?"

"Not really. It is what it is." She finishes applying her makeup in the mirror, snaps her palette shut, and tosses it in her bag. "Want to go down and get breakfast?"

"Yeah," I say, throwing my hair up in a messy bun. "I do."

Together, we go downstairs to the cafeteria.

Together.

I've been a third wheel with Erica and Zoey all year, but not anymore. As long as I don't mess it up with Jade, I might have someone.

I get my food first and find a seat, when Mr. Gutter approaches me from behind.

"Ready for a long day?" he asks, an inch too close for comfort. The man means well, but he will forever be awkward.

"I wouldn't mind a nap later."

"You'll have to get used to a busy schedule with those practices next year," he says, and I laugh a little, but he obviously can tell I have no idea what he means. "I heard Trinity University invited you to play for a full ride! That's incredible."

I set my juice on the table. "Yeah, it's great news. For my sister, Grace. She plays volleyball. I don't."

"Oh, gosh!" he says, first smacking his head and then stroking his overly long—and let's be honest, creepy—beard. "You're Maddy. I'm so sorry. I do that all the time, don't I?" This isn't strictly true, but I was fortunate enough to take Mr. Gutter's history class without Grace, which significantly decreased the number of mix-ups. "Well, be sure to eat plenty and get enough energy for the day." He smiles under his bushy beard and moseys away to torture another senior with small talk.

"That man is so weird," Jade says, taking the seat next to me with a plate full of fruit and a cup of orange juice while the room fills with other students. "Too bad Holtsof got sick."

Mr. Holtsof, a new, young computer teacher had quickly earned the nickname Mr. Hot Stuff and single-handedly increased enrollment in the tech program among female students.

He was at our pre-trip informational meeting last Wednesday with Mrs. Sanderson but was absent Thursday and Friday. Jade was not the only one disappointed to see Gutter board the bus yesterday morning instead.

"I wonder if Principal Avery has figured out who released that picture of Gutter." She lowers her voice. "Any ideas who might . . ." She trails off with a meaningful expression.

"What? I didn't do it!"

"No, not you." She laughs and stabs a strawberry on her plate. "I thought Grace did."

"That doesn't sound like something she would do." Grace rarely makes a mistake, much less an intentional decision that could jeopardize her reputation.

Jade pops the strawberry into her mouth and chews thoughtfully. "I don't know. She was pretty mad in homeroom because he gave a test the day after a quiz. She kept saying he didn't know how to teach. The picture dropped the next day."

"You better not let her hear you drumming up those rumors." Grace hates rumors ever since we had to leave our old school.

"Okay, okay." Jade raises her hands in surrender. "I just figured she would have told you. That's all."

"We don't tell each other everything."

"I always thought you were these supertight sisters, like on TV or something."

"Definitely not." I laugh, but I think even Grace believes we're closer than we are. "We don't fight, but we don't . . . talk. Only about school or schedules or chores at home. Not about *real* stuff or anything that matters. We're in different circles."

Jade leans in. "But you must still know more about her than anyone else, right?"

"Time to finish up and head into the main room," Mrs. Sanderson announces from the front of the cafeteria. My conversation with Jade dies when we clear our trash, but her question stays with me.

Grace doesn't know me better than anyone, so I doubt I know her. She could have secrets of her own, ones I'd never discover unless she confessed.

Even though the sun should already be pretty high, rain clouds keep the main room dark, leaving us to rely on the wrought iron chandeliers with lights mimicking candles. We are not at the same tables we were assigned to yesterday. Today, I'm sitting with Caleb, Nicole's boyfriend; and Chloe, a girl on Grace's volleyball team.

Mrs. Sanderson speaks from the podium with far too much enthusiasm, even if she did drink a pitcher of coffee. "Our second day of Sabbatical focuses on remembering. We can't become who we want to be if we don't stop to reflect on who we've been." She explains the instructions for our first activity. Everyone has to plot the major events in their lives on a graph in our notebooks. The highest point, ten, represents the highlights, and the lowest point, negative ten, is reserved for the worst moments.

After some deliberation, I put moving to FLA at 0, completely neutral, because my life or status didn't change too much. The scholarship rejection goes to a negative six. The high point in my life is a seven, when we rescued Fizzy three Christmases ago.

I'm not sure how to plot the last few years of general emptiness at home, with Dad working all the time and Mom always running errands or going to Grace's games. It's quieter when they're not in the house, so I end up somewhere in the middle.

Once we've finished plotting our points, we connect the dots, and it's not surprising to find everyone's endured ups and downs, but Mrs. Sanderson adds, "Your line might resemble a heart monitor with peaks and valleys, but that means you're alive. Making it through lows to discover the highs is part of living life."

I add one more dot on my graph, a ten, but I don't label it. I don't know what it will be or when it will happen, but the promise is enough for now.

Rain splatters against the large windows, forcing Mrs. Sanderson to speak louder than usual. "Now you will pick one dot you've drawn and expand on it. Write every detail. Fill the page. You should spread out. Go to your rooms, the cafeteria. You're allowed to stay here if you'd prefer, but this will be a time for you to spend with yourself. It's time to remember the moments most important to us."

I climb the stairs up to the dorms with a faint hope that we'll be blessed with sunshine for the last few days. This is, after all, the Midwest, where weather is known to be unpredictable and change quickly. One year we canceled school for ice, fog, and floods all in the same week.

I head for the end of the hallway to a tall rectangular window with a wide ledge, and by pulling myself up and shifting sideways, I'm as close as I can be to sitting outside while staying dry.

A few others enter rooms, but no one else takes the hallway, and in a few minutes, the footsteps fade. Like me, they probably know exactly what they need to say.

Mrs. Sanderson most likely expects us to write some sort of journal entry, but I have different plans. There's something I need to confess. Something I've never written about before. Something straight from the heart.

I put my pencil on the page.

Dear Grace,

My head knows my
parents still wanted
me, even though I
was a surprise.

My heart wonders
if it's true, or if they
dream of how easy their
lives could have been.

My head knows my
friend must have wanted
me around, or we wouldn't
have survived those years.

My heart looks back
and questions if I was
lying to myself and only
saw what I craved.

My head knows I have plenty
of time to feel accepted,
to experience true love,
to become the person I dream of.

But my heart feels time
ticking by with every beat.
Another day waiting.
Another hope gone.

CHAPTER 13

Grace: May 2

I need to escape this house. Too much life's been sucked out of us for this to still be a home. It's too sleepy and calm, but I hope it means Mom and Dad got to sleep through some of their grief.

Ryan Jacobs hasn't responded to any of my other messages. If Nicole has her phone privileges again, she hasn't reached out, not that I've recovered my social media accounts anyway. And I can't stop hearing the fear in Jade's voice.

No one is checking on me like my parents' friends are checking on them. Maybe that should bother me, but I don't care what people think of me right now.

Maddy and I disappeared and no one saw us. Someone attacked us. No one knows who or how or why. Or maybe they do and they're too scared to tell.

Suddenly, their silence seems suspicious.

It's all I've been able to concentrate on after coming home from Dr. Cramer's office yesterday, but when I told the police about Ryan's message, I only got a vague "We'll look into it."

Adrian, on the other hand, seemed much more alert when I told him about it.

When I check my messages, one's waiting from him: *I think I've got something on Ryan Jacobs.*

What? I type back.

You said Jade confirmed he was there when they reported you, right?

Yeah, and he said he came out of Clyde's room when she was talking with Tori in the hall. I leave out the part where Jade didn't want to talk to me at all.

Well, Clyde was my roommate, and I'm pretty sure I would have noticed another dude sleeping in a room made for two.

So, I type out, drawing the only logical conclusion, *either he lied or Jade did.*

Adrian's response is prompt. *I have a plan to find out. Pick you up in twenty?*

My fingers hover over the keypad. I've been out of the hospital for four days, and I spent two of them in bed. Despite the cops' pleas for me to update them with any information, they aren't returning the favor. I'm ready to get out of here, to *do* something. To finally be useful. But something holds me back.

Yesterday Dr. Cramer asked how I'd feel if I never remembered what happened, but I can't let my fear stop me from moving forward. I have to do this for my sister.

No matter what I find.

Just don't tell the rake, I respond.

He confirms with a zippered-mouth emoji.

First Ryan's last to arrive when Gutter and Sanderson gather everyone from the trip, then he calls me a "psycho" and blocks me when I try to message him, and now he might have lied about where he was before he reported us missing.

I finger the stitches on the back of my skull. I'll be first to admit Ryan's usually a jerk—self-absorbed and quick to laugh at someone who panics during a class presentation—but I wouldn't have pegged him for being violent. Still, something isn't adding up, and I'm ready for whatever Adrian has in mind to find out exactly what that is.

When I walk into the kitchen after getting ready, my parents are too distracted to notice. The counter is covered with papers: hospital bills and insurance information for me, funeral plans for Maddy.

"Cheryl said she'd help write the obituary." Mom moves her reading glasses to the top of her head. The circles under her eyes are darker, from stress on top of lack of sleep. "And your brother called. He can't get a flight out for a few more days."

"The funeral home said we could make arrangements for next week if we wanted to." Dad's dressed in a navy blue polo with his company's insignia on it. Last night, he mentioned stopping by work to sign some checks this morning. Mom rolled her eyes behind his back, but she's accepted, for now, that he can't stay at home all day.

"Will that interfere with the memorial the school wants to organize?"

"I'm sure they'll be flexible." Dad opens the back door for Fizzy to come in and notices me. "No sleeping in today, huh?"

"I'm going to breakfast with Adrian." I scratch Fizzy's ears.

"Who's Adrian?" Dad asks.

"A guy from Forest Lane. We're getting breakfast before he has to go to school."

"Are you sure that's a good idea?" Mom sets aside the paperwork in front of her. "We have a meeting with your counselors at school this morning," she says, clearly appealing to logic for a reason I should stay home. She doesn't mention that we're supposed to pick up the contents of Maddy's locker and notes and cards from the office.

"Okay," I say. "Instead of coming back here, he can take me to school with him, and I'll meet you there. I'll be gone for less than an hour." There's more they want to say. The unspoken worry hangs in their shared glances. "I haven't seen any friends. I don't even have their numbers in this old phone. Adrian was on the trip. He wants to help me remember."

"Okay," Dad says as Mom opens her mouth to protest. "You can go, so long as you're not late for your appointment."

"Thank you," I say and walk away. Their whispers chase me to the front door, where I wait for Adrian so Mom can argue with Dad without me.

He pulls up only a minute later in a sedan that's clearly been on the road since the early '90s. The window is rolled down, and he waves as he puts the car in park. He cleans up nicely without the ripped hat and dirt smeared across his face from helping in his grandmother's yard. His neatly styled hair emphasizes his new cut and complements his jawline.

I climb in and am immediately impressed with how clean he keeps it. Not what I was expecting.

"I thought you said your car was a classic," I say.

"It is." He covers his heart with his hand, as if I've mortally wounded him. "This," he says, his deep voice pouring out the announcement like gravy, "is Betty White."

"How'd you come up with that name?"

"Well," he says, backing out of the driveway, "I bought it from my grandma last year, and with this beautiful coat, she couldn't be anything but a Golden Girl."

I could easily argue that the exterior is more tan than gold, but I let it slide. My parents always told us we had to save up for our own car. Maddy and I were supposed to do it together, but I'll admit I've never been much of a saver. I smile sadly, remembering Maddy complaining that I could drive months before her. By that logic, I should have more saved for that car. Instead, I bought a new purse and too many morning coffees with Nicole.

"So where is Betty taking us?" I ask.

"To a place where breakfast dreams come true." He says it with a completely straight face.

"And then you'll tell me what you know about Ryan Jacobs?"

"Even better. He'll tell you himself. He's meeting us there. Well, he's meeting me there. You'll be a bit of a surprise."

After a short drive, he pulls into a parking spot behind The Grove, a small restaurant tucked in an old building downtown.

Inside, the walls are thick and tacky, suggesting they've been repainted every other year for the last several decades. Some of the patrons might've been eating here just as long. The two of us certainly bring the average age down. Except for three or four other people spread among the booths, everyone has gray hair.

Each plate we walk past is, first of all, enormous and, secondly, filled to the edge with eggs, bacon, pancakes, and sausage gravy.

"You okay?" Adrian asks as we take our seats at a booth in the back.

"Hm? Yeah, yeah. Why?"

Adrian studies me, a shadow of the concern I usually see in Mom's eyes darkening his own. "I don't know . . . you seem different." His face immediately colors. "It makes sense with everything you're going through . . ."

I swallow. "It's just weird being out. It's the first time I've been in a restaurant since . . . since we got the news." Adrian's the one person who doesn't seem to mind talking about Maddy head-on. I don't want that to change. "Do you really think Ryan will know something?"

Adrian reaches across the table and covers my hand with his. His calluses are rough, but his touch is soft. "Someone must know something. If you can't find answers, the police will. It will happen."

His strong voice reinforces my dissolving hope, and he squeezes my hand, sending a reassuring warmth up my arm.

"You're right. And even if it seems impossible, I could still get my memories back."

"Right. Of course." Adrian clears his throat and pulls away, then opens the plastic menu. "Now don't get distracted by all the options. Waffles are the obvious choice."

"What if I want pancakes?" I ask, skimming the various breakfast items on the menu.

"I'm offended," he says, holding his hand to his chest. "How can you support pancakes? They're so rude."

"That makes no sense? What are waffles? Polite?"

"Absolutely. Waffles are like, *Oh, I see you have butter and syrup in your hands. Here, let me hold those for you in my twenty-five square pockets.*"

"You're ridiculous," I say.

"And you're smiling."

It's true, but realizing it only makes the smile slip from my lips, because I'm not sure I should be allowed to smile. Not when Maddy can't.

Adrian must notice because he folds his menu and asks, "Are you sure you're ready to go into school today?"

"Yes." I place my menu firmly on top of his. "It's not like I have to go to class. I'll only be in the office."

"Fair enough. Just . . . remember there are no rules on how to grieve. Cry if you need to cry. Laugh if you want to laugh. Don't worry about what anyone else thinks."

I sink into the comfort of his words, but when I'm about to ask where all his wisdom comes from, the waitress arrives, and Adrian orders for himself before raising one brow, as if questioning if I'm up for the challenge.

I don't break his eye contact when I say, "A water and one waffle with strawberries, please."

The waitress repeats our selections and walks away. Adrian says, "Respectable choice."

"You had nothing to do with my decision."

"Of course not," he concedes, but he's smiling too.

We sit silently, but the chatter of the busy restaurant surrounds us.

"I should—"

"What do—"

We laugh.

"You go first," I say.

He takes a long sip of water, but when he speaks, I have the sneaking suspicion that his words aren't the ones he originally intended to say. "I was thinking about how much changed on that trip. I mean, before Sabbatical, I thought the Stoll sisters were twin girls in my history class from freshman year."

"We're not twins."

"I know that *now*," he says. "My point is, I didn't expect to get to know you both so well, but I did. And now I know how special you are." He shrugs, entirely unaware how bizarre it is to hear that and yet not remember the same moments that brought us closer. "So, what were you going to ask?"

"Detective Howard mentioned reading through our notebooks from the trip, but I have no idea what he might find. Did we share them out loud?" I ask, unrolling the silverware and putting the napkin in my lap.

"Umm . . ." Adrian looks like he's about to say something, but this time the words don't pop out like gumballs from a machine. The waitress returns in record time with two massive plates heaped with waffles, mine with a pile of fresh strawberries and Adrian's with blueberries. Both are topped with swirled dollops of whipped cream.

"Thank you," Adrian tells her. He holds his knife and fork vertically in each hand and wiggles his eyebrows at me.

I wait.

"What?" He spins his plate to a different angle and digs in.

"Did we share the stuff we wrote in our notebooks?" I repeat.

He takes his time, as though the use of his knife requires all of his focus. "Some people did, yeah." He takes his bite, makes a show of savoring it, and points at my plate. "Aren't you going to even taste it?"

I cut a piece with a little butter, a touch of whipped cream, and at least a small bit of strawberry. Adrian watches me like he's waiting for the final pitch in a World Series game.

"Mmm, good," I say.

"Good? Just good? Stoll, you're killing me. These are the best waffles in town."

"I said they're good!"

"You're worse off than I thought. Oh, here he is." Adrian waves to Ryan, who's looking around by the door. He nods when he catches sight of Adrian and heads for the booth, but stops when his eyes land on me.

"Not happy to see me?" I say as Adrian moves over to make room for Ryan, who looks about as comfortable as someone sitting on a chair of needles.

"No, it's just . . ." Now that he's looking at me, he can't pull himself away. "It's like seeing a ghost." He blinks and shakes his head. "Sorry. I shouldn't have said that."

A self-aware and apologetic Ryan Jacobs? That's new.

I lean forward the way Detective Howard does when he thinks I'm keeping the truth from him. "I think you know something."

"You too?" Ryan rolls his eyes. "First that detective or whatever was on me and then that post went up. I promise, I didn't do anything to you or your sister."

"What post?" Adrian asks.

Ryan grabs Adrian's cup and drinks without asking. Much more like the Ryan I remember from before Sabbatical. "That stupid Stoll Sisters Theories or whatever," he says. "Gutter still hasn't been back to school since the trip. People say he's getting fired because of everything online. And if I lose my scholarship for next year because of that dumb site, I swear . . ." He trails off but bends the fork in his hands in half.

Adrian gently takes it from his grip, and Ryan lets go, like he didn't even realize he'd done it. I haven't checked the blog since reading about Mr. Gutter. Maybe I should.

"If you're innocent, why did you block me?"

"I didn't," he declares, but then looks off and his tone softens. "Or I don't know, maybe I did. I've been blocking a lot of numbers. I had someone text me the other day saying he was Caleb," Ryan says, "but when I messaged him on another app, he told me it wasn't him. Turns out it was just someone trying to get information. Maybe they were even from the media. I don't know. That's when I deleted all my socials and started autoblocking."

"People are messed up," Adrian says.

Maybe it's a good thing the police still have my phone.

"Like I said," Ryan repeats, "I didn't do anything."

"How come you told Jade that you were in Clyde's room? Right before you reported us missing?"

"Yeah," Adrian says, unbending the fork and placing it out of Ryan's reach. "I was his roommate, and I would have noticed you there."

Ryan massages his fist before answering. "Fine. I wasn't with Clyde, all right? Jade and Tori caught me in the hall, but I was afraid they'd rat on me, so I said I was in Clyde's room. No one would think I was doing something wrong if I was with him, ya know?"

"So, what were you doing instead?"

Ryan leans back and puts his hands in his hoodie pockets, shrugs.

"Silence, huh? Interesting choice." I pull out my phone and rummage in my bag until I find Detective Howard's card.

"What are you doing?" Ryan says as I start dialing.

"I was just going to check in to see if you've been any more helpful with the police. If not, I'm going to suggest they ask for information from . . . who did you sign with for football next year?"

"Whoa. Hold up." Ryan takes the card from my hand, but I've already entered the numbers. I hold the phone up with my finger hovering over the Call button. "Fine, I'll tell you, all right? But you gotta promise not a word leaves this table, because I cannot risk losing that scholarship."

I set the phone down to show I'm listening. Adrian nods in agreement, too.

"Caleb was really messed up after he heard Nicole was cheating on him or whatever. So, he asked to dip into the stash I brought." He looks from me to Adrian and explains further. "Alcohol. I brought some bottles of vodka on the trip."

"Not too worried about losing your scholarship when you did that, were you?" I mumble.

"So," Adrian says, diverting from my sarcasm, "you were getting drunk with Caleb Thursday night?"

"I didn't end up drinking anything on the trip, I swear. But Caleb did. Not wasted or anything, but enough to numb him, ya know? When Tori and Jade saw me in the hall, I was afraid they'd rat on him, so I said I was coming out of Clyde's room. I didn't even know you were both missing at that point. I swear I didn't do anything to you guys."

"Later that morning," Adrian says, "you were the last one to walk into the main room when Sanderson and Gutter took roll. How come?"

"I was ditching the bottles."

"Outside?" I guess, remembering what Detective Howard asked me about the broken bottles the police found on the grounds.

"I knew they were going to be searching while we were all down there. I didn't have a lot of time, so, yeah. I just opened the door and chucked them as far as I could."

"This can't be a dead end. There are answers out there somewhere." I pick up my phone.

"Hey," Ryan says, reaching for it. "I told you what you wanted to know."

"I'm not calling the detective," I say, holding the phone out of his reach. "And before you're off the hook, you should never call someone a 'psycho.' People dealing with mental health issues deserve the same amount of respect as anyone else."

Ryan sits back, confusion and surprise on his face, maybe for being put in his place or maybe because he's honestly never considered his harmful language before.

I return my attention to the phone. "I'm checking that theories blog. Maybe one of those stories actually has a piece of truth."

"Uh," Adrian says, sounding nervous. "I don't think that's such a good idea."

"Yeah," Ryan adds, "Gutter still isn't back since they posted about him. Maybe you . . ."

Too late. My mouth drops when the page loads. The newest post is titled "Sisters by Blood: A Sisterly Squabble Turned Fatal."

> When a woman goes missing, it's always the husband. Or the boyfriend. Or the ex. Or at least that's the theory most crime shows are based around. But there is some truth to police looking at those closest to a victim as a lead suspect.
>
> And who's closer than a sister?
>
> The Stoll sisters were last seen alive, together, on Thursday night. Sources on the trip say it was hard to miss the shouting and yelling when the two were locked in a verbal war. While the cause of the argument is unknown, it certainly begs the question of why police aren't looking a little closer to home for a motive against . . .

My vision blurs and I can't read any more.

"You can't take anything they say seriously," Adrian says. "It's an anonymous poster. They have no credibility. They're throwing spaghetti at a wall, trying to see what sticks."

"Yeah," Ryan adds. "Yeah, another post on there says I got mad neither of you would go on a date with me, so I got revenge. It's total garbage."

Both boys across from me look uncomfortable, afraid. Too much like Jade looked in Dr. Cramer's lobby. Did she read this too? How many others have? How far has our story—*this* story, these *lies*—spread? Are people across America sitting in their homes, drinking their coffee, scoffing at the police for not investigating me as a suspect?

I grip the edge of the table until my knuckles turn white. "What aren't you telling me?"

Adrian brushes his hand over his ear as if he isn't used to the shorter cut and still expects to push his hair away.

"Adrian?"

"There was a fight," he says quietly. "Between you two. The day you disappeared."

I lean back in my seat, letting the words wash over me, but they still don't make sense.

The last fight I remember having with Maddy was in eighth grade when we wanted to wear the same pair of shoes to a dance. I can't imagine that would've been the issue on Sabbatical.

"What did we fight about?"

Adrian fiddles with his straw. "Old stuff, built up. I don't remember the specifics."

I can't imagine what *old stuff* means. Though, I guess I can believe it was *built up* since Maddy and I never did more than bicker over using up the conditioner in the shower or borrowing a charger without returning it. We squabbled. Argued. But a fight?

"Maybe," Ryan says, hedging around the words like he's not sure if he'll be helpful or make things worse, "maybe if it's old stuff, someone else knows. Like one of her friends or something?"

One of Maddy's friends?

Maddy's only friend.

Erica.

CHAPTER 14

Maddy: April 23

When I'm done with my letter to Grace, I wipe my cheeks and sniffle, hoping anyone who might walk by my spot on the window ledge will assume my nose is running from the chill in the air. I don't bother fixing the words smeared by the teardrops on the page. Grace will never read it anyway. I wrote this for me, to say how I truly feel. I could never bring myself to say it to her face.

Mr. Gutter comes up the stairs to wrangle everyone back into the main room. Once we're there, he breaks us into groups of five. Surprisingly, I'm in a group with Grace. Unsurprisingly, she's already talking to two other people when I sit down.

"Number four? Number four?" Adrian walks up, wiggling four fingers on both hands. Grace laughs with him. Mrs. Sanderson distributes a small lit candle to each group, and Mr. Gutter dims the lights and presses play for soft instrumental music.

It's a testament to the power of Sabbatical that no one imitates holding a séance.

"In your groups," Mrs. Sanderson says, "you will have a chance to share your thoughts. It can be the life event you wrote about, or something else you've been pondering these last few days. No one *has* to share in your group, but I encourage you to."

I exhale. I don't have to share, and I won't, especially not with Grace in my group. Still, I anticipate the silence that usually emerges when we're instructed to share something personal with other people. I hate the uncomfortable, itchy pressure to say something when I don't want to. The feeling doesn't come, though, because Adrian speaks without waiting a beat.

"I wrote about my grandpa," he says, nudging his notebook but not opening it to read. "My grandpa was the real deal. He lived in town, and my mom used to bring us rugrats over." He laughs to himself. "He used to give us each a Tic Tac from his pocket when we got there and then another one if we behaved or didn't destroy anything valuable before we left. I'm pretty sure we never earned our second one, but he always coughed it up anyway. I learned how to be funny from him. How to keep a straight face. He had me solidly convinced for at least two years that Oscar the Grouch lived in his neighbor's trash cans. When he died, I was in middle school. I blamed the doctors. I thought they could do more. We had"—he looks at his hands and clears his throat—"some other stuff going on as a family. It was . . . really hard."

Something passes over his face, and his lips tug up in a half smile. "Middle school's the hairy, sweaty, nasty armpit of growing up," he concludes, leaning back. His humor is an obvious distraction from getting too deep, but it works.

"No joke," Grace blurts. I expect her to say how much better high school is or share some of the high points in her life—Senior Night or being on homecoming court last year—but she doesn't.

"In eighth grade," she begins, "we had this dance, the Snow Ball."

With that one sentence, I know. I know exactly how this story ends. She focuses on her audience, because of course they don't know. Grace never mentions it.

Neither do I.

The Snow Ball was a fundraiser the school put on when our basketball team made it to the championships for the first time in our district's history. They had a spirit week leading up to that night in the gym. They'd purchased new bleachers in anticipation of the big game. Someone's dad was a DJ and donated his time for free so that all the proceeds from the dance would go directly to the team. Supposedly, scouts for a big travel league were going to be at the game, ready to offer scholarships. Everyone was going.

The mournful note in Grace's voice tells me she's not excited to share this, more resigned. "I was sitting on the bleachers talking to this guy I'd finished dancing with. He was the star of the school basketball team, super popular. All that." She gives a half laugh, maybe at the nostalgia of it. "He was the prince of eighth grade." Her voice trembles. "Mateo."

That name. A rock presses against my lungs. I pull my knees up to my chest to hide my hands from shaking. Mateo, the kid with a smile for everyone. Mateo, the kid whose single mother showed up to every awards ceremony so proud of her only child. Mateo, the kid who was a shoo-in for the travel-league scholarship.

I know *exactly* how this story ends.

Everyone else waits for Grace to finish.

"Mateo stood up." Her eyes glaze over, like she's visualizing it all happening in front of her again. "We were five or six rows up from the bottom. I don't know what happened, but all of a sudden, he fell. There was this loud crash as he tumbled to the floor, and everyone in the gym was staring at us."

I remember it only took a few seconds for the music to stop and teachers to rush over to Mateo, crumpled on the gym floor, his hand bent back, like he was a puppet cut from its strings.

"I felt awful for him," Grace continues. "But everyone blamed me."

"Why would they blame you?" Adrian asks solemnly.

"They said I pushed him."

The flame flickers, sending light and shadows dancing across Grace's face. Her simple statement hangs heavy in the air like the candle's smoke. It permeates everything.

I remember the stares and whispers. Everyone wanted to know what happened, but everyone saw something different. Only one thing was clear: Mateo had been with Grace on the bleachers one minute, and the next, he was sprawled on the ground.

"There were all these rumors that I tried to kiss him, and

supposedly I got mad when he said he didn't like me, so I pushed him." Grace's voice catches, and tears spring to her eyes. Grace never cries. Not anymore, but she cried all the time that year.

"It was the worst year of my life," she says, tears now streaming down her cheeks. "People bullied me every day. They sent me horrible text messages, told me to kill myself."

I remember those messages. I felt each one like the prick of a knife. I tried to delete them all from our phone before she read them, but she still knew. Some people slipped notes into her locker. No one else would sit with her at lunch. Someone stole her clothes during PE, and Grace had to wear her gym uniform the rest of the day. Supposedly the school they did everything they could, but between broken security cameras and students refusing to confess, they claimed they couldn't prove who did it.

Grace shudders. "I had to go to therapy for months. People don't realize how rumors can destroy lives. I begged and begged my parents not to send me to high school with those kids. That's how we ended up at Forest Lane."

She reaches for my hand. "Maddy was by my side through it all. I never told you this before," she says to me, "but as horrible as they all were during that time, I never felt more loved, thanks to you. Trying to make me laugh. Braiding my hair. Passing me tissues. I wouldn't have survived without you."

I squeeze her hand, playing the supportive sister like I did in eighth grade.

I want to throw up. If I open my mouth, I'm sure I will. I swallow, fighting to keep the truth inside.

"Today, I'm letting go of the regrets—of everything spoken and unspoken."

Forgiving someone isn't as simple as snapping your fingers and declaring it. That's only the first step. It's a process.

Grace has finished, but the story isn't done. She's not telling them everything, omitting a very big truth.

And no matter how easily Grace believes she can forgive the ones who tortured her, I know she would never, ever, forgive me if she knew the truth about that night.

By dinner, I'm still shaking. I was not prepared to hear Grace share her trauma about Mateo from four years ago. I wasn't prepared for her to dredge up mine without even knowing it. I want those memories to disappear into soot and ash like the paper of regret I wrote his name on.

Grace thrived when we transferred to Forest Lane. Her grades skyrocketed. Her friend group swelled. Her athletic ability flourished. Because of all that, I had no idea she still dwelled on eighth grade. Hearing that pain in her voice this afternoon, still as raw as it was when she was thirteen, rips through me.

Following Mateo's accident, she cried herself to sleep every night. Every afternoon, I sat in the back seat on the way home while she sat in the front, a paper cutout of the girl she used to be. The school tried to help, I guess, but you can't force people to be kind, especially not middle school girls.

"You okay?" Adrian asks. I didn't notice him approach.

"Yeah," I lie. I'm at a table in the lodge's cafeteria, but everyone else is standing in line for food. If I eat, I'll throw up. I'm sure of it. "Not much of an appetite right now."

"Me neither. Come on." He extends his hand.

It's such a simple gesture. Casual, for most. To me, it's like a gentle tap on my shoulder awakening me from a bad dream. My fingers slide between his. A slow warmth creeps up my chest, and I hope it doesn't reach my cheeks.

But then shame flicks on the light, blinding me with the truth: I don't deserve this. I don't deserve a moment of happiness after causing my sister that much pain. Even if she doesn't know I'm to blame.

Besides, the last time I let myself fall for a guy, it only led to a mountain of regret.

Adrian squeezes my hand and smiles. His hair falls across his forehead but doesn't cover the energy in his eyes. He doesn't see the past running through my mind; he only sees me.

I'm too desperate to fight it. I want this too much—an invitation. A moment of unknowns. A reason to hope.

I grab my notebook and follow him.

I'm not naive, though. This is no big deal. Adrian, a funny, attractive boy, is holding my hand in his. But it's no big deal. Totally normal. Adrian is flirty, outgoing. He probably holds hands with girls all the time, and this is no big deal. Not to him.

Hope is dangerous. I refuse to let it swell out of control.

I'm too busy battling my doubts to pay attention to where

he's leading me until he drops my hand and folds into a squashy armchair. It's not a room, exactly. Closer to a nook or an alcove. A small wooden arch, detailed with the same ivy carvings from the entryway, separates it from the rest of the main rooms. There are a few potted plants near the tall window and floor-to-ceiling bookshelves on either side, with red chairs in front of them.

"These are comfier than they look," Adrian says, swinging his legs up over the arm. I flop into the other chair and ignore the small plume of dust that rises. Only the sound of the rain gently tapping against the window, asking to be invited in, fills the space between us.

My pencil drops to the floor when I curl my legs under me. Adrian grabs it before I can reach and hands it back to me. His smile sends another flash of warmth, and this time I know it shows in my cheeks. But he smiles at everyone. No big deal. Totally normal.

He reclines in his seat. "This is where I came to write about my grandpa."

"I'm really sorry you had to go through that."

"I've learned it helps to voice my emotions instead of trying to keep them inside."

"Very wise." It feels like a gift, getting to see his serious side instead of watching him try to hide behind a joke or a laugh.

"I noticed you didn't share in the group," he says.

"Oh." He noticed me? Sort of. I mean, he noticed a lack of participation from me, but he still noticed me. "I don't think people would really be interested in what I write."

"How come?"

"Well," I say, and try to laugh naturally, tucking my hair behind my ear. "The moaning and groaning during poetry units every year is a pretty good indication that most people hate poetry."

"You write poetry?"

"I *try* to write poetry," I correct. "I'm not very good." Or at least the Dorene Williams Foundation agrees that I'm not.

Adrian sits up. His picture would appear under the definition for *charisma*. "Will you read me one?" he asks.

"What?"

"I want to hear one of your poems."

"You—you don't want to hear a poem." This time I'm laughing for real. But he's not. Adrian always laughs, but he's not. He's watching me expectantly, leaning forward with an interest I'm not used to commanding.

"And how do you know what I want?" he argues suggestively.

Holy butter on a cheese biscuit. He's so close to me that I could stare into his deep, brown eyes, say something flirty and funny, softly flutter my lids closed, and lean in to kiss him.

Instead, I make this unnaturally high-pitched sound that could be a laugh and begin to sweat profusely. I'm pretty sure he'll notice the rings under my arms in a few minutes. I lean away from him.

"I'm serious. I want to hear one. Please?"

I clear my throat and read a poem. My voice trembles. I barely process what I'm saying. I'm hyperaware of his presence so close to me. Halfway through I can't remember why I agreed to read anything. I probably gave in to avoid getting lost in his eyes.

When I finish, the rain still taps against the window. The sun still hides behind the clouds. Nothing else has changed.

But Adrian is looking at me. And it is a very big deal.

"Look," I yell to the sun,
in the moment it sinks for the night.

"Look," I shout to the lightning,
gone in a blink from my sight.

"Look," I scream to the glowing moon,
covered in a blanket of cloud.

"Look," I plead to my parents,
heads turned away yet proud.

"Look," I beg to my reflection,
but she leaves me in the dark.

"At me," I whisper in the silence.

CHAPTER 15

Grace: May 2

People are going to stare. And whisper. The whispering will be the worst. More rumors will surface, and once they take root, they'll never be destroyed. No matter what happens from now on, our family will be looked at with suspicion. No one will feel satisfied that they got the "whole story," forgetting the fact that they aren't entitled to it.

But maybe it's selfish to even worry about that, when so many other people with missing family members are left searching for answers by themselves. Maddy's face looks good on the news, and the attention is a privilege not everyone gets.

"Here we go," I say as Adrian turns at the light by school. He squeezes my hand, offering reassurance I didn't know I needed.

He parks his car near the back of the lot, and we walk into the school, which was built on tradition and mortar, equally. The silver FOREST LANE ACADEMY letters still shine, and suddenly it's like I never left, like this is any other Thursday morning. The sun is already up, teasing us with the countdown to summer. A lot of people are walking in with friends, and the ones walking alone are checking their phones. No one notices me.

Inside, I'm met with the familiar musty smell of not-quite-clean halls and too much freshman cologne. It's bizarre to think the rest of the student body and staff have been carrying on with class the last week. People have mourned, sure. But their lives haven't been torn apart like mine.

"Stoll. Hey, Stoll." Adrian tugs on my hand. "You okay? Mrs. Miller is calling you."

"What?" I look over my shoulder to see the secretary waving me over from her desk. "Oh. I didn't hear her. My mom said she'd be waiting for me in the office," I tell Adrian.

"And my mom said I better not be late to Ms. Stroud's first period anymore," he says, forging a path through the hall while I stop at the office doors. "Homemade waffles next time," he says, waving. "I'll convince you yet."

I face Mrs. Miller at the main desk. Mom's already next to her.

"Here she is now," Mrs. Miller says, stepping away from the phones and computer. "Right this way. They're waiting for you."

They? The meeting, I thought, was supposed to be with Mrs. Richardson, the counselor who's scheduled my classes the last four years. Instead, we pass her office and enter a big conference room. Mrs. Richardson is at the table along with Principal Avery and two other staff members whose names I don't know.

They're scared of a lawsuit. Definitely.

They all stand and introduce themselves, the ones nearest my mom shaking her hand. Mom turns to me. "I'm going to talk with your administrators for a few minutes about the—the memorial." She nearly chokes on the word, but retains her composure. "And then you can come back in."

"Sure." I'm not ready to face that conversation anyway. Other students are walking through the main doors as we speak. I might be able to catch the one I need answers from.

Once in the hall, a wave of people I don't recognize floods off a bus. Freshmen and sophomores, probably. Most seniors drive themselves. Student after student pours in, chatting with friends or distracted by a screen in their hand.

A short blond girl bumps into me. "Oh sorry, I—" Recognition lights up Erica's face. "I didn't know you were coming back." When she throws her arms around me, I stiffen and pat her shoulder a few times before she withdraws. "This is my first day back at school too. I keep replaying all those memories together, all those hours spent at your house." Her eyes well up with tears.

Erica was Maddy's best friend, so of course she's upset. But she also might know why Maddy fought with me.

She clears her throat. "My mom said I could stay home because I've been so upset, but she said if I couldn't make it at school then I can't go to prom on Saturday."

Prom. The word sounds foreign. It's unbelievable that there could still be things like a dance happening this weekend, that girls could be worried about hair and nails and dresses, instead of trying to survive a raging storm of grief.

"I tried texting you a bunch last week." She smiles feebly. "I heard you weren't coming back for the rest of the year."

"I'm here with my mom trying to figure that all out. I'm not sure what's happening yet." Mrs. Miller's returned to her chair and is answering a call. "And the police haven't released my phone, so I have to use this old one," I say, taking it from my pocket.

"That makes sense," she says somberly. "I wish there was something I could do to help."

"Maybe you can," I say. "Did my sister ever tell you she was mad at me about something? Something from a long time ago?"

"Me? No, she never told me . . . Wait, is this about the fight on the trip?"

"You know about that?"

"Yes," she says, grief giving way to eagerness. "Actually, no. I mean, I wasn't on the trip, obviously, but people have been asking me nonstop for updates. My phone is blowing up every day. Next to Nicole's big day-after-prom party, it's all people are talking about. They're dying for information."

"Yeah, me too."

"You don't know what happened?"

"I can't remember anything from the trip."

Erica's eyes grow round, but where I expect sympathy, there's only fascination. "Nothing? I thought you would be able to set the record straight. You can't remember anyone who's been acting different? Weird or—"

"Jade." The name jumps out of my mouth like an answer to a quiz I'm miraculously prepared for. "Jade was acting strange when I saw her earlier."

"Jade Coleman?" She crinkles her nose. "I'm not surprised. She's been weird ever since she moved back here. I think she's still mad at the school because of freshman year."

"Why would she be mad at the school?"

"I guess they called her parents and said she had an eating disorder or something? I don't know the details, but she said her dad blamed her mom and used the phone call to get custody of her."

Maybe that has something to do with why she was at a therapist's office. No, never mind. That's not my business.

"She didn't mention anything from freshman year. Or anything else. She made it very clear she did not want to talk to me."

"Oh," she says quietly, and then, as if grasping for something to fill the space, "Everyone else on the trip's been coming up with these wild rumors." She's already pulled her phone out, scrolling and tapping. "But maybe there's truth to one. Here, I've been tracking them."

She hands me her phone to swipe through a series of screenshots.

They got lost in the woods. The school knew about it and they're covering it up. The school never cares about anybody.

The Stoll sisters knew Nicole Harris cheated on her boyfriend, Caleb Jones. They threatened to tell him, and she tried to take them out before they could.

Sixteen years ago a woman was found dead on that same road from a hit-and-run. It's been haunted ever since. No one living did this.

Mr. Gutter thought Grace spread the scandalous picture of him online. He couldn't tell them apart, so he took them both.

Mr. Holtsof was never sick. He got fired, and he drove out to the lodge to take revenge on anyone he could find.

My heart drops when I reach the last one.

I heard one of them attacked a kid at their old school, but it was all hushed up, so someone finally got justice.

"I didn't hurt Mateo." The words are automatic. It's a sentence I've told myself so many times it's buried deep in my memory, never to be forgotten, no matter how hard I hit my head.

"Wait, Mateo?" Erica leans over my shoulder to confirm which one I'm reading. "Is that the kid's name? It's true?"

"She—these—these are ridiculous," I say. "This is the kind of stuff being posted to that trash theories blog."

"It isn't trash," Erica says, snatching her phone back. "Crime blogs have helped find information police have missed in a lot of cases the last few years. It's the same as canvassing people for information."

"No, it's not. It's ruining people's lives based on rumors. Mr. Gutter could lose his job forever."

She flips her hair back and tucks her phone away. "He deserves to if he did it. There's a whole group defending him online. They say he's such a great teacher and he's been here forever, as if those things somehow clear his name."

"Yeah, and if he didn't do it? Nobody wants answers more than me, but stirring up rumors for clicks and turning us all into suspects without any evidence isn't helping. Whoever is posting that stuff is . . . Wait. Why do you have all those messages from people anyway?" But even as I ask the question, the answer crystallizes before me. "You're the one writing those blogs, aren't you?"

"Other people write them. I'm just curating them."

"Are you kidding me? You're using my sister's death to build clout!"

"I'm doing this because I care. People are invested. I care about catching whoever did this—"

"Even if it means accusing me? How could you suggest I'd hurt her? You know I loved my sister. I would never do *anything* to hurt her." My voice is rising now. Some people around us stop to stare. A few take out their phones.

Erica shouts right back. "I care about her too! She deserves for everyone to know the truth."

"You don't care about my sister or our family. You just want new followers."

"Wait—"

I storm away from her and march back toward the office. I always knew she was too immature and selfish to be a good friend to Maddy, but I had no idea she was so cruel. Or maybe she's simply stupid enough to believe she wouldn't be hurting people.

Hopefully the police have more leads than the garbage gossip Erica is spreading online.

I suppose the school could know more than they're letting on, but then why haven't the police been able to uncover it?

And Nicole. If we knew she cheated on Caleb, that could be a motive for . . . something. But I can't believe that petite, barely 115-pound girl is capable of murder. Plus, she didn't seem upset to see me at the police station.

I know I haven't had my phone, but Nicole could've come by my house. She could've visited me in the hospital. She could've found a way to reach out. In fact, I can't imagine a single reason she wouldn't contact me since I've been home.

Unless she's hiding something. I thought I was her best friend, but could she be keeping secrets? Is that why she needs a lawyer?

"Ms. Stoll?" Mrs. Miller steps into the hall. "Your mom's ready for you to come in now."

I follow Mrs. Miller back into the office, where the fate of my diploma will be decided, but my thoughts linger on my conversation with Erica. I never knew Jade's history. What else don't I know about her?

Maybe I'm making up wilder theories than those in Erica's posts.

Inside the office, the school personnel all sit with overly welcoming smiles. I take my seat next to Mom and try to imagine I'm simply sitting in this room waiting for a team picture to be taken for the yearbook.

"Glad you're feeling a little better," Principal Avery says. I assume she's referring to being discharged from the hospital, and not the emotional pain of losing my sister. "Your mom and I have made some arrangements for your sister's memorial next week, and I've already spoken to all of your teachers." She indicates a set of papers in front of her. "Your performance for the year has been satisfactory."

"How much time will I have to complete my makeup work?" I imagine the dozens of notifications piling up in my school email, ready to smother me once tech support resets my password.

"Most of your teachers are quite flexible. We all know what a hard time this is and will continue to be for you. After talking with your mom, about your . . . mental struggles, I think we can all agree that schoolwork is not the most important issue, given the circumstances."

I overlook her avoiding the topic of my memory issues like I might break at the mention of it; I'm too struck by a school administrator actually acknowledging that there's something more important than school. I knew Forest Lane Academy said they believed in "educating the whole person"—it's the central philosophy driving Senior Sabbatical in the first place—I just never expected them to back it up less than a month before graduation.

"But I still want to graduate," I say, fighting panic. I'm one of the oldest in my class as it is. I don't want to be here an extra year.

"And we want you to graduate, too," Mrs. Richardson says. "Your teachers verified that you've completed enough of the coursework to get credit for the last quarter. Many teachers are using these last few weeks to review for the finals instead of covering new material anyway." Somehow, I doubt this is true in pre-calc, but I don't interrupt. "Given the circumstances," she says, carefully, "your final exams will be waived, and your semester grade will be the average of your third and fourth quarter."

Before I'm able to confirm that I will not, in fact, need to complete a mountain of classwork while missing part of my memory, regularly battling debilitating headaches, and mourning my sister's death, a radio crackles on the table calling for Principal Avery. A laptop dings with an email. Mom's phone goes off.

One of the administrators I don't recognize speaks up. "There's an update in the news." She glances at me quickly, before tilting her screen to face Principal Avery.

Mom gasps at her phone. I lean over her shoulder. It's a message from Dad with a link:

"Arrest Made in Forest Lane Academy Murder Case."

CHAPTER 16

Maddy: April 24

Adrian liked my poems. The thought still makes me giddy the next morning in the bathroom. He might've liked them only because *I* wrote them, and somehow that makes it better. It's different from my parents, whose compliments ring hollow with obligation. He saw me. He heard *me*. And he wanted to stay with me. I smile wide enough that a glob of toothpaste falls on my shirt.

Tori appears at the sink next to me wearing a mint-green button-up pajama set with a repeating pattern of cats and yarn balls. I give a small wave with my toothbrush hanging out of my mouth while I wipe off my shirt with a paper towel.

She yawns in response. "Sorry, Grace and I stayed up late talking." She runs a brush through her not-quite-curly hair, giving it an extra half inch of frizz.

I nod and try not to drool again.

"She, uh, told me about your small-group session and Mateo."

Without meaning to, I stop brushing.

"Grace kept saying how supportive you were of her." Her face glows with admiration behind her oversize glasses. "I'm glad she had someone like you to be there for her."

"Uh-huh." I gargle, and bend over to spit. I rinse and rinse and rinse, but the bitter taste of guilt won't leave. When I stand straight, Tori's already popped in her own toothbrush, but it's easy to see she expects a reply. "Thanks. I'm glad she has you too." I leave the bathroom before she notices my hands shaking.

I'll never be able to escape what I did to Mateo. It will always return to make sure I never forget. It doesn't matter how nice I was to Grace after it happened. That doesn't erase what I did.

I must be an especially horrible person to regret being kind, and to my sister of all people.

Jade's in the room, bent over the bottom bunk, digging through one of her bags. Except when she stands, it's not Jade at all. It's Nicole.

"What are you doing?" I ask.

"Oh, um," she squeaks, jumping away from the bag like it suddenly tried to bite her slender fingers. Her ice-blue eyes dart from me to the bags to the door. "Grace was searching for her straightener and couldn't find it. She thought you might have one in your bag." She circles me, edging for the door.

"Those aren't my bags. They're Jade's."

"Oh, sorry. I'll tell Grace you don't have one." Her voice returns to normal, but she nearly trips over herself.

"Wait." I dig in my bag and extract my straightener. "I have it." But by the time I reach the doorway, Nicole is gone, without a trace, her pin-straight blond hair whipping around the corner.

"Don't think you'll have time to do your hair," Jade says, emerging from the stairwell. "Sanderson wants everyone downstairs in five."

I drop the straightener to my side in defeat. "No, I came into the room, and Nicole was digging through your stuff. She said Grace—"

"What?" Jade doesn't wait for my explanation. She pushes past me into the room and dives into her bag. T-shirts and socks litter the ground surrounding her as she pulls everything out.

"She said Grace wanted to borrow my straightener," I tell her. "She mixed up the bags."

Jade ignores me, focused on her mission. Suddenly she sits back, the phone she snuck past Mrs. Sanderson in her hand. Typing. Swiping. "That little—" She releases a low growl and shoves everything furiously back into her bag. Her face grows as red as the streaks in her hair.

I flatten myself against the dresser to stay out of her way until she rips the zipper shut.

"So, I take it this wasn't about the straightener?" I ask, setting it aside.

"No." She drops onto the bed and releases a string of cusses. "She was searching for my phone. And found it."

"Why would she want your phone?"

"Because I—" Jade stops and growls again. She tenses her

shoulders and shakes her muscles loose before speaking. "I don't know. Probably thought it would be funny. Another prank. She's the one who made that picture of Gutter with the horse. That's why I thought Grace might have been in on it with her—those two are best friends, right?"

"Yeah, they're close," I say.

Jade doesn't blink. "You think Grace could do that?"

I stop to consider it thoroughly. I wouldn't have suspected Nicole of making the pic and tagging it with *I like them young and wild,* so Grace could have . . . maybe? "No," I decide. "She wouldn't."

Jade's face falls, but I know Grace well enough to know she wouldn't risk her future by sending out a picture like that because of a test or quiz or whatever.

"Why are you so invested in Mr. Gutter's picture?" I ask.

She peers up at me and freezes. Her dark eyes betray nothing until she bursts into a laugh. "I'm not," she says, standing up and linking arms with me. "Come on, Mrs. Sanderson is waiting."

I'm not dumb. I know Jade isn't telling me everything. She doesn't trust me enough to be honest. Erica sometimes acts the same way when she doesn't want me to know what she's doing with her boyfriend. I've always heard that best friends tell each other everything, but in my experience, that's a myth to make for good TV, like when they hire thirty-year-olds to play seniors. It's a false expectation of reality.

Instead, Jade's arm looped through mine, walking down the stairs together: That's real. It might even be the beginning of a stronger friendship. I'm not about to test its limits by prying. Jade doesn't have a group of friends she's clinging to here. In fact, I can't recall who she hangs out with at school. This might be the beginning of a friendship for us both. Sabbatical is changing things, changing me, and for once I'm not alone.

Downstairs, in the main room, the morning is as gray as it's been the last two days. The wall of windows seems permanently speckled with raindrops.

"Make sure you're ready to go outside today!" Mrs. Sanderson stands at the door, catching everyone who walks in.

"In this?" I ask, pointing to the dreary windows.

"Especially in this," Mr. Gutter replies, with a weird little smile twisting under his beard.

"The forecast has taken a turn for the worse, but we can't let a little rain stop us from doing all our outdoor activities!" Mrs. Sanderson says, stepping in front of him. I definitely need to ask her what brand of coffee she drinks to ooze this much enthusiasm all the time. Still, I take a seat, because my athletic shorts and T-shirt will be fine in the rain.

"All right, everyone!" Mrs. Sanderson says when the room fills. "Our theme for today is to ACT!" Mrs. Sanderson claps as she shouts the last word. "As some of you may know, even if you're not supposed to"—she shoots a withering stare across the room for anyone who has heard Sabbatical secrets from other seniors—"today we were supposed to use the zip line course. However, Shady Oaks's liability insurance doesn't cover us in the rain."

I join the groans on this one. Adrian dramatically thunks his head against his table. When I laugh, he smiles over his shoulder at me. I have a long history that proves no one is interested in me, ever. But maybe, just this once, there's hope.

Mrs. Sanderson raises her hands. "Mr. Gutter and I knew you'd be disappointed, so we have our backup plan ready to go." Mr. Gutter walks into the front of the room holding a laundry basket filled with bottles of dish soap and what could be shampoo. "The hill on the east side of the building makes the perfect"—she pauses as she wrestles out a big blue tarp from under the dish soap, and what I now realize are bottles of baby oil—"slip and slide!"

Her theatrics unleash the intended effect, and most of the room jumps and hollers, rushing to leave the lodge.

"Let's go," I say, grabbing Jade's arm.

By the time we make it outside, the tarps are already lined up, and Ryan Jacobs is helping to cover the surface with oil. The hill is around the corner from the main drive, where the bus pulled in. Fat, heavy drops fall to the ground and hit me sporadically like hiccups.

"Wait, wait, wait!" Mrs. Sanderson calls, extending her hand to stop a few boys who are ready to charge down the tarp. "You know how this works. Nothing fun during Sabbatical without a life lesson." She waits to ensure everyone is paying attention. The dark trees silhouetted in the distance cast an ominous shadow on the grounds, and she commands even more attention than usual. "You've all reflected on your pasts this week. You've opened up to new people, but you can't simply stop there. To grow as a person, your words need to be followed up by actions. Sometimes those actions are going to look pretty miserable, like standing out in the rain." She raises her hand as the drops fall more steadily. "You might even be scared of falling down and getting hurt." She points to the slippery tarp next to her, and her voice changes for only a moment. "At this point I'd also like to remind you of the safety waivers your parents signed before you came here. But seriously," she says, her voice returning to her usual instructional tone. "You're going to fall down in life. You're going to get caught in the rain. You could let that stop you from living, or you could go along for the ride and pick yourself up when you reach the bottom."

She lifts a can of shaving cream from the basket and sprays it all over the top of the tarp. "Now go have some fun!" she shouts and releases the first two people to go. Clyde and Alyssa take off running, until they reach the edge of the tarp and throw themselves on their stomachs, leaving a trail of bubbles and white froth as their bodies fly down the hill, shooting them several feet past the edge and into the soggy grass at the bottom. They barely clear the way before the next set charges for their run.

Only a moment later, a dull thud reverberates from the bottom of the hill, followed by an echo of *oohs* and one loud *ouch*. Caleb and Clyde are both on the ground, one rubbing his head and the other gently massaging his ribs.

"Are you okay?" Mrs. Sanderson calls, jogging down the hill with her hands out at her sides to keep her balance. "Do you know how to check for a concussion?" She calls to Mr. Gutter, who meets her at the bottom. She gingerly inspects Caleb's head and checks his pupils. "Where's the first aid kit Nurse Sanchez sent with us?"

"This would never be allowed in a public school," I say with a soft laugh as both boys get up amid a round of claps and cheers from the others. "Too many risks of lawsuits. Then again, a public school would never allow a week off, in case it hurt test scores."

But Jade doesn't appear to hear me. She watches Nicole, who's pulling her silky blond hair into a ponytail and telling Grace she's going in to use the bathroom. Jade's face transforms with a devious smirk.

"What are you thinking?" I ask.

"Oh, about Sanderson's words." She doesn't tear her eyes away from Nicole disappearing back into the main doors. "You know, how important it is to *act*." She sidles next to the laundry basket of supplies and tosses a can of shaving cream in the air, catching it again easily. "What do you say? Ready for a little prank of our own?"

I wait for her to laugh like she's joking, but her face tells me she is dead serious. I bite my cheek. Hard.

The Maddy who signed up for this trip would have said no. Actually, the Maddy who signed up for this trip wouldn't have been asked at all. I would have been forgotten or intentionally uninvited, like when Grace went to Alejandra's thirteenth birthday party, and I stayed at home watching *Home Alone,* wondering how Kevin could ever want to be by himself.

Jade waggles her eyebrows at me. An open invitation to take

part in the level of fun I've missed out on for years. She *wants* me to join her. I'm *wanted.*

"Let's do it." I grab a can of my own.

Mr. Gutter and Mrs. Sanderson are too busy supervising the sliding students to even notice us sneak back into the lodge. We race through the hall, Jade whispering the plan in between laughs. We grind to a stop outside the bathroom doors. I hold a finger up to my mouth, barely able to suppress my own laughter long enough to shush Jade. She pulls the door open, and we tiptoe inside.

One stall door is closed in the middle of the row. Jade waves me to the left while taking the right. Nicole's shoes shuffle on the other side of the wall, and then her toilet flushes. I leap atop my own toilet seat, and Jade's head is already floating above the other wall. Before Nicole's hand reaches for the stall door, *schhhhhhk.*

We spray her. Shaving cream foam pours from my can and Jade's, covering Nicole's long hair in a frothy white mess of bubbles. Nicole shrieks, the massive volume of foam swallowing her petite shoulders and covering her face.

"Run!" Jade screams. I drop my can and bolt. Nicole releases a frustrated cry and fiddles with her lock, which I imagine to be impossible to find under the shaving cream, much less open in the slippery, slimy mess. Jade throws open the door, and we shoot outside.

"Go, go, go," I yell, pushing Jade forward. We hit the crowd in front of the slip and slide, but don't slow down. I knock Grace's elbow, shoving my way through until Jade and I are at the top of the tarp. My body hits the ground hard, but I'm sliding so fast, I don't have time to register pain. We slide, slide, slide all the way down with screams and squeals and more laughter than I've ever let myself peal out.

At the end of the tarp, covered in oil, soapsuds, and foam, we slide through the grass. I stop, and Jade crashes into my legs, both of us laughing so hard, no sound escapes at all. I fight to stand, only to slip some more, clutching Jade for support. She snorts, sending us both into another fit, barely able to raise ourselves off the ground.

Nicole stands on top of the hill, streaks of white covering her hair, shirt, and neck. It only makes me laugh harder, until Grace frowns at the two of us. I have a moment of guilt, but by the time Jade pulls me down again, still laughing, it's gone.

I've never lain on my back in the rain before. Each drop rinses a spot of soap from my body. The residue washes my face, my hair soaking wet. I'm breathing hard. From the run, from the fall, from the high of being so wrapped up in a joke with another person that the rest of the world falls away.

I'm contemplating how long I can stay in this moment, when Adrian stands over me, rain already soaking his shirt so it sticks to his chest.

"Looks like you might've made a new enemy," he says, snapping me back to reality.

"She can't be that mad," I say, grabbing his hand and pulling myself off the ground. "She would have been covered when she went down—whoa!" I slip on my way up, and Adrian catches me. His arms, impossibly warm in the cold rain, grip my elbows.

"Easy," he says, helping me get steady. Our eyes meet. Wet hair hangs over his brow, his curls more defined in the water.

"Thanks," I say breathlessly. He helps Jade up too.

"She'll get over it," she says, wringing some foam from her hair. "A little fun never hurt anyone."

Mirror, mirror on the wall
Who is this person I've become?

I don't recognize her voice.
I don't know her laughter.

I've been locked in a tower
Waiting for a rescue

But now that I'm free
I see the life I've been missing.

I'm not the princess to protect.
I'm the dragon spreading its wings.

My chains are broken and I'm alive.
My story could end with a happily-ever-after.

CHAPTER 17

Grace: May 2

Arrest made in the Forest Lane Academy murder case.

The words haunt me. By the time I leave this police station, I'll know who killed Maddy.

But right now, no one tells us anything.

Officer Jones shows us into Detective Howard's office to wait. Unlike the bare interview room from my last visit, this room is more informal, personal. Without a window, the space is especially cramped, with a cluttered desk and two worn chairs across from it. A photograph sits on the desk, and a Cubs banner is pinned to the wall above an empty space. A broken clock hangs next to it, permanently stuck at 7:28.

If Nicole's lawyer wasn't still forbidding her from contacting me, I'm sure she'd be sending me messages, asking if Mr. Gutter is the one arrested. Unlike Erica, she'd actually care about the truth, not the rumors.

I don't know if it's Mr. Gutter. I don't know anything, because no one will tell us anything.

I search the web for updates. The original report is only a few sentences long, saying police came to a French Lake home and drove away with one of its residents. A name, however, is not listed. The rest of the article covers the details of our case again, offering nothing new.

"What's taking them so long?" I poke my head out the door.

"I'm sure we'll get answers soon," Mom says. Her jiggling leg betrays her—that and the way she shouted at a young officer for updates when we arrived, before Jones showed us into Detective Howard's office. Mom's no more patient than I am, but if she's trying to make me feel better, the least I can do is play along.

I flop back into the chair and refresh my search results.

Mom's already disposed of old receipts and expired coupons from her purse. She's moved on to pulling a tissue from the box on Detective Howard's desk and wiping furiously at a black streak running across the fake leather. Waiting isn't easy on either of us. She cleans and I research. Both of us avoid discussing the what-ifs.

When the door opens, I expect it to be an officer, someone who will tell us the unreported details from the media release.

Instead, Dad comes in, still talking on the phone with, it sounds like, someone from work. He hugs Mom and kisses my forehead in between giving instructions to whomever is on the other end of the call, and then hangs up.

"I'm sorry, I got here as soon as I could," he tells Mom. She doesn't say anything, but I know she's filing this instance away in her mental drawer of Things to Yell at Husband about Later. Dad ignores her irritation. "The officer in the hall said Detective Howard should be in soon."

"He should be here already," I say. I shouldn't expect a man with a broken clock to respect people's time.

The door clicks open, and Detective Howard comes in, laptop under his arm. "Sorry to have kept you waiting," he says, taking his seat behind the desk. "It's been a busy day."

"Is that because you arrested someone?" I ask.

Before he's able to answer, Mom says, "I thought you were going to report any major developments in the case to us."

"That information wasn't supposed to be released to the public. I don't know how the local media got hold of it." Our local media *and* the paper from French Lake. Both towns are following developments closely.

"The articles didn't give a name," I say. "Who is it?" I don't know which name I'm expecting to hear. One I recognize.

Detective Howard takes a long sip of coffee. "The article is misinformed. We brought someone in for questioning, not on any charges."

After all this waiting, we're no closer to an answer than we were yesterday.

"Questioning still sounds like a development," Dad says over my shoulder. Detective Howard does not respond or apologize. He opens his computer and types a few things without giving the screen too much attention.

"But who is it?" I ask. Mr. Gutter still isn't back at school.

"Someone who lives near the lake. He had a prior offense involving a minor."

Definitely not Mr. Gutter. He doesn't live an hour away from school, and if he had a prior offense, he'd never be employed as a teacher. But then . . .

"An offender? Like a pedophile?" Mom expresses my thoughts, her voice high and tight.

I clutch my arms. Maybe the head injury didn't affect my memory. Maybe my psyche is protecting me from things too horrible to remember—hands grabbing, mouths screaming . . .

I squeeze my eyes shut. No. I can't go there.

Detective Howard doesn't answer Mom's question. Instead, he says, "We are conducting a thorough investigation and covering our bases, but the person in question has an alibi."

If it wasn't this sicko, was it another? Missing my memory's always been . . . disorienting. Frustrating. Confusing. For the first time, it's terrifying. The echo of Maddy's shout. Our feet running. Cold sweat breaks out across my forehead.

What happened to us?

Sh. Sh. Sh.

"So, it wasn't him?" Dad asks, fists clenched.

"As I said, we are doing a thorough investigation," the detective repeats. I squeeze my arms and rock back and forth.

Dad paces. "You told us you would keep us updated on progress. How come we weren't notified?"

"I assure you, when there are concrete developments in the case, you will be informed."

"How much more concrete do things need to be after my

sister drowns by some sicko's house? How do you know he's not lying about an alibi?"

Detective Howard studies me carefully for a moment. He's decided on something, but I don't know what. "We brought him in for questioning, but his alibi's been confirmed by several trustworthy sources." He draws out the last three words. The room grows quiet. He turns to his laptop and types while he says, "I was actually planning to call you down to the station later today before we got a hit on this person of interest."

Dad stops pacing, and Mom clutches her purse more tightly.

"The medical examiner's report came back with a cause of death." Detective Howard refers to his screen. "We found water in her lungs, indicating she drowned as we suspected. But there was also distinct bruising on her chest and arm."

"Distinct?" Dad asks.

"May I?" The detective's hands are positioned to show us.

Dad swallows slowly, but nods.

Detective Howard rotates his laptop to show us: Maddy's skin, dull and pale and white, against a dark deep-purple bruise. A handprint. Four distinct fingers meeting a thumb, wrapped around the arm in a vise grip.

She must have been in pain. So much pain. She might have screamed. Did I hear her?

"Someone gripped her arm pretty tightly to leave a dark mark like that. Notice the size, though. The thumb and forefinger barely meet." He points to the gap between the bruising and then faces me, despite directing his next statement to my parents. "Whoever grabbed your daughter's arm was small."

The detective's eyes drop to my hands, and I fold them in my lap.

"Another student?" Dad asks, squeezing the back of Mom's chair.

Detective Howard swings his computer back around and clicks a few more times. "As you know, we didn't get many details from the other students when we questioned them on that Friday. However, we've had more time to go over the items collected on the school trip. Do you recognize this?" He rotates the laptop forward again to show me a marble composition notebook with *Grace* written on the cover in black marker. Black Sharpie.

"It's one of the notebooks from the trip," I say. "We wrote in them a lot."

Detective Howard cocks his head.

"A friend from Sabbatical told me about it."

Detective Howard sets his coffee aside. "So you have no"—he waves his hand in the air as if he's searching for a word, even though his tone tells me he already knows it—"personal recollection of this notebook or its contents?"

Mom grabs Dad's hand.

"No."

Detective Howard examines me the same way Dr. Cramer does when she's waiting for me to say more.

"Is it possible you can't remember that week because you don't want to?"

"No." I clench my jaw. "I'm trying to remember."

Is that skepticism I detect? Or resignation? He clicks to another image. "This letter was found in the last page of the notebook, separate from all the other writing from the trip. Do you know anything about it?" We all lean closer to read. After a minute, Mom gasps.

Dear Grace,

Why are you so obsessed with being perfect all the time? You put all this energy into making the best grades and becoming a team hero on the court and never doing anything wrong . . . and for what?

If people knew the real you, the one you try so hard to keep hidden, they'd be disappointed. That truth's too hard to handle, isn't it? Think for yourself for a change and stop caring about everyone else. You're not as smart as they think or as talented. I know it. You know it. Why can't you just accept it and move on? Your life would be easier for it. You might even be a better person for it.

You have circles and circles of friends, guys messaging you all the time, parents who have sacrificed more money and time than should be legal . . . and are you even worth it? Who are you, really, without the grades or without volleyball? Do you even know what you want to do with your life? Get it together!

"I don't understand," I say. Someone hated me enough to write this letter and put it in my notebook? Who would be so cruel?

"Why are you showing us this?" Mom asks. The pain from each day since the first missing person report stays etched on her face, the redness already swelling in her eyes.

Detective Howard locks his jaw, like he's steeling himself. "Mrs. Stoll, were you aware of this conflict?"

"N-no," Mom stammers. Dad runs a shaky hand over his face.

"What do you—" But then I recognize the handwriting, and I can't believe it. I genuinely can't. "No, it can't be," I whisper.

My sister's handwriting stares up at me from the page, as familiar as my own.

Detective Howard clicks one button to reveal the rest of the letter.

You're the older sister. You're supposed to set the example. That's what Mom always says. Accept who you really are and be happy for it. Stop pretending to be something better.

Sincerely,
The Stoll Daughter No One Sees
When You're Around

The word *hate* never appears in the letter, but her resentment stains the paper like the ink her bitter words are written in.

The Stoll Daughter No One Sees When You're Around.

We were always different, no matter how much people said we looked the same, but this intense hostility? It can't be real. Maddy filled her notebooks with poetry and stories. Fiction. This . . . this must be fake. An example of one of those literary terms like *irony* or *satire* or something. Not *evidence*.

I push the laptop away. A noise escapes my throat, something caught between a cry—from the sheer and utter pain tearing through me—and a laugh—from the absurdity of questioning Maddy's hatred, when it's printed here in black and white.

You're not as smart as they think or as talented. I know it. You know it.

This letter is real.

"These are strong emotions here," Detective Howard says. "We believe it may be connected to how your daughter died."

I cover my ears. They think . . . they think it means . . . I don't want to finish the thought.

They believe I took revenge on her. Hated her. Hurt her.

"I've never seen this letter before," I say, pushing my chair back from his desk.

"Forgive me, but as you've stated several times, you've been diagnosed with a traumatic brain injury and have experienced memory problems, correct? Can you be sure you've never seen this letter before?"

"I—I don't—"

"But you did know she drowned. Even though that official cause of death only crossed my desk this morning."

Mom pales. "What are you suggesting?" Dad's confusion surrenders to horrible understanding and realization. He stumbles back against the wall. Detective Howard ignores them and focuses on me. I know exactly what he's thinking.

This man believes I killed my own sister.

And I can't remember enough to prove him wrong.

"She obviously felt strongly while writing this," he says. "You were able to tell us where her body was. You knew how she died."

"She was found in a lake! Of course she drowned!" I yell and find my hands tugging on my hair. "If I knew more, why wouldn't I have told you about it?"

"Now just a minute," Mom says, but Detective Howard keeps pushing like she never spoke at all.

"You and your sister argued during Sabbatical."

"I don't remember."

"Several students reported it. Could she have attempted to act on these feelings? Perhaps you tried to stop her. Perhaps in the struggle, things got out of control." He points to my head, to the stitches none of us can see beneath my hair but know are there.

"No." She wouldn't have given me these stitches. I wouldn't have killed her. "It wouldn't have led to this!"

How could it? Maddy and I hardly ever fought.

The beginning of a headache radiates against the base of my skull until it's right behind my eyes. I push back on it with the heels of my hands and rock.

"So, you remember arguing with her?"

Dad leans over the desk, fists planted firmly on top of it. "What are you getting at, Detective?"

Detective Howard leans around him. "Do you or do you not remember arguing with her?"

"No," I say, shivering. "I don't remember it. But other people told me we did."

"What else did they tell you?" He doesn't wait for an answer. "Who left the lodge first? Was it her? Was she still upset like she was in this letter, and you went after her? What did you say to her?"

My throat goes dry. I can't speak.

"We received the results of that blood test from your clothes. Some of it is hers. Do you know how it got there?"

I was with her. I know I was. I was with her in the water. But why were we there? The headache pounds against my skull, and I pound back with my fists. Remember. Remember. Remember.

Sh. Sh. Sh.

Dad throws open the door. "We've had enough questions for one day."

Detective Howard doesn't break eye contact with me while he slowly leans back in his chair. His voice is low and calm. "I'm merely suggesting your daughter may know more than she claims."

But I don't. I can't. I want to tell him again, but only a sob escapes.

"I think we need a lawyer," Mom says.

"You're free to go at any time," Detective Howard says, waving his hand.

"You're supposed to be investigating my dead daughter's

murder," Dad says, a vein I've never seen before popping out of his neck. "Not interrogating this one."

"My job, Mr. Stoll, is to discover the truth of what happened that night. And if your daughter isn't able to remember, we only have the evidence in front of us to go on."

CHAPTER 18

Maddy: April 24

We clean up all evidence of the slip and slide before we shower and spend the rest of the afternoon indoors, gathering in the main room, killing time before the teachers call lights out.

It's hard to concentrate when Nicole keeps shooting suspicious glares my way. My notebook is open to the sixth draft of a poem I've been revising but can't seem to get right.

"I could totally go for a slushy," Ryan Jacobs says.

"We could probably walk to the gas station and get some," Nicole says, squinting at the clock. "It's only, like, a mile down the road."

"How do you know?"

"We have a house on French Lake, and after a whole day on the boat in the summer, those slushies are the best." She throws her head back so the light catches the little diamond stud in her nose.

Caleb scowls from across the room. It's the first time this whole trip he hasn't been attached to Nicole's hip.

"Need I remind you that you're not allowed to leave?" Mrs. Sanderson asks, getting up to address the group.

"Hot Stuff would have let us if he was here," Nicole mumbles.

"Well," Mr. Gutter says, coming up behind Nicole. "Mr. *Holtsof* isn't on this trip. We are."

"But it's so boring," Ryan whines, either oblivious to Nicole huffing at Gutter and his stern glare in her direction, or else actively trying to distract them both. "We were supposed to play capture the flag outside tonight, weren't we?" The rain still splatters against the window, the reason no one's having fun.

Tori sits behind Grace, braiding her hair. I shouldn't let it bother me. I won't be able to do it for her next year, when she's at Trin U, anyway.

"I hope we still visit the caves tomorrow," Grace says. The longing in her voice is deeper than only wanting to have fun.

Ryan plasters a charming smile on his face, the one that he tries to use to avoid consequences but that never manages to appear sincere, and addresses Mrs. Sanderson. "Come on, we need something to do."

"We still have all the flashlights from capture the flag . . ." Mrs. Sanderson's voice trails off as she goes to the corner of the room, unburies the box, and kills the lights. Darkness cloaks the room until *click*. Mrs. Sanderson flicks on a flashlight and shines it directly at the group.

"Hide-and-seek, anyone?" Nicole says, jumping up and grabbing another flashlight.

After promising Mrs. Sanderson many times that they'll stay indoors and not go anywhere off-limits, Ryan and Nicole recruit virtually everyone else to play. Caleb sulks in the corner.

“One. Two. Three.” Ryan and Nicole count together. Nicole staves off giggles, and Ryan shouts like he’s calling a play on the field. The rest of us scatter.

I race up to the second floor where everyone sleeps. “Thirty-four. Thirty-five.” Nicole’s and Ryan’s voices echo up the stairwell, picking up with the intensity of the rain outside.

It would be weird to hide in someone else’s room, but Grace’s room is on the left. She won’t care. I fling open the door, and a light whips into my face, blinding me. I raise my arm to block the beam, but I can’t see who’s holding the flashlight.

“Maddy?” When it lowers, I recognize the red-and-black hair pulled into two low buns.

“Jade?” I gasp, my heart in my throat from the surprise. “What are you doing in here?”

“Sixty-seven, sixty-eight.” The counting rises and falls with bursts of energy.

“Hiding,” she whispers. She drops a cat-shaped pillow and dives across the room to the closet. “Come on.”

I maneuver inside with her, then push the door shut so the darkness wraps around us like a blanket. We crouch on the floor, and I quiet my breathing, which suddenly sounds like a roaring wind tunnel.

“Ninety-nine, one hundred!” Ryan’s and Nicole’s shouts drift faintly through the floors. “Ready or not, here we come!”

Jade stifles a laugh, and I bite my lips trying not to fall into the same fit. “Shh,” I plead.

“Okay, okay,” she whispers, shifting into a more comfortable position. I pull my knees up to my chest, waiting.

Someone screams in the dark, and Ryan’s voice booms from

another room, "Found one!" Thunder rolls outside and rattles the windows of the old building.

Another few minutes pass in silence, and then, "Who's Mateo?"

Jade's question, whispered quietly and innocently, screams in my ears.

Not again. Mateo. Will he ever go away? I never mention him.

"How do you know that name?"

Her face is invisible, a black hole next to me. "You kept calling it out in your sleep last night. You sounded really upset."

Silence surrounds us, except for blood pounding in my ears. I wouldn't be surprised if Jade can hear it too. I can't remember any of my dreams from last night, but I know I fell asleep thinking about him. No one had spoken that name in four years before yesterday.

"So, who is he?" The words are small, but the question is heavy.

Mateo is the secret I've been hiding. The piece of my story I've worked so hard to forget. It's appropriate that she questions me about him here, in a dark closet, tucked away in shadows. That's where it all started. That's where I've been fighting to keep him ever since.

Mrs. Sanderson's words come back to me. If I want to change, I have to be open. I have to remember. I have to act.

"My biggest regret," I finally say.

Jade waits. She can't see me. I don't need to look her in the eye. It's almost as if she isn't here at all. I could be whispering to an empty room. But if silence hasn't eased the guilt these last four years, maybe it's time to finally confess the truth.

"Mateo Ramirez-Hernandez." Most other girls were writing Casey's or Chris's names on their notebooks, but I preferred Mateo's dark hair swooped to the side and his darker eyes. "I had a huge crush on him all through elementary school. I thought that if I kept it secret for long enough, he would actually notice me. But in junior high, at the winter semiformal, with my new dress, and my hair done, and makeup on, I believed I looked pretty enough to *make* him notice me. So, I asked him to dance."

I remember it like someone snapped a picture and tacked it up in my mind, a twisted achievement framed forever and mocking me. I was so confident when I asked and already dreaming of his hands lingering on my waist. His eyes would find mine as we swayed to the music, and he would feel the same thing I'd been feeling for so long.

"He said no?" Jade whispers. I could've forgotten she was here at all, but now that the story is unraveling, I don't know if I can stop.

"Worse. He said, 'Hang on a second,' and disappeared. The next song started, and he didn't return." I stood there, in the middle of the gym with couples swaying around me, alone. Mateo never came for me. I was dumb enough to think he'd gone for a drink or couldn't find me. Anything would have been better than the truth. "I went searching for him, and I found him. On the dance floor. With another girl."

"Don't tell me . . ."

"Grace."

If he had chosen any other girl that night, I would've been hurt, but he chose Grace. I knew, somehow, with 100 percent certainty that he hadn't confused us. He'd left me to ask her for a dance, and she'd said yes. And there they were, his hands resting on her waist instead of mine. It destroyed me.

Our dresses and hair may have been different, but our bodies, our faces were nearly identical. If Mateo had chosen her over me, it wasn't for some superficial reason like looks. It was because of *me,* of who I am. I could change my looks. I could learn about makeup or curl my hair, but I didn't know how to change *me*. Because I didn't know what was wrong with me.

But there must be something wrong to make a boy, an otherwise nice boy, run to the other version of me. The better version.

The most embarrassing piece is that all these years later, I still don't know what it is. I don't know what's wrong with me that I don't have more friends. I don't know why I've never had a boyfriend. Somewhere along the way I decided that if I hid more of myself, no one else would discover what was wrong with me either.

"What did you do?" Jade asks gently.

"I went under the bleachers and cried. Until they sat in the seats over me."

I'd recognized her shoes first. They were the black heels that I wanted, but I'd let her wear them because I got my first pick of the dresses. Grace was laughing, her gentle giggle that charms everyone around her. And then I heard his voice.

"He told her how pretty she was. I think she asked him about his next basketball game." I couldn't be sure because I was too focused on the sound of my heart shattering and fighting back tears. "Grace's purse was at her feet, and inside she had our cell phone. I didn't want to stay at the dance, so I reached up to get her purse and text my parents, but at the same moment, they stood up . . . and he tripped."

I imagine it all in slow motion. His toe catching on the strap as I pulled the purse down. Grace's gasp as he flung forward. Her arms outstretched behind him. She kept telling everyone later that she tried to catch him, that it only appeared as though she'd been the one to push him.

"He fell. Hard and fast. The music stopped. The lights came on. The teachers rushed to his side. Someone called 911, and in the chaos, no one noticed me under the bleachers."

No one looked at me.

No one ever looked at me, but they should have.

"At first, everyone seemed to accept that it was an accident. The teachers and chaperones didn't believe Grace would purposely hurt someone, and it was an accident." I repeated those last four words to myself a million times over the last four years with varying inflections:

It was an *accident*. You couldn't have done anything to stop it.

It was *an* accident. Don't punish yourself forever.

It *was* an accident. Why can't you accept that?

It was an accident. . . . But never telling Grace the truth? That's a choice.

"The other students wanted someone to pay. They glared at Grace in the classrooms and whispered about her in the hall, pointing, not even trying to hide it. Someone even took her name and picture out of the yearbook, but the editors claimed to have no idea how it happened. They left notes in her locker telling her she was worthless, she deserved to die."

That's when Mom and Dad decided to transfer schools, to move, to switch our phone plans. After all those changes, it would still take months of therapy for Grace to move forward from the guilt and shame.

Or so I thought. But she's still dealing with the trauma.

And it was all my fault, not hers.

"Wow," Jade whispers. "That's so messed up. And you've never told anyone?"

I shake my head before I remember she can't see me, but Jade seems to know.

"No wonder you never said anything. When I was thirteen, I wouldn't have been brave enough to take on a mob like that either. That's a huge overreaction to thinking a kid was pushed."

Before I can correct her, before I can work up the courage to tell her the rest of the story, she speaks again.

"But you should tell Grace."

"That's not an option."

"No, seriously. My dad didn't tell my mom that he wanted a change in their marriage and it ruined them. When he finally said something, it was too late for them to move past." Her low voice quivers in a way I never imagined her confidence would allow, but she recovers so quickly, I'm not sure I heard it at all. "It changed them both. For the worse. He said I had an eating disorder and blamed it on my mom. Said she was obsessed with her diet and exercise and it was rubbing off on me. That's how he got custody of me."

For a moment, I don't even know what to say. Somehow, I know that if the lights were on, if Jade could see me, she might not have confided this truth, just as I might not have admitted to what happened with Mateo.

"I'm so sorry he did that to you. He never should have lied about something like that. Don't they check that kind of thing?"

She shifts in the dark. "It doesn't matter. He convinced the judge. What matters is he could've done things differently and he didn't, and it ruined all our lives."

Even though the darkness hides everything surrounding us, I face her. "Then it's probably already too late for me and Grace. She believes I was a saint during that whole time. I could've left her alone, ignored her. But instead I—"

"Was a good sister," she finishes.

"No. Instead I was the worst sister. Instead, every hug, every tissue, every comfort—everything was a lie. I let her believe I was this saintly sister who'd stick by her through her darkest valley. But I was the one who kicked her down in the first place."

"You weren't trying to make her think you were an angel. You were trying to acknowledge her pain."

"I was trying to make my guilt disappear." I don't bother to whisper any more.

"You still need to tell her." Jade's volume matches mine, the game forgotten. "It's not fair that she doesn't know."

"It won't make anything better. If she found out—"

The closet door flies open. Grace stands over us, her flashlight flicking from face to face.

"What are you arguing about? If who found out what?"

I jump to my feet. "Nothing."

Grace studies me skeptically. I know her well enough to know she's putting puzzle pieces together in her head, and I need to stop her.

"Fine," I say, making a big show of flopping my arms to my sides. "If Nicole ever found out we were the ones who sprayed her this afternoon."

Grace laughs and puts a hand on her hip. "There's a *distinct* possibility she already knows. It's not as if you were subtle about it."

"Wait," Jade says. "Where *is* Nicole? She's supposed to be finding people."

Grace points into the hall. "She's not one to forgive and forget," she says. Jade pushes past Grace, and I follow her. People who have already been found are in the narrow hall, but there's a group gathered around our doorway, whooping and laughing. Something hangs from the ceiling above our door.

"Excuse me," I say, nudging my way into the middle of the crowd. Something flies through the air and hits me in the chest. The hall light flicks on. I pick up the item that fell at my feet. Purple fabric.

Underwear.

Jade breaks through the crowd first with a shriek of colorful expletives.

Three more pairs of her underwear are tossed and flung among the crowd to more catcalls and jeers. Two bras hang from their straps directly over our doorway. The people who aren't participating stand around acting shocked while poorly containing their laughter. Nicole stands a little ways down the hall, leaning nonchalantly against a doorframe like she's watching an old show she's seen a thousand times but still finds amusing.

Jade tries and fails to jump and pull her items down, but with her height, her fingertips don't even graze the edge, and her desperate efforts only elicit more laughter.

I snatch a purple polka-dotted pair from the air and shout, "What is wrong with you people?"

Jade, with a deep blush spreading up her neck and into her cheeks, makes another stunted swipe for her bras, but Adrian breaks through from the other end of the hall and pulls them down with a good stretch on his toes. Jade snatches both from his hands and slams our door shut as a black thong singshots into wood behind her.

"Gutter on the stairs!" The whisper-yell scuttles up the hall, and everyone dives into the closest room, Nicole disappearing like a snake in the grass. Grace helps me gather the last few pairs of underwear before Gutter reaches the top, but when I duck in our room, Jade is already in bed, face to the wall.

Most of the contents of her bag are strewn around the floor, so I quietly place the underwear back in her bag. Maybe it will be easier if she can pretend it never happened. I get ready for bed and climb into the top bunk.

In the dark again, the silence around us once more, Jade says, "Thank you." When I don't respond she says, "You're not the same kid you were. You just proved it."

She doesn't say the last part, that I should tell Grace, but I can hear it threaded between her words.

I fold the pillow over my ears so I can only hear the sound of my heartbeat. She doesn't know what she's asking. She wouldn't be saying that if she did. She wouldn't even want to be in the same room with me if she knew.

It takes me a long time to fall asleep, as it has so many times in the last four years. The same thoughts play over and over and over again in my head, no matter how many times I tell them to stopstopstop.

His toe catching on the strap as I pull the purse down. Grace's gasp as he flings forward. Her arms outstretched behind him. The music stopping. The teachers running. Someone screaming. The chaperones kept everyone away, but I still remember seeing his hand between their feet. His fingers were half-curled. Still. Like he was waiting for someone to reach down, take his hand, and whisper that everything would be all right.

So many things went wrong so quickly. He should've caught himself on the railing, not gone over the side. The railing should've held his weight, not crashed to the ground. The metal should've been strong and sturdy, not shoddy and loose. The fall should've broken his arm, not snapped his neck.

He should've gotten up and walked away.

He shouldn't have died.

i never meant to hurt anyone and i never wanted anyone to die. the pain i caused is like a razor blade **SH**aving away any joy, always threatening to pierce the delicate surface until the truth bleeds out. it lurks in the **SH**adows of night, stares me in the face every day, and i cannot hide. its watchful gaze will not let me sleep. i cannot **SH**ut my eyes without those memories haunting my dreams, reminding me of the death i saw, of how i destroyed the lives of people around me. my guilt does not blink, never tires or grows weary, but keeps a **S**teady watch for any moment i might dare to forget the damage i have done. the **T**ruth whispers to me, the gentle breath of death brushing against my ear **A**t the close of every day and the break of every dawn. and the whisper grows, worming its wa**Y** into my thoughts, burrowing deep so it can pounce on any moment of bliss, rise in a howl of pain and anguish, of mourning and de**S**truction. no matter how hard i try to deny the truth, no matter how hard i pretend i am innocent, **I** don't deserve a moment of peace, when i am the one who brought discord and death. the rea**L**ity of what i have done stays buried deep inside, but it is screaming, shouting, crying to com**E** out, to escape, to be known. i shove it down to the depths of my memories, block it out whe**N**ever i can, deny its existence, and when the truth begins to bubble up, i burn it out wi**T**h lies.

CHAPTER 19

Grace: May 2

I would never hurt Maddy.

She was my sister and I loved her and I would never hurt her.

No matter what she did or said, I would never ever hurt her.

But I can't remember for sure.

Despite what I want to believe, from what Adrian said, Maddy and I did fight that night. Maybe she gave me that letter, and I was so hurt that I left. Maybe she followed me.

Or maybe I made her so angry that she stormed out, and I was the one who went after her. Even if I never meant to hurt my sister, her death might still be my fault.

The whole conversation from Detective Howard's office plays over and over in my head while we drive home. Mom doesn't say a word. She thinks I won't notice the tears falling down her cheeks if she doesn't wipe them away. I can't tell if she's surprised to know how much Maddy hated me or if the letter simply confirmed a truth she's been struggling to ignore. There's a chance she observed the distance growing between her daughters and had been crying quietly all along.

I lean my head against the window. Maybe I didn't know Maddy like I thought I did. She was in my life before I was a year old, and we shared a room since we moved to this house four years ago, but I never . . . I never knew she felt that way about me.

I can't believe the words. *Accept who you really are and be happy for it. Stop pretending to be something better.* They hurt because I'm afraid they're true. I'm nothing special. I've devoted my life to volleyball, to trying to be the best off the court and on. But I wasn't a good sister.

My head thrums with pain. I wince and suck in air between my teeth. The cool glass of the window offers a distraction.

I don't understand what happened. I don't know how my sister died. But maybe the worst part is not knowing why I survived. I don't deserve to be here any more than she does, and maybe even less. Yet here I am. My heart's still beating. My lungs are still breathing. My sister is going to be buried six feet under the cold, hard ground, and I'm still moving forward.

It's not fair. She didn't deserve to die, and now it feels like I have to prove I deserve to live, that I deserve this future facing me, that I'll become the person she never got a chance to be.

I don't even know who I am now.

When we park in the garage, I climb out before my mom kills the engine. I leave the door open for Fizzy to greet her and take the stairs two at a time.

This morning I thought it was impossible when Adrian told me Maddy and I had fought during the trip, but that letter was filled with *old stuff*, just like he said. If Maddy hated me, it had been long and simmering. The evidence will be in more than a Senior Sabbatical notebook.

If I can't figure out who I am, I'm going to learn who she was once and for all.

I shut the bedroom door and grab the stack of notebooks off the shelf. Two are filled with blank pages. Another with what could be the start of a story. A third has the first quarter filled with Spanish notes from sophomore year, but nothing personal.

I cast the notebooks aside, scanning the room. She wouldn't leave her journal out. She never revealed her real feelings to me, so she wouldn't risk me finding her notebook. She would hide it. Somewhere. Somewhere in this room.

I try to see the space from Maddy's perspective. We share our closet. But not all of the dresser. I plunge my hands into her drawers but find only clothes: underwear, swimsuits, T-shirts, and pajamas. No journal.

Under the bed.

I throw my hair into a ponytail and grab my phone for light, but there's no notebook there. I stretch my arms between the mattress and the box spring. Nothing. It's too obvious. She wouldn't hide it there. I lie back on the floor, the headache pounding strong against my eyes.

I need to know. Now. No more waiting for answers. I have to know what she thought of me, what she really saw when she looked at me. I have to know if those words are true. If I'm as awful and disappointing as she said. I need to know what I did to make her write them.

As much as Maddy's letter pounds through my skull with every streak of pain, it's closely followed by the horror on my parents' faces. During the last week, worry has clung to their limbs, weighing them down as they sat next to my bed in the hospital. Then their faces would light up with hope that I might remember something and bring Maddy home safe, only to be darkened by disappointment when I failed.

They think I don't notice Dad's face, thinner than it was two weeks ago, or his shoulders, hunched and sagging. They think I don't hear the broken notes in Mom's voice or see the tremble in her hand when she stands in front of our family picture in the hall. Staring. Studying the broken family that will never be the same, the smiles that have disappeared.

I thought the anguish of hearing Maddy is dead would be the worst, the lowest.

But I was wrong.

Nothing will compare to their faces in Detective Howard's office when they heard I might be the one responsible. They told Detective Howard he was mistaken, but they couldn't hide the doubt on their faces or the fear flashing in their eyes.

I never want them to look at me like that again. And the only way to ensure that is to find the truth. I *need* to know. The harder I try to remember what happened, the murkier that week becomes. But if I can't know what happened on the trip, then I need to know *her.* I need to find her notebooks. I need to think like Maddy.

Pain.

It slices through the base of my skull and rises. I push my

palms against my temples and squeeze my eyes shut, breathing through the throbbing. If I take Dr. Thelsman's prescription now, I'll be asleep before I get answers.

Inhale. Exhale.

Where would she put a notebook?

Inhale. Exhale.

Where would she hope I wouldn't look?

Inhale. Exhale.

When I open my eyes, I'm staring up at the bottom of a drawer. She wouldn't hide it *in* the dresser, but then again . . . I jump up and wrench the top drawer open again. There. Yes! Underneath, balanced between the center slide and the bottom wood, is a notebook.

It's small with a sturdy green cover. Inside, each page is dated. Maddy's loopy scrawl fills nearly every line. The pages crinkle from her pen pushing to the corners, using up every inch.

I'm seeing Maddy in a new light.

She had plans with Erica to watch a movie last July, but when she arrived at the theater, Erica didn't show. She got a text saying Erica and her boyfriend had decided to watch a different movie and would meet up with Maddy after. Maddy went into the theater herself. And still she writes that she understands: *Of course Erica deserved to spend time with her boyfriend alone.*

She was hurting and she never admitted how badly, but it's here, between the lines.

In November, she wrote about a concert she and Erica discussed getting tickets for. Erica went to that show with Zoey and didn't mention it to Maddy until after, like she didn't remember they'd made plans. And Maddy said nothing about it. She sat at the lunch table listening to their stories, and only cried later that night.

I don't remember hearing her cry. I didn't know any of this happened. Was I truly that absorbed in my own world, or was she that good at hiding her secrets?

There are plenty of entries featuring me.

Mom noticed my silence in the car today as Grace talked about Jackson liking her and maybe asking her to senior prom, even though she's only a sophomore. She doesn't know if she wants to go. Why would you not? I can't get a guy in our grade to look at me, and she's turning down requests for prom *already.*

Several more entries rant about me not inviting her places. The beach. The movies. A basketball game. By the end, the picture is pretty clear.

I didn't know Maddy at all.

I always thought she was happy to be with Erica, that she didn't want to go out with my friends, that she never enjoyed the big parties and sitting in the student section. But I was wrong. She only hated the way people made her feel when she was there: ignored.

And I ignored her too.

I stopped inviting her long ago and accepted that was who she was and who she wanted to be. Instead, she was someone else entirely. I was as much the cause of her pain as anyone else. Maybe more. And it wasn't because I was doing something *to* her. I didn't call her names or steal her stuff or tell people at school embarrassing stories.

I let her slip into the background. Be a wallflower. Hover on the edges of everyone else living their lives without ever inviting her to join.

As that guilt settles in, something else rises.

Anger.

It screams to reach the surface.

Why didn't she say anything? Why did she never tell Erica what a crappy friend she was? I wouldn't have sat through lunch, nodding and smiling like a puppet while Erica laughed and squealed about the concert *we* were supposed to attend together. *I* would've said something instead of being a doormat. Why didn't Maddy? How could she convince herself something was wrong with *her* or that friendships sometimes hurt that deeply? She should've *said* something. She should've told me she wanted to hang out instead of being hurt when I didn't invite her. She shouldn't have let her jealousy fester and tear us apart.

She shouldn't have made me the villain in her story.

I slam the notebook shut and throw it across the room, where it crashes into my volleyball trophies. They tumble to the floor and land in a pile, burying the notebook.

If she did tell me during Sabbatical, I wouldn't have reacted in anger.

Would I?

Did I?

Another headache blossoms in the back of my head, creeping up my skull and inching toward my forehead.

I wouldn't have hurt my sister.

I wouldn't.

I wouldn't.

I wouldn't.

But maybe I did.

Sh. Sh. Sh.

I try to silence the images flashing in my mind, but they keep coming.

Sharpie. Shoes. Shouting. My fingers wrapped around her cold wrist.

I measure out the number of pills Dr. Thelsman prescribed and swallow. I shut off the lights and shut out the thoughts. With my head on the pillow—of my own bed—I allow sleep to comfort me.

Sh. Sh. Sh.

CHAPTER 20

Maddy: April 25

The next morning, Jade grumbles about Nicole under her breath as she gets ready. Twice now Nicole has come in and gone through her things, first in secret and then very publicly.

Jade shoves her sweatpants into her bag but doesn't speak a word to me the whole time we get ready and walk downstairs, not even to push me about airing my own dirty laundry to Grace.

Then again, I don't need her to. Her voice has been playing in my head since I woke up. *It's not fair that she doesn't know.* Jade's right. I know that. But it's a secret I've been keeping for so long that I don't know how to say it.

Even if I can accept Mateo's accident wasn't my fault—a big *if* that comes and goes in waves, one that requires reminding myself that the manufacturers of the bleachers paid his family a settlement for faulty materials—I still can't forget the pain and cruelty Grace endured from those other kids.

Things would be different if Grace was over it. If it didn't bother her anymore. But I heard the pain in her voice. Old wounds aren't a scratch on skin. They're a poison contaminating our blood, traveling through our minds, infecting our hearts.

Confessing to her won't be an antidote. It will set that poison on fire.

And still, that voice keeps tugging at my conviction.

It's not fair that she doesn't know.

"You look as tired as I feel," Adrian says, sitting next to me as everyone gets settled for the first activity of the day. Mrs. Sanderson and Mr. Gutter stand at the back, riffling through some papers.

"I didn't sleep so well," I say, sliding over to make more room at the table.

"Yeah, it took me a while to fall asleep too. How can people stand around watching that without stepping in to stop it?"

I know he's referring to what happened to Jade, but I can't fight the fresh wave of guilt washing over me because I did the same thing to Grace years ago. She was being tortured after Mateo's death, and I only stood by and watched.

"Yeah, this whole trip has made me rethink a lot of things."

"Like what?"

"Things I've been holding on to for years. Well, one thing in particular. It's something I want to say, something I need to say, but I don't want to be the one to say it."

Adrian leans back in his chair, his dark hair falling over his forehead. I resist the urge to brush it back and run my fingers through its wave. He started this conversation with me. That matters. But probably not. I've gotten my hopes up before.

"That usually means it's a hard truth," he says.

I nod dramatically. "A very hard truth."

"About yourself?"

I scrunch up my nose. "I cringe just thinking about it."

"I've noticed you don't like to open up much. Not with specifics, anyway."

He's right. It's part of the reason I like poems. Even if someone thinks they know what I'm writing about, I don't have to confirm it.

"I guess I like to be in control of what people know about me."

"Maybe write out all your thoughts first," Adrian suggests. His voice is gentle, void of judgment. Perhaps I don't need to hide myself in the dark all the time. He points to my notebook, open to an already-filled page. "Let it out."

"I wish that's all it took. I've written it down already." Writing a letter to Grace that I never intended her to read is completely different.

"So, it's the actual speaking that's the problem, huh?"

"Absolutely." An attempted poem mocks me from my open notebook. Maybe I'll write something new to tell Grace.

"Would it help to picture me in an orange Speedo and swim cap?"

I laugh, secretly amazed he remembers that moment from freshman year. "No, not this time."

"Ah. So, it's almost like," Adrian says, "you'd rather someone grabbed your voice and made the words come out for you?"

"That would be great," I joke. "Do I get to leave the room while they do it?"

"Only if you want to."

Before my brain processes what he's doing and before my heart starts beating again, he takes my notebook and walks to the front of the room.

"Hey, everyone," Adrian says, calling the attention of the entire audience. "I know I'm not one to be serious all the time . . ." He pauses, and sure enough someone calls out, "Never!" Adrian points at whoever it is and winks, mimicking a stand-up comedian. "Okay, you got me," he concedes. "But I wanted to share something serious with all of you today."

Oh no.

"Now, I didn't write these words," he says, flipping through the notebook. *My* notebook. "But when I heard them, I knew they were meant to be shared. And I know, I know!" He drops his head and raises his hand as if giving them time to applaud, even though we're all still sitting here. Correction. Everyone else is sitting here. I'm about to throw up.

Stopstopstop. My brain screams, but my throat closes and my legs freeze. This can't be happening. It can't. This isn't what I meant. I'm suddenly light-headed.

"You might not all enjoy poetry when we're forced to read it in class," he says, "but I'm telling you, *this* you are going to enjoy." He lifts my notebook in the air like a trophy, and several people cheer and clap. He lowers his arm, waits for the room to fall quiet, clears his throat, and reads, "This is who I am / I've accepted what I tried so hard to deny . . ."

My brain doesn't process the rest of the poem, *my* poem, *my* words pouring from his mouth for everyone to hear. The blood pounding through my ears blocks everything else.

I slink out of my seat. Black stars dance in front of my eyes. I have to get away from this room. Away from the podium. Away from Adrian. I don't know if anyone notices me leaving. I can't see anything but the exit.

I'm so embarrassed, I could die.

this is who i am
i've accepted what i tried so hard to deny
i will always be different
it's easy to see that
even if we look the same
only one attracts every eye
you can't convince me
i'm worthy of love
i know the truth:
i was a mistake
and i'll never accept
i can be loved the same
i'm second-born and second-rate
in my heart i will never believe
someone could still want me
when i reflect my true identity

CHAPTER 21

Grace: May 3

Dr. Cramer sits in the chair across from me. She wants to know how I've been coping with my sister's death, but that hardly seems to matter when we still don't know how she died. I pull a throw pillow under my arm, not sure if I want to hug it or punch it.

"Can't you do some kind of hypnosis therapy or something?"

"Like they do on TV?" Dr. Cramer smiles as if she's surprised I hadn't asked sooner.

"I need to remember what happened. This is taking too long."

"Why the sudden rush?"

I confess Detective Howard's accusation and the secrets I found in Maddy's journal yesterday.

"She's the one who kept pretending everything was fine. She could've talked to me about it, given me a chance to make things right. Now I can't."

Dr. Cramer nods along while I talk, implying she's truly processing what I'm saying. *Active listening*, I think it's called. It's what my English teacher told us we should do during our classmates' presentations.

"And why do you believe she stayed silent?" Dr. Cramer asks.

"I don't know. I'll never know now that she's gone." Dr. Cramer doesn't nod along this time. She only waits, and I know my answer isn't enough. "She was probably scared. She didn't want anyone to think she wasn't happy." I punch the pillow down. "She still could've said something. She could've said she hated me. How could things have gotten any worse?"

"Excellent question," she says, leaning back this time. "What could she have lost?"

I know what Dr. Cramer is hinting at. Yeah, she could have lost something with me, because I still would have been ticked. I *am* still ticked. But if Maddy told me she hated me, I wouldn't have killed her for it.

"She wouldn't have lost her life," I shout.

Detective Howard sees a motive in that frustration. He believes I killed her. And he's not the only one. I'm sure thousands of people have read Erica's post by now. The comments are probably blowing up with people screaming that I did it. They don't need evidence or facts when there's a juicy story to spread.

I know how mob mentality consumes the truth. It devoured me in junior high, and it will come for me again. Only this time, my parents can't make it disappear with a simple transfer of schools. I can't erase the past with good grades and volleyball stats. This time, I'll have to live with the whispers forever.

This time, I could be sent to jail for my sister's murder.

Dr. Cramer says something. I don't know what.

I blink.

Her lips move, but nothing registers.

"What?"

"Did you find anything in those journal entries to suggest your sister might have been participating in self-harm?"

"What do you mean? Like she would cut herself or something?"

Dr. Cramer nods. "It's a common struggle for many girls. If someone was feeling as lonely and isolated as those entries suggest, it wouldn't be unusual to have intrusive thoughts about death or suicide."

"No." It comes out loud and firm.

"If she did," she says gently, "it wouldn't mean anything was wrong with her, not that she was weak or broken."

"I know," I say, more calmly this time. "If anything, it would mean she was stronger for surviving those thoughts. It's just . . ." I rack my brain, recalling every word and line I read, making sure I'm not wrong before I finish my statement. When I'm sure I'm right, I say, "She never even considered it an option."

It's odd how I can feel like I don't know her and yet know this to be true.

Dr. Cramer crosses her legs. "Let's experiment with a new tactic. Rather than fixating on the past, let's direct our attention to the present. How have you been coping?"

This feels like a secret test I didn't study for. "I'm doing my best. Trying to be normal."

"*Normal* is an interesting word. What does it mean to you?"

I pull the pillow onto my lap. "Doing the same things I used to do, I guess."

"What are some of those things?"

A few months ago, I would've said volleyball, but I haven't touched a ball, not on the court or in my own driveway. School doesn't dominate my days anymore. I used to be busy hanging out with friends, but they've all disappeared.

"Everything I used to do for fun doesn't matter. Nothing matters from before because everything's changed."

"You didn't only lose a sister, you lost a piece of yourself," she says slowly.

"I lost all of myself." My words ring hollow; they'll fall over if I breathe too hard.

Dr. Cramer tilts her head with satisfaction. "We can't control other people, and we can't change them. Even if you had known, you could not have changed your sister's opinion of you. But you *can* change how you view yourself now. You can accept who you are or change. Those are your two options."

Only two options. Accept who I am or change. It sounds so simple, but not at all easy.

For the last twenty-four hours, I haven't been able to focus on anything but Detective Howard's accusation, with a few flashes of anger whenever I remember Erica's theories. Now the time has come to focus that attention on myself. I haven't been able to think of anything but Maddy for a week.

No, that's not entirely true. There have been moments when reality's slipped away and I've been free to live, to relax. The only one who's been able to distract me from any of this is Adrian. I can so easily picture his smile, dark eyes crinkled, or the sound of his laugh, always seconds away from escaping. Many guys have tried to get my attention in the past, but not one of them held my interest for long. Adrian is the only one who's made me laugh by simply being himself.

Still, I can't shake how Detective Howard leered at me, suspicion injected in every question. It's like he knows something about Maddy's disappearance that I'm missing, that I'm forgetting.

Dr. Cramer crosses her legs. "This week I want you to find *one thing* you can do to reconnect with yourself. Something that feels like *you*. Maybe not the old you, but something you can do to feel more . . . complete. Whatever that may be. As you try to get to know your sister, I want you to center your consciousness on getting to know yourself."

I suppress the urge to huff a sigh. "How long will that take? To rediscover myself?"

"That depends. But it sounds as if you need to figure out a few things before the police do."

I nod at Dr. Cramer.

If I want to know what happened to my sister, I have to start searching within myself. I have to reconnect with who I am so I can reconnect with my memories.

I won't let Detective Howard discover the truth before I do.

CHAPTER 22

Maddy: April 25

I don't breathe again until I'm in the lobby, taking great gulping breaths of cold air. I can't believe Adrian did that. I edited that poem for hours. I poured my pain onto the page. It was *mine.* I don't write for anyone to see. I trusted him and he—

"Maddy?" The sound of my name spins me around like a high-speed car wreck. Mr. Gutter holds open the door from the main room and asks quietly, "Are you sick?"

"No, I was—"

"Then I'll remind you that on the first day we discussed etiquette for when our classmates are sharing with the group." He waves me back in.

"I wasn't walking out—"

"I know you may not see it that way, but Adrian took a risk by speaking in front of everyone, and we need to show him respect."

"I—"

"Come. Back. Inside. Mrs. Sanderson is introducing the next activity."

He shuffles me into the main room. I bite my cheek to keep from arguing. *I'm* getting in trouble for Adrian reading *my* poem.

My notebook waits for me at my seat. I can't decide if I want to hug it to my chest or hurl it across the room.

"Is everything okay?" Grace tips her chair back from the next table.

"Yeah," I say, glaring at Mr. Gutter in the back of the room. "I had to go to the bathroom." Grace is the last person I want realizing I wrote that poem. I know exactly how she'll react. She'll believe I'm blaming her. She'll build a wall and shut me out. She does it with Mom and Dad for days every time they accuse her of not cleaning the kitchen when it's my fault the sink is dirty.

If she realizes I wrote that poem, she'll only hear me accusing her of causing my problems.

Grace pats my arm. Affection is not something we do in our family. I'm instantly preparing to be told bad news. Instead, she says, "You don't have to tell me what's going on, but I hope you know that I'm here for you if you need me. You were there for me when I needed it most. I want to do the same for you."

Her sincerity stings. I force down any temptation I had earlier this morning to confess. She wouldn't be comforting me if she knew the truth about Mateo.

I can't break. I know how to do this. I've been doing it for years. Smile first. Then look directly at her, and do not blink. Believe the words, and they'll be true.

"I'm fine. Really."

Grace settles her chair flat on the floor again, returning her attention to Mrs. Sanderson, who's standing at the front of the room.

"Be prepared to get up and move around. You'll start on the left side of the room and make your way to the right." Adrian's trying to catch my eye, but I maintain my focus on Mrs. Sanderson. "You'll have to work together to move your entire team from one side of the room to the other."

"What's the catch?" Nicole asks.

Mrs. Sanderson smirks. "The floor is lava."

"Let's gooooo," Ryan Jacobs shouts, and the room erupts as everyone lines up on the left. Mr. Gutter removes some of the chairs from the playing field as Mrs. Sanderson groups us.

"Maddy, Chloe, Tori, Clyde, Ryan, and . . ."

Not Adrian. Not Adrian. Not Adrian.

"Adrian." And she moves on to the other seniors.

"No worries," Adrian says, coming over. "I'm a lava pro. When I was six, I didn't touch the floor in my house for three days."

I clench my jaw. I will not look at him. I will not acknowledge him. He does not exist.

"All right," Mrs. Sanderson shouts. "We're ready to . . . begin!"

Ryan Jacobs leaps atop the nearest tree-trunk table and swings a chair backward for Tori to follow.

"Stoll?" Adrian steps aside to let everyone else go first. I ignore him. He fluffs his hair. "Stoll? Hello?"

He does not exist. My shoulders tense. *He does not exist.* I wring my hands. *He does not—*

"Why would you do that?" I blurt out in a whisper-yell.

"Do what?"

"You know what. Steal my writing and read it in front of everyone."

He holds his hands up in surrender. "I thought you wanted me to."

"Why would you think I wanted you to read my personal writing to a roomful of people?"

"Team," Ryan calls. "I'm out of furniture. Pass it up!"

Adrian steps up onto a chair and then the table.

"You said you had something you needed to say but you hate talking in front of people." He extends his hand to help me. "So I thought—"

"No, you didn't." I step firmly on the table, ignoring his hand. "You didn't think or you wouldn't have walked to the front of this room with my notebook."

"Chair, dudes!" Ryan calls again.

I grab the back of the chair and shove it toward Adrian.

"Whoa," he says, passing the chair up to Clyde without so much as glancing at it. "I wasn't trying to hurt you. I thought I could be that voice for you. That your words could be heard if I took the attention away—"

"Well, that I believe." I throw my arms into the air. "Any excuse to direct the attention back on yourself." I stretch my legs across to the table Clyde vacates. "That sounds about right."

Adrian steps back like I slapped him. He makes the same stretch to my table, but when he speaks, his words are slow and measured. "I wasn't *trying* to get attention. You said you wanted someone to be your voice. I was *helping* you."

"I didn't mean sharing something with the entire group." I lower my volume to a hiss. "I was talking about *my sister*. One person! And I didn't ask you to do it for me. I was *joking*. Don't you know how to tell when someone is joking?" Clyde moves onto another chair with Chloe, and I use the chance to leap away from Adrian.

Adrian doesn't wait for me to move on. He lunges to the chair, forcing me back. His toes barely grip the edge, and I'm millimeters away from falling off. He grabs my shoulders and pulls me toward him. We're chest to chest—both of us panting slightly, breath warm between us—with nowhere for me to look but into his brown eyes. If I wasn't so furious, I'd be wishing we weren't surrounded by classmates so he would kiss me, and maybe he's thinking the same because his eyes drop to my lips before flicking back up. "I know how to be myself. It's something you might want to try more often."

I steady my balance and push his hands from me. "Sorry if I don't take advice about authenticity from the guy who's always putting on a performance, acting happy and cheery to keep people from getting too close."

Adrian barks out one harsh laugh. "Look in the mirror. You're putting on an act every day. I can see it. You doubt yourself where you should be confident. You don't believe in yourself when you're fully capable of more than you know."

He leaps two chairs ahead, leaving me to climb atop the middle one and pass the remaining chair up to him.

"Don't turn this around on me," I say, refusing to move onto the chair with him again, refusing to be that close.

"It is about you." The edge in his voice disappears. He

stretches his hand out for me. "Your poems focus on being lost and abandoned by Grace. You don't believe you're worth people's time or attention. But I'm telling you that you are. I tried to help people see the real you."

I grab his hand, stepping onto the seat of the chair with him. I'm too mad to back down. "They were *my* words." My voice cracks. "*I* should have shared them."

"But you wouldn't have, would you?"

"Come on, come on!" Ryan calls from the floor on the other side of the room. The rest of our team is already across safely.

"I guess we'll never know." I leap off his chair and leave him behind.

"That's not an answer."

"You don't deserve an answer." I make the final jump to the ground.

A chair in the middle of the room clatters to the floor. People, those safely on the right side of the room and those stranded in the lava, stop to find the source. Jade is sprawled on her backside between Grace, ahead of her, and Nicole, behind.

Nicole's hand covers her mouth, but her laugh is loud. Jade mutters something under her breath. I half expect her to tackle Nicole, but instead Jade's glare flicks to Grace, who simply stands there. Jade springs to her feet but doesn't attack. She storms out the door. The whole thing happens so fast, Mrs. Sanderson hasn't even noticed.

Adrian lands next to me, but I move over to the other side of our group. Minutes later, the last senior lands on the ground safely, and Mrs. Sanderson climbs onto a table in the middle of the room.

"We're nearing the end of our trip, and today is one of the most significant. Actions are important, but they mean nothing if we don't have genuine motives. So many of our actions come from old wounds or pain that we can't let go. But we can't dwell on what's behind us. Your teammates got stuck without any stepping stones, until the items from the back were passed forward. We need to keep moving forward in life, and sometimes that means using what's in our past to get there. Those old wounds and that pain will keep holding us back, unless we forgive and move forward."

Adrian's stare burns into me. Or, at least that's what I imagine as the cause of the heat rushing to my face. I refuse to look at him, so I can't know for sure.

"We have to examine ourselves," Mrs. Sanderson continues, "and decide who we are withholding forgiveness from. Is it someone close to us? Someone we used to be close to? Sometimes, the person we need to forgive the most is ourselves, or we need to seek forgiveness from someone else."

I scoff, and those nearest shoot me a look. Mrs. Sanderson's convinced of what she's saying; she believes you actually can—and should—forgive someone because they ask for it, or even if they don't.

But you can't let go of the pain they caused as if it's a balloon slipping from your hand that simply floats away. I can't . . . I won't forgive Adrian for what he did. I won't forgive myself for what I've done to Grace. And there's nothing that could make her forgive me if she discovers what I did.

Mrs. Sanderson might imagine we'll all line up to drink her

wisdom without question, but I'm more likely to jump into a pit of real fiery lava.

Following lunch, I sit in the upstairs hallway window frame again, skimming through a photo album from past Sabbaticals. The tiger-stripe highlights and butterfly clips from the 2000s are comical enough to distract me for a while. The back of the album is more recent. The last few pictures are from this year: seniors on top of the mountain, some hanging off a bunk bed, and then some overly bright photos distorted from using the flash in the dark.

One of them is of Erica and Zoey. Cheek to cheek, their faces glow from the flash and Zoey embraces Erica's shoulders, a Sharpie in her hand. A big rock dominates the background, the wall of a cave with names written all over the surface, including *Erica and Zoey BFF.*

Four days ago, that picture would've made me want to throw the book across the floor. So much has changed in such a short time.

Yet, it's not enough.

I've been sitting in this window, fighting to avoid one simple truth: I have to talk to Grace. Each day of this trip's been leading me here. I haven't been open with her. I've let all the bad memories fester and mold, poisoning me without acting on them. I've tried to justify it, ignore it, deny it, but the truth weighs on me like a pile of rocks and I can't move until it's gone.

Mrs. Sanderson's words from earlier float back to me: *Those old wounds and that pain will keep holding us back, unless we forgive and move forward.*

I don't want to face my old wounds or admit what I've done, but I can't keep sitting here, either. I needed time alone to smother my rage so I could see clearly. Now I do.

I can't keep hoping someone else will change my life for me.

Abandoning the photo album in the window frame, I find Grace's room and rap my fingers on the open door. Tori lies on her bed, pencil flashing across a page filled with sketches of cats in every position: curled into a ball, leaping to an impossible height, walking away with tail high in the air.

"Have you seen Grace?"

She shifts the big frames resting on her nose. "No. Was she up here earlier?"

"Yes, but now she's not?"

"Right."

"Thanks." I peek into other open doors on the off chance Grace is chatting in someone else's room. I stop at a closed door on the right.

Adrian's room.

Grace isn't the only one I need to talk to. If I want Grace to forgive me for my actions, then I know I'll be a hypocrite for not forgiving Adrian too. Relationships don't get better with secrets or grudges.

I hesitate to knock. When I recall him saying those words—my words—to everyone, the panic rises again. Imagining my words being shared in front of everyone makes me want to scream. It took every ounce of confidence I have to share my poem with Adrian. If I wanted to share it with other people, I'd apply for more scholarships. At least then the judgment would come from a stranger instead of a roomful of classmates.

No, if I tell Adrian I forgive him right now, my heart won't mean it. I'm not ready for—

"Whoa." Clyde swings the door open and jumps back in surprise. He clutches his chest and takes some deep breaths.

"Sorry," I say. "I'm looking for Adrian. Well, I was, but then I wasn't and— Are you okay? Do you need your inhaler?"

"I'm fine," Clyde wheezes, holding up his finger. "Adrian grabbed his notebook." He inhales and exhales deeply. "And went downstairs."

"Thanks."

"No problem."

It doesn't really matter where Adrian is. I'm not ready for him, for *that*. I scamper down the steps to search for Grace and nearly run into Mr. Gutter on the landing.

"Oh, sorry," I say, stepping to the side.

"I was coming up to let everyone know to head to the meeting room for our next session in five minutes."

Five minutes? Any conversation with Grace will take longer than five minutes. I decide I'll have to wait until after dinner . . . when her laugh dances from around the corner. Rather than heading for the main room, I make a right, toward the little nook with the red chairs, the ones I sat in with Adrian.

And there—with her radiant smile and contagious laugh, with her confidence and charm—sits Grace, facing Adrian.

She points to something in a notebook on his lap, whispering so he has to lean closer to hear.

She might as well be standing in the middle of a poorly

decorated gym with his hands on her hips and hers around his neck. It doesn't matter that we're not in eighth grade anymore. With a single smile, she can still steal every gaze, including the only eyes that glanced my way.

I will never forgive her for this.

The truth is a rose
Delicate in form
Seductive in smell
And bright in beauty

It grows on a stem
Strong and true
Until it's ripe
For the picking

It endures the harsh sun
The cold winters
The crushing breeze
Waiting to be plucked

But thorns of reality
Prick my hand
Blood drips out
Staining me red

The truth is a rose
Waiting to be plucked
But my fingers can't
Escape the pain of reality

CHAPTER 23

Grace: May 4

My thoughts are like a prison I can't escape.

Maddy.

The case.

My parents' disappointment.

Detective Howard's suspicions.

Four walls locking me away from Dr. Cramer's directive to get to know myself. I let myself believe my friends were distant because they didn't have my phone number and I'm locked out of my social media accounts, but I was in denial of the truth. They think I'm a murderer, that I hurt Maddy. It's the only explanation, and I should have seen it sooner.

I stay up most of the night, plagued by a Sharpie, shoes running down a dark hall, a shout. The result is that I sleep most of the day until Adrian picks me up.

He drives through the back of the neighborhood, to a street I know I must have been down before but that's only vaguely familiar. I checked multiple times to make sure he didn't mind missing prom to hang out with me, but he said he had something else planned that was better than an overpriced meal and a sweaty dance floor.

He parks at a playground. The mirror on the side of Betty White reflects the confusion on my face.

"I didn't know this was here," I say.

"It was built a few years ago."

"But I must have run past it before. I should remember it." Shouldn't I? Everything lately feels like I'm walking in someone else's shoes, living someone else's life. I can't even tell what gaps are from my memory problem and what's simply living with the hollowed-out shell of existence without my sister.

"Give yourself time," Adrian says with a sympathetic smile. "My grandma walks us down here for my younger siblings to play."

The colors of the slide are still bright and unfaded by the sun. Swings stand between a smaller structure designed for littler kids and a bigger structure for the adventurous ones. Everything is empty now, quiet. Parents have their children at home for dinner or in bed, not playing at the park.

"My Grandma Patty used to take us to a park too," I say. "My sister and I always played on the swings and had jumping-off contests."

"Who usually won?"

"It was a pretty even split until she jumped off and broke her arm when we were six."

Adrian sucks in a breath. "Ouch."

The brush of a headache tickles the back of my skull. I squeeze my eyes tight, fighting it off. I don't want anything to ruin this.

We climb to the tallest structure. From this height we can see the small creek winding its way slowly along the edge of the park, like it knows time will push it forward even if it wants to stop. The sun sinks into the tree line. I perch on the edge and Adrian plops next to me, our legs hanging over the side, where a pole runs to the ground.

"You look too serious to be on a playground," he says.

I sigh without meaning to. I checked Erica's blog before we left, and she hasn't posted since I confronted her at school, but even without that, there are too many other sources of frustration to ignore.

"I can't help but think there's something missing in all this. I need to know what we fought about during Sabbatical."

I need to know I didn't hurt her.

"I thought we weren't supposed to mention that today," he says.

Dr. Cramer's recommendation to get to know myself and reconnect with my memories suddenly seems infuriatingly indirect.

"But there has to be something there."

"Nicole's having that day-after-prom party at her house tomorrow night before senior skip day. Everyone in our class is invited. I wasn't going to go since we're not at prom, but we can if you want. It would be a good chance for you to talk to everyone."

He says *everyone,* but I know that's not true. He means

everyone who is typically invited to big parties. After reading Maddy's notebook, I know how hurtful it must be for the people who aren't.

Now that I think of it, *I* wasn't even invited to this. What kind of friend is Nicole? She either believes the rumors that I killed Maddy or she's listening to her lawyer to stay away from me to help keep her reputation safe. Regardless, she's throwing away four years of being my best friend when I need her the most.

Well, I know where her lawyers *won't* be.

"Yeah, that's a good idea," I say. A party doesn't sound like fun considering the emotional Olympics I've been competing in, but if it means getting answers for Maddy, it will be worth it.

"Maybe Tori knows something. Roommates usually get surprisingly close during Sabbatical." He takes out his phone. "I have her number. We were in the same English group for that project." It's not until he offers the last sentence that I recognize the small spike of curiosity—jealousy?—that rose in me after he said he had her number. He scrolls through his phone, but then stops, considering. "Are you sure you want to dredge up everything from that week? Maybe your missing memory is a gift."

I kick my legs back and forth with anxious energy. If I want to keep feeling like myself with Adrian, I have to be honest with him. "I wondered that too. Until the police started questioning me as a suspect."

It takes half a second before he recovers and shifts his customary charm back into place. "Yeah, I could see how that might light a fire under the motivation." He tilts his phone so I can type

Tori's number into mine. "Hey," he says, bumping my knee with his. "There's no way you did anything to hurt her."

I slide my phone back into my pocket. "How do you *know*?"

"Because I know you. Whether you remember it or not, we got tight during Senior Sabbatical. And if those officers knew you, they'd know you wouldn't hurt her."

Not intentionally.

"I wish I could be as confident as you right now." I sigh.

"Yeah," he says, brushing imaginary dust off his shoulder, "most people do. Except my therapist. She calls it a mask."

"You go to therapy?"

"You sound surprised. Should I be flattered or insulted?"

"Sorry, I just never would've guessed you struggled. You're Mr. Charming Confidence and Sense of Humor all the time."

"Hmm, charming," he says slowly, as if he's tasting the word. "I'll have to add that one to my résumé. And I don't have to go to therapy. It was offered and I accepted. But you don't want to hear about all that." He rotates his body and pushes himself down the slide, waiting at the bottom. I scoot over and do the same, landing with my legs wrapped on either side of him.

"No, I do," I say and find myself resting my head against his back. I want to know him more. I want to know someone else suffered a dark moment and made it through. I've been extending a piece of myself to Adrian, but I want to be trusted with his burdens too.

He rubs his thumb across my knee and talks easily. "My mom was pregnant. I was in sixth grade, and my brothers and sister were in, I don't know, fourth and second, and kindergarten," he rattles off. "My parents were always really intentional about what was happening with the baby. They didn't keep it a secret for months like some people do. My mom told us how the baby had the beginning of a heart the week after she found out she was pregnant and when it got fingernails. Stuff like that. At night, she'd lay on the couch, and we'd take turns shining a flashlight on her stomach and watching the baby move."

His voice is calm and strong with my ear pressed against his back. I didn't have his same experiences. Our school's online health class is severely lacking, beyond technical information. I remember one day Maddy and I were joking with Mom about how she got pregnant so soon after having a baby, and she said, "Remember: Breastfeeding is not always an effective form of birth control." We were instantly mortified and never brought it up again. Listening to Adrian makes me wish we were the sort of family who didn't get embarrassed about things.

His voice drops. "One night, she was close to six months along, and I was moving the flashlight around, but the baby didn't move. My mom tried massaging her stomach a bit. Drinking juice and lying down. All the stuff that usually causes *some* movement. But there was nothing. When she went in for an ultrasound, they couldn't find the heartbeat."

"Oh. Adrian, I'm so sorry." I cringe, immediately hating myself. Those words become so meaningless once you hear them over and over and over. I don't know what else to say. I wrap my arms around his chest, and his hands find mine.

"They had to induce her labor. We all still got to hold him. My parents named him Brayden, and even though he wasn't living, he still had these little hands." He lets go of me to examine his open palm, like he can still imagine Brayden's little body there. "When I turned eighteen, I got this." He lifts up the left side of his shirt. I lean back to get a clearer picture of tattooed text trailing up his ribs: BRAYDEN DREW CLEMENT. Then in smaller text underneath, a single date for when he was born and died.

Another life gone too soon.

Adrian loved his brother and lost him, just like I loved and lost Maddy. Our pain isn't the same. No one's is. But grief and suffering don't discriminate.

"It was a really hard time for all of us," Adrian says, pulling his shirt down. "But especially for my mom. Postpartum hormones and grief. She was depressed, and that depression affected the rest of us. She knew it. She simply didn't know how to fix it. So, she took us all to therapy instead."

"Did it help?" I ask, leaning my head against his back again.

Adrian pulls my arms tighter around him, sinking into the moment like this intimacy is the most comfortable thing in the world. "It didn't take away the pain or confusion, but it was comforting to know I had someone to listen to me without having to worry whether or not I was being a burden. Like, my parents lost their baby. I didn't want to make things worse for them."

He expresses what I've been experiencing. I'm supposed to be thankful to be alive, but now I'm an only child with grieving parents who are learning how to live with their own loss.

He shifts so I have a full view of his profile. "Actually, my therapist helped me a lot. You know how sometimes I'm annoying?"

I laugh at him. "I thought that was called *being funny.*"

"I am funny. I'm simply acknowledging that I am also sometimes annoying, even when I'm being funny." A hint of laughter returns to his voice, breaking the tension but also bringing us closer together. "You need to take this admission while you can."

"All right, I take it. Taken." Silence settles again. His eyes move from mine, down my cheeks, until they rest on my smile, my lips. "So, you said you are sometimes annoying," I say softly.

"Right." He hesitates, but I'm still smiling at him, still content to gaze into his brown eyes, still comforted by his warm hand in mine. "Turns out making people laugh was the only way I knew how to deal with the grief. I started getting my family's attention and making them laugh. I never learned how to stop."

"You learned all that at therapy, huh?" I find myself leaning in.

"Yeah." He tilts his head and moves a fraction closer, speaking softly until it's barely a whisper. "She tackled that early. Have you ever been caught trying to make your therapist laugh? Let me tell you, unpleasant results."

He's so close his breath dances across my cheek. I close my eyes and whisper back, "I'll keep that in mind."

His lips touch mine, both of us smiling until we relax into a light, enchanting, true kiss of understanding and comfort. Of trauma and grief. Of new joy and laughter. Of forgetting everything else and being truly happy and—

And then he pulls away.

"Sorry, umm." He laughs nervously and stands up. I slip the last foot or so to the bottom edge of the slide. He grabs my hand. "I don't know if this is the best time."

I let him pull me to my feet and try to force a laugh but sense my cheeks growing red instead. "Because a mom and her kids might see us?"

"Well, that too." He scans the empty playground and scratches the back of his head. "No, I mean it might not be a good time with everything going on." He brushes his hand over his ear. "People react differently when they're grieving. It's why I suggested we could get waffles 'as friends.' I didn't want to take advantage of you or anything."

I thought the "friends" excuse was part of his infamous commitment issues.

He takes both of my hands in his. "I genuinely like you, and I will be here for you, but if this becomes . . . something, I want it to be something that matters, and if that means I have to wait to make sure you're in the right headspace, I will."

He doesn't glance away, or smile, or try to make me laugh, and maybe it's the combination of all three that convinces me he's telling the truth. This, between us, *is* something different. Neither one of us could deny how *right* that kiss was. Instead, I'm oddly reassured by his restraint. He knows I'm in a screwed-up place, and he doesn't want to be *that* guy.

He is the good guy I imagined him to be.

"I think I want that too," I tell him.

"So, we can still have this," he says, swinging my hands, "and wait for the other stuff?"

"Yeah." I smile. "We can."

He's looking at me again, my eyes and lips, and I sense it building. The attraction. The closeness. Why is a guy respecting me as a person so incredibly attractive?

"I have something I want to tell you," he says, popping the intensity between us. "But first, are you hungry?"

I groan and roll my eyes. "The waffles were *good,* okay? You don't need to give me more."

"We'll get you to say the waffles are *phenomenal,* but that's not what I mean. Come on." He takes my hand, and we walk back to his car. I'm thankful things can still be easy between us, and there's a promise of hope, that he's willing to stick with me through this and he'll be waiting for me on the other side. Adrian pulls out his keys. "Betty White would like to serve us a picnic."

"Really?" Respectful and romantic. Funny and serious. Adrian is more than I could've dreamed.

"I'll grab the food out of the back seat if you want to grab a blanket out of the trunk." He pushes a button, and the pop of the trunk latch punctuates his sentence as his head disappears in the car.

His trunk is littered with all kinds of loose items. A flashlight. One shoe. A gym bag. Several packages of fruit snacks that probably slid out of a box. And, yes, a blanket.

His muffled voice floats from the car, fighting to be heard above the crinkle of several plastic bags. "I hope you aren't expecting a five-star meal, but I promise I brought all the essentials."

I grab the blanket, then freeze. There—underneath the blanket, next to an empty water bottle and a crumpled receipt—lies a notebook.

It was presumably thrown open when Adrian turned a corner or something. In the middle of his messy trunk, it's open to two pages. The left is covered in doodles of a cactus and a sun, but at the top of the right page is my sister's name.

"What is this?" I ask, grabbing it. I already know the answer.

Adrian comes around the back, carrying two yellow Dollar General bags. "—some barbeque chips, cheddar whales, which are far superior to Goldfish, by the way, and— What?" His face falls, but I've already gotten halfway down the page.

Maddy,

I'm better at making jokes in person than being serious. It's something I'm working on, so I thought I could maybe try writing this to you instead. You're funny and brave. You're passionate about your poems, and I love how they give me a glimpse of what's going on in your head. I've never wanted to get to know a person more than I've wanted to get to know you.

"That's not—" Adrian makes a swipe for the notebook, but I spin my body to finish the last bit, cracking as the knife of deception wedges in my heart more deeply with every word.

I screwed up, and I never meant to hurt you. I'm sorry. I care about you more than you know and I hope you'll forgive me, but I understand it may take some time.

—Adrian

I refuse to cry. Not over him. Not now.

"Were you ever going to tell me?" I ask.

"I—" He stands there stupidly next to the car, the bags anchoring his hands to his side. I've been trying to cope with the death of my sister, with being accused of her murder, and he . . . He was what? With her on Sabbatical?

"I thought you said you wanted something that matters," I hiss at him. "I guess my memory loss is a convenient way for you to hide the truth, huh?"

"No," Adrian says emphatically. "No, it's not like that."

"Whatever," I say, shoving the notebook and blanket into the trunk and stalking out of the parking lot.

"Wait—" Adrian calls. The bags crinkle, but I don't watch him throw them in the back. The trunk slams shut. "I want to explain!" he calls after me. I resist the urge to flip him off over my shoulder, but I bolt away, cutting through yards to get home sooner and knowing if he jumps into his car, he won't be able to follow.

I was stupid to believe anyone wanted to be around me right now. He's worse than Nicole and all my other friends. Their distance feels like a betrayal, but it's better than using me, than getting close to me only to hide the truth.

Maddy dies, and now he pursues me? It's sick. What am I? A consolation prize, since my sister isn't an option anymore? I could spit venom with all the things I want to shout at him. The imaginary conversation plays out in my head, fueling my anger like gas on a grill.

What kind of guy switches his interest to a girl's sister not even a week after she dies? And what kind of stupid sister falls for it? I want to scream!

My phone buzzes in my back pocket, but I ignore it. I don't want to listen to his excuses. The wind picks up, and I need to reach home to avoid wandering in the dark. These street names aren't ones I recognize, but I know if I keep heading in this direction, I'll get somewhere familiar soon.

And that's all I want. Somewhere familiar. Somewhere I'm not a suspected killer or mourning sister or leftover daughter or lonely girl. I want to go back to before. Life was easy with a busy schedule filled with practices and homework and friends. Nothing's prepared me for all of this, and I don't care how many medications Dr. Thelsman prescribes or how many sessions I sit through with Dr. Cramer. It's not enough to handle this. Nothing is.

If this is the *normal* Dr. Cramer wanted me to find, I've had my fill. Everything's different. It's not like before, not like what it's *supposed* to be. I should be getting ready to head to campus early and train with the team for the fall. I should be packing to move into the dorms and scoping out the best price for a minifridge.

Everyone else has gotten the time to mourn Maddy, but I'm stuck in this shadow life mourning everything else that was meant to be and never will. And I don't want to be dead like her, but I don't want to live without her either. I don't want to live as myself. I still don't even know who I am.

By the time I reach my street, the sun is gone. The streetlights are on, and the temperature has dropped. I go into my house through the garage, but Mom and Dad must not hear me, because they're still talking.

"Dr. Cramer's office isn't open until Monday," Dad's voice carries from the other room.

"What do we do until then? She isn't—" Mom gets interrupted by Dad again.

"I know. We'll call Dr. Thelsman in the morning. And a lawyer."

"Robert."

"Just in case."

Fizzy races around the corner, announcing my presence. When I come into the kitchen, Mom's mouth hangs open and Dad's clamps shut.

They won't admit their suspicions to my face, but they obviously believe I'm guilty enough to need legal defense. I suppose I should be thankful they're getting me a lawyer before the police make it necessary.

"We were trying to plan ahead." She points to the calendar spread across the table with other papers. "The school's having that memorial service, and we wanted to bring some of your sister's things to set out. Can you go through your room and pull out anything she might want there?"

I stop cold, then turn to the pantry and open the door. "How would I know what she wants? And why does this pantry never have anything good to eat in it?" I slam the door shut and move on to the fridge.

"Is everything okay?" Mom asks.

No, Mom, I'm being investigated for my sister's murder,

and now you want me to pick out items for a little display so everyone can pretend they cared about her? "Why wouldn't it be?" I do not need this right now. Not on top of everything else. I take out my phone, delete Adrian's messages unread, and then put it back in my pocket.

"Your mom is only asking for your help," Dad says. "We've all been under a lot of stress, and we need everyone to help out."

I point at myself. "I *have* been trying to help out! Sorry for having debilitating headaches and needing to lie down for a few hours every day. Believe me, if I could do more, I would."

"Where is this coming from?" Mom says.

"What do you mean? I come in here and ask one question, and then I get accused of not helping out."

Mom scoffs, insulted. "Your dad and I have been pretty patient with you this last week. Working with the school, taking you to doctor appointments, communicating with the police. All we're asking for is a little patience in return."

"Sorry I've been such a burden." I roll my eyes.

"You know, if you're going to act like this, maybe you don't need to go out and be around any friends for a while. Maybe you should stay home and rest more."

"So, what? I'm grounded now?"

"This isn't like you," Dad says.

"How would you know?" The first tear falls, and the silent screams are scratching to escape my throat.

"Excuse me?" Mom shrieks.

Dad rests a hand on her shoulder and takes over. "I know you're going through a hard time, but this is not—"

His words remind me of Adrian. Everyone *knows* it's hard. Everyone *knows* what it's like.

"You don't know anything. You didn't know her! None of us did!" I point a finger directly at Dad. "You work so much, how could you? And for what? So I could play volleyball?"

They both look as though I've slapped them across the face.

"You're making the same mistake again. I'm not the same person I was before. I'm not your same daughter—"

"Settle down—" Dad says, too loudly.

"You're not listening! You don't even know me! You—"

"You're not making any sense," Mom yells.

"I know who you think I am! I see it when you look at me. It's not the same. You believe them—the police. You believe I killed her!"

"Just stop, Maddy!"

The name knocks me down like an avalanche, sweeping away my breath as quickly as snow and ice wipe out acres of trees and life. She *does not* get to make that mistake anymore; I don't care how stressed she is. I press back and glare at her, my shoulders squared and neck straight.

Tears well in her eyes and she turns away before racing up the stairs to her bedroom and then shutting the door, not bothering to slam it, though it feels like she did.

She doesn't have to say it. I still know what she's thinking.

She doesn't need words to tell me Maddy never would've fought with her like this. Maddy would've laughed and smiled sweetly. Maddy would've been the dutiful daughter.

At least on the outside.

Mom never knew the daughter who fought with herself in her diary, who stood silently so no one would suspect her real feelings, who shined bright enough to keep people looking exactly where she wanted them to. Mom never knew the girl Adrian apparently fell for.

Dad and I stand in silence, but I'm begging him to yell at me, to hint at continuing the fight. All I need is a reason to keep screaming, and not even a good one. Only the breath of anger will ignite me again.

But he slumps into a chair at the table, his head hanging in his hands. His shoulders move a few times before it registers that he's crying. Softly. Finally.

He doesn't stop to watch me walk up the stairs alone.

CHAPTER 24

Maddy: April 25

In the private nook, Grace and Adrian are illuminated like they're under a spotlight. Her soft laughter floats across the room like a siren alerting me of the danger I don't want to discover.

I didn't know I was still whole before this moment, but my chest crystallizes. Frozen. Hard. Still. The truth hits me all at once: Grace's playful banter with him on the hike, the way she's looking at him now. She likes him. The one time a guy shows *any* interest in me at all, and she can't leave him alone.

She's the sun, pulling everyone into her orbit, her warmth, her light.

The realization—that she likes *him,* that she'll always be the better version of me, that she'll always have everything I want, that my hopes for anything different were naive and foolish and wrong—cracks me open. I can practically hear the pop, like warm water poured over ice cubes in a glass.

A strange hush falls over the room, as if they heard it too. Both look up at me and stare.

I bite my lip and spin.

"Maddy," Adrian says, but it's Grace's hand gripping my arm, pulling me to a stop.

"Maddy, wait," she says.

"Why, Grace?" All the years of being ignored and overlooked light up like a fuse. I'm tired of being in the background. "Why do you always have to do this?" I shout.

"Do what? Adrian told me you were mad at him—"

"You what?" I practically scream the question at Adrian.

"I didn't tell her why," he says, taking a step forward from the red chairs.

"We were just talking," she says, ignoring him.

"You can't 'just' do anything without making people fall in love with you," I spit at her.

"What are you talking about?"

"Mom and Dad. Teachers. Coaches. Friends. Everyone! You don't know how to exist without getting people to like you, to be dazzled by you."

"That's not true. I—"

My laugh cuts her off. "You're right. I've been such an idiot all these years thinking you wanted them to look at you. The truth is, you couldn't care less, because that would mean you'd actually have to notice someone other than yourself."

Grace's jaw clenches, but she manages to growl, "I wanted to *help*."

"Everyone is suddenly so interested in helping me. I said I was *fine*." The tremble in my voice betrays me.

"I didn't do anything wrong."

There it is. The classic Grace wall of deflection.

"Of course you didn't." I meet her eyes without blinking, but I can't put on the smile anymore. I can't keep lying to her or myself. "You never do anything wrong, and heaven forbid anyone suggest otherwise."

Adrian clears his throat. "We weren't—"

"You've said enough," I say at the same time my sister swings around and snaps, "Stay out of it."

Adrian shuts his mouth and takes a seat.

Grace rounds on me. "Stop being so sensitive. I know you, Maddy, and you're—"

"You don't know me. You haven't known me for years." The words tumble out of the dark little room I locked them in and rise to the surface. I can't take them back. I can't even try to hide them and more keep coming. "You don't know how hard it is to see our differences every day. Or what it's like to have Mom and Dad rushing off to watch your games every weekend. Or how I feel eating dinner at home alone while Dad works to pay for your club fees and Mom drives you to practice. You don't know how hard it is to be left behind every weekend when you go out with your entourage of friends."

"I invited you to come with, but you were always busy babysitting," she says, and the edge of defense breaks through her voice.

"No, I *made* myself busy with babysitting because being in a house with a four-year-old who enjoys my company is better than tagging along with my sister and learning new ways to be ignored."

"You weren't ignored—" Her gaze flicks over my shoulder at the footsteps stampeding down the stairs and echoing chatter. "Can we discuss this somewhere else?"

"Right here is fine," I say. I sense the presence of classmates hovering behind me, even without the color draining from Grace's face. "And I *was* ignored. You were too blinded by your friends' attention to even notice. They didn't talk to me. They talked to you while I stood next to you. They didn't even look at me."

"Maddy, please," she begs, still looking over my shoulder instead of at me.

"Now you're going to Trin U next year and leaving me at home. I'm sick of being forgotten. Do you remember when everyone went to Nicole's house after the movies?"

"You got sick and called Mom to come and get you."

"No. I didn't get sick, Grace. I went to the bathroom, and everyone decided whose car they were riding in and no one remembered to make room for me."

"I didn't know—" Grace mutters at the floor.

"That's not an excuse. You could have known. Look at me!" I shout. It doesn't surface as the plea I always imagined. It's a command, and she obeys. "If you cared enough, you could have looked around and noticed me, but you were too busy with your friends, just like they were too busy with you."

"You have friends," she whispers. "You have Erica."

"You wouldn't understand. I have no one, Grace. Not even you."

I turn my back on her and face the crowd that's clogging up

the hall and spilling from the stairwell. They all have the sense to get out of my way.

I march past every turned head, every eye focused on me, and I keep my head held high.

They all see me now.

~

I stomp up the stairs and imagine everyone staring at my back, but it doesn't embarrass me. In fact, the anger and pain shake off more with every step, like old mud cracking away from my shoes. By the time I reach the top of the stairwell, I've transformed.

I've never been so honest in my life. Not with Grace, not with anyone. The thrill thrums through me. I feel weightless, like I could float in the air if I try hard enough.

Everyone was staring at me, and I didn't even care.

Everyone was listening, and I only shouted louder.

Who have I become?

Whoever she is, I like her.

This must be what Fizzy experiences when the door is carelessly left open and she zooms outside. Total freedom.

"Ahhhh," I half shriek and half sing as I bounce into the room. I nearly crash into Jade as she's coming out with her head swallowed in a sweatshirt she's pulling on. "I did it. I actually freaking did it."

"Did what?" Jade asks when her head emerges.

"I told Grace how I've felt the last four years."

"Told her everything?" She sounds suspicious.

I twirl once and flop backward on her bed. "I was myself. For once. I didn't hold back. I'm surprised you didn't hear me. I didn't hold back the volume either." I laugh and can't stop.

"How did she take it?"

My laughter fades, and I lie in quiet. "She— I don't know. She tried to avoid it, I guess."

"But you didn't let her."

"No. I laid it all out."

She digs in her bag. "I had no idea you had all that anger built up."

"Honestly, I didn't either." The energy pulsing through my veins was more electrifying than any adventure or activity Sabbatical could have planned, but it's wearing off, and my body goes heavy. I sit up. "Do you think it was too much? Part of me feels bad for her."

"She deserved it," Jade says, a slight sneer in her voice. "Did she feel bad when she went to parties without you? Or when you didn't get that scholarship? Or when you were sitting at home alone?"

"Wait, what did you— How do you know about the scholarship?"

Jade freezes. Only for a moment. "You said it the other day." She speaks with that same tone she had when I walked in the first day and caught her with a phone, as if I'm incredibly dense. "When Mr. Gutter asked you about volleyball."

"No." I shake my head. "No, I didn't say anything about the

scholarship. Grace doesn't know about that. No one knows. Except . . ." Everything locks into place like the final three pieces of a jigsaw puzzle. *Click, click, click.*

"I've shared a room with Grace for the last four years." I stand up and cross the room. "She's never, not once in all those years, mentioned me sleep talking."

"Your point?" Jade laughs, coolly. Calmly. Naturally. As though she's waiting for some nonexistent audience in our room to laugh along with her.

"I didn't say Mateo's name in my sleep." I snatch my notebook from the dresser. "You read this." I enunciate the words slowly, each one flickering my anger back to the flames.

"I don't know what you're talking about," she says.

I flip to one of the early pages, the graph of highs and lows in our life, the heartbeat. I point at the negative six. "You read my notebook. That's the only way you could've known about the scholarship and Mateo."

I brace myself for her reply. She's going to tell me the truth. I've caught her in a lie. Whatever friendship I thought we had is broken, and she'll have to admit her betrayal.

"I don't know what you're freaking out about," she says without an ounce of anger. Her voice is soft, like she's confused but trying to be helpful. "I know fighting with Grace must have been hard for you, but honestly, you don't have to project your dysfunctional anger on me."

"That was the goal, wasn't it? For me to fight with her? You've been pushing me this whole time."

"I only encouraged being honest with her." Again, Jade's

voice is like a saint's, genuinely perplexed why I need this explained. "I didn't force you to do anything."

"The questions about her—asking if she made that picture of Gutter—you wanted me to tell her about Mateo. You wanted me to hurt her."

"Little tip? It's dangerous to accuse people of things. Tends to make them angry." She walks away.

"I trusted you," I call after her.

Jade pivots in the doorway. The red hair frames her face, but her natural color, the dark underneath, matches her eyes. When she speaks, her voice is full of pity and sincerity. "I learned a long time ago not to trust anyone, especially not so-called friends. It's time you learned the same lesson."

She swings the door shut as she leaves.

I rip the door open—except I don't. As soon as my hand grips the knob and pulls, it falls right off. I stumble back from the unexpected change in momentum.

I push my fingers into the hole left by the knob, but I can't get a grip. The door won't open.

I'm locked in.

Jade locked me in.

I fiddle with the knob, trying to shove it back in place, but the tiny screws fall to the ground with a soft tinkle, and one rolls under the door.

"Jade!" I yell, pounding against the door. "Jade! Let me out of here." I pound some more. "Someone help! I'm locked in!"

I know I sound ridiculous, but I don't care. I want to get out of here and throttle her.

I pause my pounding to push my ear to the door and listen carefully. The hall is quiet. Mr. Gutter herded everyone downstairs for the last evening session. There's no one on this floor, literally no one to hear me scream.

And that's what I do. One deep-from-the-diaphragm, gut-wrenching yell of frustration. Jade's been manipulating and tricking me this entire trip.

I try to fit the other screw back in and twist it with my fingernail, but it's not strong enough. Jade must have used something to unscrew it in the first place. I search the room for a screwdriver or nail file, anything that could be repurposed as a tool. I only hesitate for a second before checking her bag. She lost the right to privacy when she stuck me in here.

Nothing.

"Help!" I call again, my fists still hammering.

But no one is coming. Everyone is downstairs, and no one knows I'm missing. Or if someone notices—Grace or Adrian—they don't care. I pushed away the only people I was getting close to.

There's no clock in the room, so I'm not sure how much time passes before footsteps echo in the hall. I jump up from the cold ground and slam my fists against the door.

"Hello? Someone out there?" *Pound, pound, pound.* "Hello?"

The outside knob turns, and the door swings open. Tori, with her glasses so big they take up half her face, stands in the doorway.

"Maddy?" she asks. By the time she spots me, I'm gripping her around the waist.

"Thank you!"

"Have you been in here this whole time?"

"Yes, I—"

"Were you looking for Grace?"

"Grace? Wha— No."

"She wasn't downstairs, so I came up here to find her. Then I heard you knocking." Tori walks toward the room she shares with Grace. She only glances inside before suggesting we check the bathroom, but I notice a piece of paper folded on the floor.

It's been ripped from a notebook. I unfold it. My notebook? The handwriting is mine.

But . . . this can't be. It doesn't make any sense. I read the note again, trying to process it.

It's my handwriting.

That's my name at the bottom.

But I didn't write this.

"It's for Grace," Tori says, squinting over my shoulder. I fold it in half before she's able to read past the first line.

I don't want her to see the lies covering the page. That's what they are: blatant lies. I'm not dumb enough to believe them, especially not when I know I never wrote those words. But Tori might be if she reads the note.

And Grace probably already did.

I curse, and Tori jumps. "What is it? What's wrong?"

I'm tired of stupid games and silly pranks. This ends now.

No one's going to frame me for the consequences of these lies. I'm not taking the fall.

"I know where my sister went. I'm going to get her, but I need you to cover for me."

"What do you mean? Where are you going?"

I'm already racing through the hall, shoving the note in my pocket and taking the stairs two at a time.

I didn't write those words to Grace, but I know who did.

It
pierces
my back
like a
jagged
blade right
to my heart.
All the pain
twists in my
tendons and
burns in my
muscles.
You wielded your knife and plunged it in,
holding me close like a scorpion on its prey.
Your words
carve deep.
But worse
is knowing
the malice
inside your
wicked heart.
I cannot see
any other
reason for
the depth of
your be
tray
a
l

CHAPTER 25

Grace: May 5

The tension in the house remains high the next day, adding to—or causing—a new wave of headaches. The dull pain behind my eyes transforms into agony whenever I lift my head from the pillow. At least it distracts me every time I remember Adrian's betrayal. I've spent the day in bed so I'll be left alone. Mom and Dad have checked on me a few times, but I imagine they're as relieved to have me "asleep" as I am to have them close the door.

A text from Tori tempts my face from the pillow. *Hosmer St, right?*

Adrian gave up texting me, but I haven't forgotten the tip he gave me on the playground. Someone at Nicole's party, Tori specifically, might know something that can clear me. I'm taking advantage of having her number. I can't trust Adrian to be honest with me, but someone else might be.

My parents will never let me go to a party, but I already solved that problem. Once they head to their room for the night and bring Fizzy with them, I'll leave through the back door. They'll never hear me.

Yeah, by the stop sign, I tell her. Tori will meet me at the end of our street, and I'll be back before they know I'm gone. Nerves buzz through me. Not about sneaking out or going to the party, but about knowing the truth.

The sun still shines brightly outside, but it's getting late, and I should only need to wait ten or fifteen more minutes for Mom and Dad to come up the stairs.

A car door shuts outside. And there's another. Tori can't be here yet, and she's not supposed to come to my driveway.

Out the window, Officer Jones follows Detective Howard up our front path.

Oh no. No, no, no! They must've found all the evidence they need to arrest me. There's no other reason they'd be here.

I need to get out. *Now.*

If they believe I killed Maddy, there's only one way to prove them wrong. I have to figure out what really happened that night. Someone at the party must know what we fought about, or why we were outside, or *something.* If they don't, no defense will save me.

I grab my phone and sprint out of my bedroom but stop at the top of the stairs. They're already halfway up the sidewalk.

Downstairs is blocked. Next option.

The doorbell rings. Fizzy barks. I dash into Mom and Dad's room. My heart pounds in my throat.

The balcony.

Mom and Dad have a balcony attached to their bedroom.

I've never climbed over the railing or shimmied down the post, but I don't have an option now.

I hear Mom open the front door but any conversation is covered by Fizzy barking, and even that becomes muffled once I'm outside on the balcony behind the house. I grip the railing tightly and swing my legs over. The ground appears much farther away with my heels hanging off the edge, but no matter how scared I am of falling, the fear of being arrested is worse.

The balcony support beam is a few feet to my left. I wrap my legs around it and move down. This might be the worst idea I've ever had. My hands sweat. My flip-flops don't give me any traction. Almost immediately the back of my knee scrapes against the corner. Splinters dive into my skin like needles.

Definitely the worst idea. If I fall now, I won't be able to escape Detective Howard, *and* I'll have a broken leg. Or worse. And I can't handle worse right now.

I'm almost halfway down when, through the kitchen window, I see the edge of an officer's profile. If he steps a foot to the right, he'll catch me.

Screw it.

I jump to the ground. A sharp pain spikes my ankle. I wince with every step and hobble through the neighbor's yard until I emerge on Russell Street.

It worked. Walk casually. They're probably still in the kitchen, not upstairs yet.

I take out my phone and message Tori, who should be on her way. *Change of plans. There's a playground in my neighborhood where you can pick me up. I'll send the address when I get there.*

I cut through the same yards I did yesterday until I reach the park and send my location. Tori responds with a thumbs-up. The few minutes I spend waiting behind a tree pass as slowly as an hour. I keep expecting Detective Howard's car to come into the parking lot instead of Tori's. There's no reason he would come to my house other than to arrest me. If it was another update on the case he'd simply call, like he said he would.

The playground is empty, like when Adrian brought me here. No, I don't want to think about that. About him. About how stupid I was to believe anything he said.

A car slowly pulls into the lot. Every muscle in my body tightens. Its headlights are too bright. I can't tell who's driving. My phone buzzes in my hand, and I nearly scream. *Here,* Tori's text says.

I come out from behind the tree and try not to make it obvious I was running when I get into her car. I should've gone to the bathroom before I fled. My bladder can't handle these nerves.

"Sorry about the cat hair," Tori says, scurrying to lint-roll the last of the seat before I come in. "We had to go to the vet earlier today."

"It's fine," I say, practically sitting on her hand in my rush to get in and shut the door. "We can get going," I say, more breathless than I'd hoped.

Tori backs out of the spot. "So you, uh, had a change of plans?"

Suspicion undercuts her question. It's definitely weird to be picked up at a park and sneak out from behind a tree. "Yeah, I did. My parents have been really overprotective since, you know, everything. They didn't want me to come out tonight." She probably wouldn't be as willing to offer me a ride if she knew I was running from the police coming to arrest me for my sister's murder.

Tori licks her lips and taps her fingers nervously along the steering wheel. I don't know Tori well, but from what I do know, she's not the type of girl to sneak out for a party. I'm not either. Or I didn't use to be.

My phone rings. "My parents."

Tori keeps driving, but glances over nervously. "Maybe they're worried about you," she says quietly.

My phone keeps ringing, buzzing in my hand. I know they won't understand why I left, but it's cruel to disappear. They already lost Maddy. I don't want them to wonder if they've lost me, too.

I slide my finger over to answer, and Mom's voice shrieks on the other end before the phone reaches my ear.

"Where are you?"

"I'm okay, Mom! There's something I have to do."

"You need to come—"

"I promise I'll be home later! I'm fine!" I shout over her and hang up, cutting off her yells. I hate making her worry. And Dad. I hope he's only angry. Not scared. I can't handle making them afraid for me after all they've been through.

The car's awkwardly quiet without my mom shouting through the phone. If I discover what happened to Maddy and avoid being arrested, I'm going to suffer from Mom and Dad anyway.

I need to make this trip worth it.

"You can adjust the radio," Tori offers, breaking the silence. "I, uh, don't really listen to music, so I don't care."

"You don't listen to— Never mind," I say, reaching for the radio. I knew Tori Syblonski was strange, but who doesn't listen to music? "I wanted to come with you tonight so we could talk."

"I'm glad you messaged me last night. I wanted to reach out to you before, but I didn't know how."

"You did?" I ask, checking over my shoulder. No lights. No other cars.

"I wanted to offer condolences and ask if you needed anything."

"Oh. Thanks." I pull at the edges of my skirt. "I was hoping you could tell me more about what happened on Sabbatical. Especially the fight I had with my sister. Do you know what it was about?"

"So, it's true? You can't remember anything from that week?" She takes her eyes off the road for some quick glances at me.

I don't care where she heard the rumor. "Yes, it's true."

She hesitates, her hands squeezing the steering wheel at precisely ten and two.

"This, uh, isn't easy to say, but I'm glad I get the chance to do it in person." She pauses, and I have no idea what's coming. What could Tori Syblonski have been hiding this last week?

She turns off the main highway, slowing on a street bordered by cornfields with no center lines. We're the only car on the road.

"I know why you went outside that night," she says all in a rush. "There was a note in our room, and I didn't see all of it, but after reading it, you ran outside. I knew you and your sister left the lodge, but I promised not to tell anyone. I kept that promise." Tori's chin trembles and her voice cracks. "I thought I was helping, but when you didn't return, I should've said something sooner. I never expected anything to happen. I didn't know what would . . ."

She's crying and can't speak anymore through her gulps for air.

Maddy and I both snuck outside, and Tori helped keep it a secret.

"I'm sorry," Tori says, still fighting to catch her breath and turning onto another road at the same time. "Maybe if I had said something sooner, maybe then . . ." But she can't finish.

We both know Maddy might have lived.

But Tori's secret didn't kill Maddy. I need to know who did. I need to know it wasn't me.

"How far away is this party? Shouldn't we be there soon?" I ask, squinting out the window at the dark landscape. We've been driving for a while, and none of the roads are familiar. The sooner we get there, the sooner I learn the truth.

Tori sniffles but answers calmly. "It's still another thirty minutes away."

"What?" My head whips around to her. "I thought it was at Nicole's house."

"It is," Tori says. "Nicole's lake house. On French Lake."

French Lake.

I lean back in my seat, suddenly light-headed.

We're driving to French Lake. To where I was found on the side of the road. To where Maddy's body was found on the sandbar.

"You're shaking," Tori says.

I take a few unsteady breaths and pin my hands between my legs. I can do this.

I don't remember exactly what happened there, but I know it was the worst night of my life. I know I was injured enough to be hospitalized. I know I held my sister's unconscious body. I know Maddy died.

I'm going back to French Lake right now.

Unless I tell Tori to take me home.

Where Detective Howard and Officer Jones are waiting.

I can do this. I can return to the lake if it means proving my innocence. If it means giving Mom and Dad answers about Maddy, if it means we can lay my sister to rest with the truth, I can do this.

"What else do you know about the note?"

"Nothing, really," she says. "I didn't get to glimpse more than a quick flash."

"Who else knew about it?"

"No one. Except . . ." She flips on her blinker for another turn.

"Except what?"

Tori speaks slowly, like she's trying to remember the details. "When Mrs. Sanderson realized you two were missing, she checked your rooms. But Jade didn't go to her room. She followed me and started searching. She said she was looking for a paper she thought she forgot in there earlier. I didn't think much of it at the time, but I don't remember her being in our room before. Do you think she was searching for the note?"

Jade. Maddy's roommate. She was terrified of me when I sat across from her in the lobby of Dr. Cramer's office.

"Maybe." Definitely. Jade knows *something*.

When we pull up to the house, Tori puts the car into park, cuts the engine, and faces me. "I'm sorry," she says again.

"I know." But I didn't run away from the police at my house to listen to apologies. I need confessions.

I'm not at all surprised at how big Nicole's house is. It could eat two of my house for breakfast and still be hungry. A big wrap-around porch dominates the front, but the four-car garage is equally impressive. The white paint glows from the light shining through the big windows.

"Let's go find Jade," I say. Music blares and groups of people dance on the sprawling front porch. Practically everyone in the graduating class is here, and even a few underclassmen snuck in. Each glance my way lingers a second too long. I walk through the front door and tuck a piece of curled hair behind my ear. It's not styled quite the same as when I usually go out, but I'm out of practice.

Inside, the music blasts even louder. Faces I don't remember seeing in two weeks—since before Sabbatical—float past me. I know their names and recognize their faces, but they might as well be strangers.

One guy jumps over the couch and comes up with someone's shoe. A couple is pressed together against a wall. I can't believe I used to come to these kinds of parties every weekend. I feel like I walked into the wrong class at school. Everyone else is comfortable and confident, but I don't belong.

"Hey." Adrian appears out of nowhere. "I was hoping you'd be here, but I wasn't sure."

"I'm not here for you." I stand on my tiptoes, trying to catch a glimpse of Jade's black and red hair.

"I really want to talk about what happened."

"Which part? The part where you tried to get with my sister? Or the part where you lied about it?"

I can't believe how much I trusted him. But I'm not the one who should be embarrassed. He is. And that makes me the angriest of all.

What, exactly, Adrian wants to say, however, is unclear, because at that very moment Maddy's friend, Erica, spots me from the living room. She throws her head back, tipping her red plastic cup and downing its contents before passing it to Zoey. She heads straight for me with determination. She bumps into a kitchen chair and nearly falls over but doesn't appear to notice.

"I'm so glad you came!" She almost cries as she embraces me. I pull back, undraping her arms from my shoulders. "I am *so* sorry for writing those posts. You were totally right to call me out on it."

"I don't really have time to talk right now," I say, peering over her shoulder.

A little alcohol (okay, apparently a lot) and she's staring at Adrian as though she's noticing him for the first time. "And who did you come with?" She tries to wiggle her eyebrows, but instead goes cross-eyed.

"I'm not with him," I say impatiently. I have a mission of my own to pursue.

"Here, have a drink." She shoves a cup from the counter into my hand, but Adrian tries to take it first.

"This . . . this isn't like you," Adrian says. "And besides, that's probably not going to mix well with your meds."

"How do you know I'm taking meds?"

"You told me, remember?"

I don't. I don't remember, but it would've been after the accident, not before, and those are the things I'm supposed to remember, so if I don't have those memories, what else is my brain losing? What other memories have tipped into the void without me realizing it?

"We should probably get you home," Adrian suggests.

"I'm not going anywhere," I shout over the music, but a blinding shriek of pain pierces through my skull. I clamp my eyes shut and press my palm against my temple.

"Are you okay?" Adrian says, leaning close to me, his breath warm against my ear. "What's going on?"

"Leave me alone," I shout again.

"Come on," he says, still reaching for the drink in my hand. "Something's not right. Let me bring you home."

I twist away from him to Erica. "I need to find Jade. Have you seen her?"

Erica makes a face and shakes her head. Ryan Jacobs passes behind her, and I grab his arm.

"Have you seen Jade?" I yell.

"Huh?" His eyes take a second to focus, but then he leans in to hug Adrian and stays propped against him when he says to me, "Welcome back to life." He grabs a cup off the counter and raises it. "To Maddy," he cries. People all over the room echo his cheer and tip back their drinks to toast my sister.

Suddenly the room's too hot. Too crowded. The faces surrounding me start to swim. I need to get out of here. Escape. Breathe fresh air. I set the cup on the counter and stumble to the door.

"Wait," Adrian calls. "Stoll!" But Erica slips and stumbles into him, and he catches her. Her uncontrollable laughter follows me onto the deck.

Nicole must have a walkout basement, because the back deck is two stories up. A pergola wrapped in twinkle lights glows softly. The music still plays out here, but it's quieter.

Over the rail, the party thrives. A firepit lights up the backyard. Past the smoke is French Lake. The surface of the water shimmers under the moon. Somewhere out there, Maddy died. I grabbed her wrist. I held her body in the water. I—

Sh, sh, sh.

I spin around, and there she is.

Two-toned hair to match her two-faced personality. Thick black lines outline her deep brown eyes, which pop wide open when they meet mine.

"You," I say.

Jade jumps up from a glass table, knocking over the empty cup in front of her. She takes a leap for the stairs leading to the yard, but I jump in front of her. She spins to go into the house, but Tori and Adrian appear in the doorway, blocking her only exit.

"You know something about that night," I say.

"No, I don't," she says, terror in her low voice once more. "I swear." She backs away from us, toward the corner.

"You came into Tori's room searching for a paper. It was a note that led me and my sister outside."

"No, I—"

"You came to my room that night searching for it." Confidence replaces Tori's usual timidity. She edges to the left until the three of us form a semicircle around the girl who has the answers I'm looking for.

Jade's dark eyes are as wide as the moon. They jump from side to side, lingering on the blocked exits.

"I didn't do anything to her," she screeches.

"Slow down," Adrian says calmly. He inches forward. His hands stretch in front of him, like he's attempting to subdue a caged animal. "Why do you think Jade had something to do with that night?"

"Because she locked Maddy in her room," Tori says.

"What? No, I didn't." Jade sounds as surprised as I am to learn this.

"I had to let her out when I went looking for Grace," Tori says. "Then there was a note that Maddy read, and she bolted outside to find Grace. Jade came to my room searching for that note the next morning."

Jade stares me dead in the eye. She speaks slowly, emphatically. "I swear to you, I didn't lock anyone in any room. I had no idea that happened."

Incredibly, I believe her. Something genuine in her plea tells me she's being honest. At least about this.

"But then what about the note?"

"Ask her," Jade cries, pointing between Adrian and Tori.

Through the door—dressed in a tiny skirt, holding a red cup, with hair shining as bright as her smile—steps Nicole.

"She was pranking us all week." Jade's voice breaks, but her finger is eerily still, pointing straight at my best friend. "I bet she's the one who locked the door. I overheard her mention a note. I wanted to find you both, so I followed Tori to her room. I wanted to help. But she—" She shakes her finger at Nicole again. "She's the one you should be looking at."

Nicole's smile slips off her face at the same time her drink slips from her hand. It crashes to the floor, splashing its contents all over her legs. She makes no move to clean it up, only stares at the four of us, frozen.

CHAPTER 26

Maddy: April 25

"Wait, Maddy!" Tori's voice trails after me, but I ignore her and jump the last three steps to the bottom.

I have to get to Grace. I don't know why, but she's being sent on a wild-goose chase outside, and someone is framing me for it.

I pause. Someone in the main room is giving a speech. Mr. Gutter appears in the doorframe, but he's angled away from me. I dodge around the corner.

Mr. Gutter's footsteps draw closer. I press myself flat along the wall, not moving a muscle. If Mr. Gutter finds me out here, he'll accuse me of being rude to the speaker and force me inside again. If that happens, the only way I'll get to Grace is by telling him where she is, which will lead to questions about why she's there. Mr. Gutter—my judge, jury, and executioner—won't doubt my guilt about writing this note for a second.

Rereading the message adds a drop of anger to my blood with every word.

Grace,

Erica told me there's a rumor about you on the cave wall. I was embarrassed for you, but after today, I'll be glad everyone gets to see it tomorrow. You deserve what you get.

Maddy

Since our fight today, it's entirely plausible that I wrote this to her and planted it in her room. The forgery is nearly perfect. I doubt anyone else will notice the too-steep slant of the *S*s or the skinny loops in my *Y*s. I can't even blame Grace for believing I wrote it.

Erica never told me specific Sabbatical secrets, nor did she tell me anything concerning a rumor. Everything in this note is a lie.

But Grace hates rumors. One rumor about pushing Mateo destroyed her life. She'd never risk it happening again. If Tori didn't see Grace upstairs, she must be outside, heading for the caves, and I'm going to find her.

Mr. Gutter's footsteps echo up the staircase, trailing away. I exhale slowly, but my hands still tremble and sweat. Hopefully, Tori keeps her promise to cover for me. I need to find Grace before the teachers realize she's missing. This note was meant to send her outside and cast the blame on me. It will tear my relationship with Grace further apart, and Mrs. Sanderson will blow a gasket if she catches either one of us outside without supervision. In the dark. With a storm coming.

Only one person's proven herself to be deceitful and manipulative enough to mastermind this: Jade.

The coast is clear. Mr. Gutter is gone. The wind tries to pull the front doors from my grip. The rain has stopped, but black clouds block any whisper of the fading sunset and cloak the evening in darkness. Tree branches in the distance shiver like they're shaking a finger at me, scolding me for sneaking outside. I wrap my arms around myself. No one told me where the caves are. I only know it's the final tradition of Sabbatical before we leave tomorrow.

I can't see the lake at the base of the mountain, much less my sister; current visibility doesn't extend beyond the halos from floodlights surrounding the building. The muddy grass squelches under my shoes as I dart down the hill. I almost slip twice before reaching the bottom.

"Grace!" I call, cupping my hands around my mouth. Only a shift in the wind answers. The gust lifts my hair behind me, carrying my next call away. A bolt of lightning flashes an eerie glow over the dark trees surrounding the clearing. They sway in the growing storm, warning me to go back inside. Thunder rolls in the distance, shouting at me to return to the lodge.

Jade wanted me to fight with Grace, and I don't want to give Jade anything she wants. I follow the line of dark tree trunks, hesitant to enter the woods. There's no path to follow, and without any sign of her, I could be wandering in the woods for hours.

Nothing. No answer. No movement. Only the wind.

The sky opens with a rumble of thunder that rattles my bones. Buckets of rain force me to keep my head bowed and watch my step. My shoe sinks into the mud, sucking my foot down. I wiggle it free, but I'm drenched within seconds. The wind howls. Lightning explodes again.

"Gra– Ahhh!"

A dead branch crashes to the ground in front of me. I leap back, but it catches my leg, and the scrape along my shin stings even if I can't see it. My heart thumps almost as loud as the clap of thunder that tears through the night.

I'll never be able to find Grace in this. There's a chance she never found the note anyway. Jade might've only wanted me out here, stuck in the storm, in which case I should sprint back up to the lodge before—

A glimmer of light. Not lightning. The faint beam swings back and forth on the other side of the clearing.

Grace.

Her silhouette and gait are familiar even thirty yards away in the dark. She heads into a culvert at the end of a drainage ditch. The caves.

I remember the picture of Erica and Zoey and a wall behind them, but it wasn't stone from a natural cave. It was smooth and light, like the concrete inside a culvert. I take off running and calling Grace's name. The rain falls, a fast, formidable sheet. Wind whips my hair in my face, and I swipe it back only for it to fall over me again.

"Grace," I call, running toward her and panting.

She shines the flashlight on me.

"That note's a lie," I shout above the roar of the wind and rain. "Erica never told me any rumor related to you or anything written on the cave wall."

"What?" she yells.

"The note's a lie," I call again, ripping the paper from my pocket. Water hits it like a machine gun until it's sopping wet and wilting in my hands.

"Why would you lie to me?"

"I didn't. Jade did, I think."

Grace turns her back on me and marches into the culvert.

"What are you doing?" I scream over the wind, and follow her.

Inside the tunnel, the wind dies out. I clip my hair away from my face. The walls curving around us muffle the rain. The tunnel is big enough that we barely need to duck. Icy water, running in a skinny stream down the middle, soaks through my already-wet shoes, covering my toes. Everything beyond the circle of Grace's flashlight is pitch-black. She marches forward, splashing into the tunnel.

"I said it was a lie," I repeat. "Come back inside."

"Or it's true, and you want me to be humiliated tomorrow." She throws the words over her shoulder like grenades. "I guess yelling at me in front of everyone today wasn't enough for you."

"I'm telling you the truth. I didn't write that note. Jade did."

"Jade's the one who told me where the caves are."

"Grace, wait." I pull her arm and make her stop.

She throws me off. "You made it pretty clear this afternoon that you hate being my sister. You couldn't just tell me, either. You had to yell at me in front of everyone. Do you know how that made me feel?"

I wanted to be heard, but I didn't set out to embarrass Grace. I could have said all the same things in a different way, in a different place.

"I won't be humiliated again." Her eyes flash with anger I haven't seen since we were kids. "What's written on the wall? Be honest, because I'm going to find out anyway and cross it off." She waves a Sharpie in her hand.

"I'm not lying to you."

"Right. Because you never lie to me." She marches through the tunnel, her flip-flops smacking against the concrete like a popgun. I splash through the water to catch up with her. The entrance to the tunnel falls farther behind.

"You don't have to follow me," she says. "Jade told me the truth about you."

"What did Jade tell you?" I can't believe I trusted her, that I confessed to her. She couldn't have—could she?

Grace ignores me and stomps into the dark.

"What did Jade tell you?"

I know the answer, and I despise her for it. Jade kept pressuring me to tell Grace I tripped Mateo. She didn't wait for me to fold. She told Grace herself.

"Stop." I lunge forward and grab her flashlight. I know what I need to do. I've been hiding what I did to Mateo, what I did to Grace, long enough. It's time to bring it into the light.

"I should've told you the truth. I was stupid not to, and then I was too afraid of what you might say. It was an accident. I'm s—"

"An accident?" Her eyes bulge out of her head, and she snatches at the flashlight. "Oh, right. How do you *accidentally*—?"

"Can't you let me talk without throwing it back in my face?" I shout over her, keeping the flashlight out of reach. A rumble of thunder echoes through the tunnel. "I'm trying to apologize. I know you don't know what that's like since you don't make mistakes, but you're not perfect, Grace."

"I never said I was perfect."

"No, but you spend all your time trying to be. You hate to admit when you're wrong."

"No, I don't."

"Then do it," I challenge. "Admit you were wrong to flirt with Adrian."

"What are you talking about?"

I know I'm diverting from the topic, but I can't stand it. I need her to admit this. To admit she's not as flawless and innocent as the mask she wears, that I'm not the only one with something to apologize for. "You. Adrian. Sitting all close in that private little nook, laughing and smiling together."

She takes a step back and runs into the tunnel's wall at her back. Grace shakes her head and laughs. *Laughs.* Finally, she pulls herself together.

"Adrian likes *you.* Anyone with eyes could see that since day one. When you were mad this morning and he was all mopey, it didn't take a detective to figure it out. I asked him, and he was writing you an *apology.* I was helping him."

"But you were smiling and . . . and laughing . . . and . . . being you."

"I might have laughed at a joke, but I promise I wasn't flirting with him, and even if I was, I promise he would still only like *you.*"

"Oh." The flashlight drops and hangs at my side. Adrian

was trying to apologize again, even after the way I raged at him. And Grace wasn't trying to take that away. I only saw what I expected to see: Grace catching Adrian in her net.

"Yeah," she says, wrenching the light from my hand.

"I—I didn't know." My voice is small.

"Well, now you do." She wipes wet hair off her brow, but there's still a small bite in her words. "So how was lying about the scholarship results an accident?"

"What?"

"Jade told me you lied about the scholarship results. You didn't get it. Why didn't you tell me the truth?"

That's the secret Jade told. Not Mateo. I've told Grace so many lies, I can't keep them straight.

She waves the flashlight in my face. "Hello? Why didn't you tell me you didn't get the scholarship?"

"Because—because I was embarrassed." I'm tired of lying, to Grace and to myself. I slump against the wall until my back curves with it and pull my feet from the water. "I could barely look at myself after that, much less look anyone in the eye and admit it." I rub the back of my neck. "They rejected me."

Given the way I've acted today, I wouldn't be surprised if Grace rolls her eyes and runs to the caves without me. Or even if she pushes me down first.

Instead, she sighs and leans back, pulling her knees parallel to mine. When she speaks, all the anger's melted away. "They didn't reject you. They picked someone else."

"Same thing. They looked at me, they looked at someone else, and they decided the other person was better."

"You aren't your writing. I know it feels like they rejected *you,* but there are other scholarships out there."

"But my writing *is* me. It's my heart and my ideas and my words, and if they saw those pieces of me that I never show anyone else and they still said no, then who is there left to say yes?"

Grace stays quiet. The water still flows through the tunnel, carrying the occasional leaf or stick from outside. She lowers the flashlight, understanding washing over her face. "So the same day you didn't get the scholarship, I got the one to Trinity University."

"Pretty much."

"I'm sorry."

"I know. But it's not your fault." I've been mad at her like it is, like she is somehow to blame for not getting the things I wanted, but I know the truth: life isn't fair. No one can control the cards they're dealt, only how to play them.

"I still don't know how it could be an accident," Grace says.

"It wasn't." I look her in the eyes, the eyes so similar to my own. "I purposely lied to you about the scholarship. The 'accident' I was trying to apologize for is . . . I was trying to apologize for being the one who tripped Mateo."

Grace tries to speak, but I hold up my hand.

"Please. I've been keeping this in for too long, and I need to say it."

Her mouth remains closed.

"Thank you. I was under the bleachers and trying to get our phone when you two stood up. Mateo's foot caught on the purse strap, and he fell. When everyone blamed you, I was relieved I wasn't in trouble. But then they started torturing you and tormenting you, and I let them. And I'm so, so sorry."

The secret I've been hiding for four years is out, and it hangs heavy in the darkness between us. I thought I might be relieved, but it's not over yet. I still have to face the consequences.

"Why didn't you tell me any of this before?" she whispers.

"Once we switched schools, everything worked out for the best. You were more popular than ever. You got better at volleyball. I was afraid you might hate me forever if you knew the truth."

"Maddy," she sighs. "I could never hate you."

"But that was the worst year of your life."

"Yeah, that year was hell. But it wasn't because of anything *you* did. *I* pushed Mateo."

"What?" I hear the words clearly, but they don't make sense. I remember that night. It's haunted me. I grabbed the purse. His foot caught on it. He fell.

Right?

"When Mateo and I were sitting on the bleachers," Grace explains, "he started saying all this really gross stuff . . . telling me we should go find an empty classroom, putting his hand on my leg. I stood up to leave, but he grabbed me. So I pushed him."

"But you always said you didn't do it."

"I didn't *kill* him, but I did shove him. I was thirteen. The railing collapsed. He landed wrong, and everyone was in a panic. The principal asked me what happened. I was scared. Terrified. So . . . I lied. But he didn't deserve to die. He was . . . he was a kid. I didn't mean to hurt him, but once I said my lie, I stuck to it. Until right now."

After all these years, the guilt I've been carrying with me disappears, and I never needed to carry it in the first place. Grace and I both convinced ourselves we could never admit the truth to anyone. We let shame keep us from trusting each other.

One confession, shared in a chilling, dark tunnel, changes all of that.

"You know neither one of us is responsible for his death, right?" Grace says. "We never meant to hurt him, not like that. It . . . it was a freak accident. It took me a long time to believe that with Dr. Cramer. It *wasn't* my fault, but it wasn't yours either."

"I do know." I've been telling myself that for years, but it never stopped the guilt for Grace getting the blame. I stand in front of her and extend a hand to help her up. "I'm still sorry."

"Me too," she says, grabbing my hand.

And then we hug like we haven't hugged since we were kids. She holds me so tight, I can't breathe, and I don't care because for the first time in years, I have my sister back in my arms.

My sister without secrets.

My sister, who will always be there for me.

My sister, who will love me, no matter what.

When she lets go, Grace wipes her cheeks and laughs. "You look like a drowned rat."

"Except I make it look good." I strike a pose. She laughs again, and it echoes down the tunnel, filling the dark space with her own special light.

I take the flashlight and point to the left, toward the distance that leads back to the lodge, then to the right, and the never-ending darkness beyond.

"So, do we head back to the lodge?" she asks.

"Are you kidding? Jade locked me in our room, forged a note for you, and wrote something about you on that wall. We have to go find out what it is."

Side by side, my sister and I follow our circle of light, facing the darkness together.

The power of forgiveness should be
enough to right the wrongs of
this world, but unfortunately,

Truth cannot heal all wounds, nor
can it bring back the dead.
Ultimately, the bottom line

Is my desires, my beliefs,
don't matter. Joy will

Not last, but heartache won't
either. Somehow, they come
together, rising and falling.

As much as I want to forget the
pain of the past and move on,

It will always haunt me like a ghost,
torture me like a villain, pain me
like a victim, infinitely more than it

Seems.

CHAPTER 27

Grace: May 5

"I can explain," Nicole says, raising her hands in surrender. Her silvery voice catches with a distinct note of panic. The stench of her spilled beer mixes with the smoke drifting from the backyard.

"She made the picture of Mr. Gutter and sent it out to everyone," Jade says, still pointing. "She locked Maddy in her room. She tricked them both into going outside to get them in trouble."

Nicole is oddly still, her feet planted to the wood deck. Her icy blue eyes don't blink. Her skin pales under her dark eye makeup, but she doesn't deny it.

"What did you do?" Tori asks, turning on her and edging closer.

Nicole's eyes jump from one face to the next. "Okay, yes," she says, moving her hands down. "Yes, I was the one who made the picture. And yes, I hung up the underwear and rigged the doorknob to fall off, but I was trying to lock *Jade* in, not Maddy."

A breeze tingles my skin. This is it. The truth buzzes in the cool evening air. It's coming.

"After the trip meeting at school that Wednesday, Gutter came into Holtsof's room and overheard us making plans to get coffee on Saturday. He blew the whole thing out of proportion. Gutter reported Holtsof to Principal Avery, and she found a bunch of our DMs."

"You were DMing a teacher?"

"It wasn't like *that*. I'm not even underage, and he's only twenty-three. He was just being my friend! That's what I told Principal Avery, but she's a moron and suspended him anyway."

"But you're still his student," Tori says with a mix of shock and disgust at Holtsof, neither of which Nicole seems to understand.

"So? Just because Gutter's a creep doesn't mean everyone else is. If the school was investigating anyone, it should have been Gutter, not Holtsof."

She opens her mouth again—I assume to continue justifying a teacher sliding into her DMs and trying to get her to hang out—when I jump in.

"What's this have to do with her?" I ask, pointing at Jade.

"I told Caleb during the bus ride that I was the one who dropped the picture," Nicole says. "But Jade recorded me on her phone, so I snuck into her room and deleted the video. She came back at me with the shaving cream. I took her underwear, and she started a rumor that I cheated on Caleb. Which wasn't even true because Holtsof and I were just *friends*. So, yeah, I thought it would be funny if she got locked in her room. But I did not—definitely *not*—write any notes luring you outside."

Nicole's story swirls with Jade's. A dull throb sparks at the base of my skull. I didn't take my meds. The headache settles in. I don't know who to believe anymore, but someone is lying.

Someone hurt Maddy.

As if Nicole can read the suspicion sprouting on my face, she adds, desperately, "Adrian, I sat next to you during the last presentation that night. You know I didn't leave or go upstairs to drop a note."

"Yeah," Adrian says, still eyeing Nicole carefully. "Yeah, she was there."

"Can anyone vouch for you?" I turn to Jade—but Jade is gone. She peeks over her shoulder from the bottom of the stairs and takes off at a sprint across Nicole's backyard.

"Jade!" I yell.

WHOOP, WHOOP.

The siren sucks the air from my lungs. Red and blue lights flash through the night. A police car drives down the street and disappears in front of the house.

"COPS!"

Everyone shouts the same word. A torrent of seniors spills from the house. People shove their way onto the deck, throwing cups over the railing and diving toward the stairs.

I'm already three steps down and chasing Jade. Everyone else is running from an underage drinking fine. I'm running from a murder charge *toward* the person who must have killed my sister. I push my legs as fast as I can across the yard.

People sprint in every direction, like mice scurrying away from a cat. Jade's heading for the docks. Someone jumps in front of me, but I dodge them, nearly falling into the firepit. I get my footing as someone screams behind me.

A cop grabs Tori by the arm. She yells, "I haven't been drinking!" The officer doesn't release her. Someone else screams.

I can't slow down. My lungs burn. It hurts. I force myself to keep going.

Jade's still ahead, through the neighbor's yard. Maybe thirty feet. My muscles cry. My head throbs with every step.

"Jade!" I yell.

She doesn't stop but turns her head. Hair flies in front of her face and she trips.

I shoot forward with a burst of speed. For Maddy.

Jade's back on her feet, but I'm right behind her. She's hurt, limping.

I throw myself at her, and when our bodies collide, we smash to the ground, rolling in a heap. My elbow and knee scrape on dirt and rock. We tumble to the water's edge. Something slams into my back. I'm thrown across her. We stop tumbling, both gasping for air.

"Get off me," Jade shrieks, shoving her fists in my side and scrambling her legs against the ground. She cries out and clutches her ankle. I roll off her.

Adrian runs up to us, bracing his hands against his thighs, panting.

"Get away from me," Jade cries, but she's no longer making any attempt to run. She rubs her ankle and winces.

"You killed her," I shout.

"No." She shakes her head emphatically. Her tangled black

and red hair falls across her face, eyes smeared in black and bulging in fear. "It wasn't me."

"You wouldn't run if you were innocent."

We're five or six houses down from Nicole's, but the area stays lit from the police lights flashing.

Lights flashing. Siren wailing. Someone's hands under my neck. Loading me into an ambulance.

This is where they found me. I stand, breaths coming short and quick. A flash of pain spikes through the back of my head.

Right over there—I dragged myself out of the water. I crawled to the road. The ambulance parked in front of that house.

The ground sways under my feet, like I'm walking on a trampoline while someone's jumping.

Across the lake, way up on the hill, there's a glow from a lone building. The lodge from Sabbatical.

Maddy and I were supposed to be safe inside that night. Sleeping. Not here. Not in this water. She wasn't supposed to die.

Adrian's voice brings me back.

"Why did you want to hurt her?" he asks Jade.

"I didn't," she says, and sucks in a breath between clenched teeth, cradling her ankle. "I wanted to hurt Grace. But not like this. I didn't want anybody to die."

My knees go weak, and I stumble. Jade keeps glancing at me as though afraid I might leap on her again any second. I still can't breathe. Black spots dance in front of my eyes.

Maddy was in this water. She died here.

"You wrote the note that sent us outside."

Jade is silent.

"Is it true?" Adrian asks.

"Yes, okay?" Jade avoids my presence. "I forged the handwriting."

"Why?" I gasp.

"I wanted to prove a point."

My heart pounds. My hands shake. I step toward—

"Stay away from me," Jade cries, scooting in the grass.

The same terror rings in her voice that did in the lobby of Dr. Cramer's office.

Adrian holds out his hands, signaling me to stop, but I already have. Jade's terrified. Of *me*.

"Keep talking," Adrian says. The warning in his voice is clear.

When Jade speaks, her low voice is broken and cracked. "All I wanted was an apology." Tears roll down her cheeks, leaving black trails of makeup, but she won't look at me. "I wanted an acknowledgment that she *hurt* me. But she wouldn't give it to me. My life fell apart because of her. I had to leave Forest Lane. I had to leave my home. I had to leave my mom and my brother. And senior year I come back to find"—her voice rises in pitch, mocking—"everyone still loves Grace Stoll." She punches at the ground and shouts at Adrian. "She ripped my life apart, and hers got better. It's not fair."

I want to ask why she never *asked* me to apologize for anything and what I could've done to ruin her life, but the pain in my head erupts behind my eyes. I squeeze them shut and double over. My eyes stream. Adrian and Jade stare at me, one with concern, the other fear.

"So you looked for revenge instead?" I growl.

"Yeah, I did. I went looking for something to make sure I wasn't the only one who suffered. My life was flipped upside down, and someone deserved to pay."

"What did you do?" Adrian asks. His back is straight, tone firm.

"I thought since she was friends with Nicole, she might've been in on Gutter's picture. That's why I recorded Nicole on the bus, but she didn't mention Grace. So, when the chance came to get close to her sister during Sabbatical, I took it."

Her whole friendship with Maddy was a facade. It was all to get revenge.

"Then you got us outside so you could what? Hurt us?"

"No!"

"Why did you want Grace to leave the lodge?" Adrian asks.

"I only wanted to tell the teachers she was outside. When she came back, they were supposed to call her parents. She was only supposed to get in trouble. That's it. It would have been fair. It would have been *justice*."

"But we never came back." I stumble and jump when water covers my feet.

The splash. The cold.

It's like that night. My headache threatens to rip me in two.

"No," Jade repeats. "You never came back, and I panicked. I went searching for the note so it couldn't be traced back to me, but it was gone. I never wanted to hurt anybody! I only wanted Sanderson to call your parents."

Another flash. *Maddy on the ground. Not breathing. Dark. I'm shaking. Cold. So cold.*

It's hard to breathe, to see. My vision narrows.

"It's your fault my sister's not here!" I want the words to be true. Please be true. Please. Please.

"No! It's yours! I never went outside that night. I didn't hurt her. But you were there! You were with her."

The pictures from the police station flash before me, the dark bruises marring Maddy's pale skin. *My hand, gripped around Maddy's wrist. Blood on my clothes.* Detective Howard said it wasn't mine. It was hers. *Her blood.*

I hurt Maddy. I must have.

A blaze of pain shoots at the base of my skull, and a wave of nausea washes over me. I sway on my feet, and Adrian grabs my elbow to steady me.

"You two had that big fight!" Jade shouts. "Everyone heard."

Boom! Fireworks explode over the lake. Bright green and purple cascade into darkness, and the air whistles as two more rise. *Boom! Boom!* They crack through the night like thunder. Like the thunder from the night we went missing. It was raining and thundering. I was dragging her through the lake.

Sh, Sh, Sh.

Shoes running down a dark tunnel. A Sharpie. A shout.

"You were alone with her!" Jade shrieks above the fireworks.

"No," I yell. I cover my ears with my hands. "No, no, no!" I scream, but still Jade's words crash through.

"You killed her! *You* killed her!"

My mind lights up like the lake with every burst of fireworks. Image after image. Memory upon memory. *Her body floating in the water. The rain pouring down. The weight of her in my arms. The lightning flashing across the sky. Her eyes closed and peaceful.*

Stop.

Stop.

Stopstopstop.

But they don't stop.

Her hair stretched across her forehead. The thunder echoing over the lake. Her hand limp in mine. My heart pounding.

Hers not beating at all.

I didn't want anything to happen to her.

I loved her.

She was my sister.

She's gone.

She's gone.

"I remember everything."

CHAPTER 28

Maddy and Grace: April 25

"This is a night we'll never forget, huh?" Grace asks.

"How far does this thing go?"

The tunnel is cold, and my teeth have been chattering sporadically for the last five minutes. Water soaks through my shoes and socks, and I'm pretty sure it's in my bones. Or at least the bitter cold is. I haven't felt my toes for at least the last ten minutes.

"I don't know," Grace says. "It can't be too much farther."

As if summoned by the confidence in Grace's voice, the first name appears on the wall. Then another and another, until we're surrounded. Some are faded, others bright and bold. The writing spreads like spiderwebs, interlaced and locked together, up both walls, converging on the ceiling. Couples' initials stand together in hearts. Friends' names link in circles. Hearts and crosses, years and messages, scribbles and names tell the history of Forest Lane seniors for the last fifty years.

But none of them mention Grace.

"Did we miss it?" I ask, squinting back at the words we already passed.

"No, look. Here's Erica's name, and a bunch of other people from our class."

The flashlight illuminates Erica's and Zoey's names, exactly as they appear in the picture I found of them in the scrapbook earlier.

"There's nothing here," Grace says. "Nothing about me at all."

A street lamp shines through a sewer opening in the ceiling. A small waterfall trickles in from the road. I grab the flashlight and sweep the tunnel again, but there's nothing.

"Why would she lie about something we can check so easily?"

"I don't know," Grace says slowly, still scouring the names. "She was nice to me the first few weeks when we moved here. We were actually kind of friends."

"Yeah, she told me that on day two, but she said you drifted apart."

"Drifted? She ghosted me right around the time she moved."

"What about when she came back?"

"I tried to talk to her, but she acted all weird. She said I owed her an apology."

"For what?"

"In ninth grade, she kept making these comments about herself or other girls. She was always talking about her weight. Then she stopped eating lunch, so I told the counselor about it."

"And she was mad at you for that?"

"I guess. I don't even know if the counselor talked to her. Jade never told me about it before she moved away. All I know is her parents were going through a divorce at the time."

"Yeah, she mentioned that too. Her dad claimed she had an eating disorder because of her mom, because of her exercise habits and diets. He convinced the judge it was true, and the call from the school was apparently a crucial piece of evidence. Jade said that tore her life apart."

"Then she should be mad at her dad, not me."

"Yeah, she should, but . . . maybe deep down she didn't want to hate her dad, because, despite everything . . . she still loves him."

I know that better than anyone. I love Grace, so I didn't want to hate her for leaving me behind and getting all the attention and success. But the ones we love the hardest sometimes hurt us the most.

I recall everything Jade shared during hide-and-seek. "She saw your phone call as the tipping point in her dad's claim to the judge, and without it, her life could've been different."

All week Jade relished my complaints about Grace. Now I know she was jealous of her, like I was. But where I tried to swallow the jealousy, Jade let it consume her until she grew hungry for revenge.

"I didn't want to hurt her," Grace says, still confused. "I was *helping* her. Dr. Cramer helped me when everyone hated me in eighth grade, so I figured talking to someone would help her too."

I move the flashlight under my chin. "Grace, I say this with all the love in the world: You don't want to acknowledge how your actions, however well-intentioned they are, hurt people."

"No, they don't. I—"

"Grace."

"Okay," she admits. "I get it. But it's not as though I did anything *wrong*. I was worried about her and wanted to help."

"You're right. It wasn't wrong." She's repeating almost exactly what she said earlier about being with Adrian—she knew I was upset and tried to help. I can imagine what Jade might've been feeling. "Sometimes it's easier to blame other people than to accept we need help."

"And some of us are really good at blaming ourselves for everything." She squints at me pointedly and coughs.

"Yes, well," I say, and nudge her with my elbow. "Glad I have you to help me with that."

Everyone says their memories from Senior Sabbatical last a lifetime, and I know I'll never forget this. Grace and I have been through a lot together, and no matter where the future takes us, she'll always be there for me.

She was there to tuck me in when Dad was working late, even with only a few months separating us. She was always there to begin a game of Monopoly, even if we never finished. She was there to throw a pillow at me in the middle of a storm and make me laugh so I wouldn't be scared.

My sister's always been there for me and always will be.

Grace pulls a Sharpie from her pocket, takes the cap off with her teeth, and writes on the wall. She steps away, and reveals *Grace Elyse Stoll* and our graduating class year. She hands me the marker. The light shining through the sewer grate in the ceiling shifts. A car drives down the road, lightly splashing us below. I add *Madelyn Claire Stoll* and below it, *Sisters last forever.*

But I can't admire our artwork for long before my attention is pulled away.

"What's that sound?"

It's coming from above, on the street. The light disappears with a torrent of water rushing down on us. Grace slips to the ground, her flip-flop flying off and floating away.

Drenched and partly shoeless, she laughs. This is why everyone loves her. It's why I love her.

I pull her up, and we backtrack toward the entrance. I may not room with her next year, or attend the same school, but she'll still be there for me when I need her, and as long as I have her, everything will be all right.

We sing some old songs from when we were kids, to pass the time, but the minutes stretch and the tunnel never ends. Or it only feels that way because our feet are numb from the cold stream flooding up to our shins instead of our ankles. The glow of the flashlight fades, dimming more as time passes.

"We must be almost there, right?" Grace asks with a shaky voice.

I don't answer. The flashlight blinks out. I bang it against my palm, and it gets enough juice from the batteries to power up again. For how long, I don't know.

"Wait, up there," I say, pointing ahead. A glow, barely visible, signals we're close to the entrance. We trudge on, lifting our knees higher, fighting to get above the water. I'm nearly out of breath, but I can't hear myself panting over the splashing.

The rushing grows louder and louder.

An inlet on Grace's side releases a huge gush of water. It crashes into the wall in front of us. The current shifts, sucking my feet from under me, flooding over my head.

I gasp too late.

A burst of water charges into my lungs. I come up gasping for air and coughing with dirty street water burning my nose and throat. My head smacks against the tunnel, the claws of my hair clip tearing into my scalp.

"Maddy!" she screams my name and reaches for my hand. I scramble to stand. A fresh wave knocks Grace over. It sweeps us away from the opening. I kick out my legs, trying to steady myself. The cement scrapes my arm. I strive to grip something, anything along the walls. We slide in pitch black downstream. I reach for Grace. When my fingers find her wrist, I squeeze. Hard. I can't let her go. It's everything I can do to keep my head above the surface, and we're moving faster and faster and faster. My elbow knocks against something hard, and I fold it close, pulling my hand up to protect my head, but water rushes up my nose and I plug it instead, tucking my chin to my chest. A wave washes over my head again, and I swallow great gulps of it, trying not to breathe while a burning rises and squeezes my throat until the dark breaks way to faint light.

The air opens a moment before we're pulled under. Bubbles swirl. Darkness all around. Ice-cold water. So cold—like a thousand needles piercing every inch of my skin. My muscles freeze. I command them to move. *Kick. Swim. Live!* My mind screams, and they respond, straightening like a rod.

No cement scrapes my toes. No wall scratches my arm. There's no floor to propel myself to the surface. We're in a lake. A freezing-cold lake. I kick out, and stop swirling, fighting to reach the light. My lungs burn and I can't breathe and I kick harder but there's no air and I can't hold my breath much longer and I don't want to die here. Safety is so close, but so far. I have to keep going. My body screams. I'm almost there. Black spots dance before my eyes. I don't want to die. I don't want to die. I break the surface.

I can't gasp for air without coughing up more water, but Grace's hand is gone.

Grace is gone.

Rain pounds the lake as strong as bullets punching through a wall, exploding in a million shards. A small waterfall gushes from the tunnel's mouth behind me. Off to the right—

Grace.

She's floating face down and I can't get to her fast enough even though I'm trying and kicking as hard as I can but the water won't let me and my limbs move too slowly and I see her but I can't get to her fast enough. The slithery tendrils of her hair wrap around my fingers first. I flip her over, but she's not coughing and oh God is she not breathing? Out of the water. I have to get her out of the water. I have to get Grace out of the water. Grace needs to be on land.

It's the only thought my brain forms as I kick us toward a small island suspended in the middle of the lake, a weedy sandbar. I don't feel her weight dragging me beneath the surface. I don't try to calculate how many minutes she's been without oxygen. I don't feel the burning of my lungs still fighting to recover.

My feet slip along the rocks, but I pull from under her

shoulders, ignoring the way her head lolls to the side. I tilt her chin back, straight toward the sky. Her airway is clear. I clamp my hands together and push on her chest. One. Two. Three. Four. I'm going too slow. Nine, ten, eleven. I have to go faster, faster than I think. Fifteen, sixteen, seventeen. I have to get to thirty. My arms are already screaming, but when I get to thirty she'll be breathing. Twenty-eight, twenty-nine, thirty.

But she's not. Her chest isn't moving and there's no air coming out of her mouth and oh my God, Grace. One, two, three,four,fivesixseveneight. Please let it work. Please let Grace be okay. Please let her breathe. *Breathe, Grace, breathe.* I can't feel the tears running down my cheeks any more than I feel the rain or hear the thunder, but I can detect the aching sense of dread and panic welling up within me and closing off my lungs as tightly as the water did earlier.

Please. Please, God. Please, Grace. Please please please let her be okay.

I don't know how many times I count to thirty before I stop, before I fall over, before the blackness overtakes me and I pass out, before my hands slip from her chest but grasp her wrist, knowing she's already gone.

Grace is gone.

I am not the person you thought I am.

All I ask is, will you still love me?
Me, the one I am inside,

Me, the one I can't trust others to see?
And if I'm not her,
Do you think I'm still worthy of love?
Do you think I'm meant to be?
You have to know, know the real me.

CHAPTER 29

Maddy: May 5

"Grace is . . . gone." I can't tell if I'm saying the words out loud, but I need to hear them. I have to understand them. "She—she died."

My legs crumple beneath me and hit the shore.

Grace is dead.

"Shh," Adrian says, wrapping his arms around me. "It's going to be okay."

"She died." The words are hollow. My chest is empty. No air. No tears. Nothing. "Grace is dead."

Adrian might take my phone from my pocket. I'm not sure. He might call my parents and tell them where we are. I don't know.

All I know is my sister died on April 25, but reliving the memory makes it feel as though she died today.

A piece of me has died, too.

Flashing lights. No sirens.

Two patrol cars.

Officers approach.

"I only wanted the school to call her parents," Jade cries, still cradling her ankle, begging me for something I can't understand or give. "I wanted someone to tell on her like she told on me. That's all."

Grace reported Jade to the school counselor freshman year. The school called her parents. Her dad used it against her mom during the divorce.

She blamed it all on Grace.

Grace is dead.

I remember everything, and I already want to forget it all.

"Why didn't you report Grace right away on Thursday night?" Adrian asks the question my mouth can't form. "If you hadn't waited until the next morning, then maybe Grace—"

"I know," Jade wails. "I didn't mean for this to happen. When Maddy didn't show up that night, I didn't want her to get in trouble too. It was only supposed to be Grace. So I waited, and I . . . Nothing went like I planned. It wasn't supposed to turn out like this."

Jade's cries continue until the officers move her into the back seat of a car.

Adrian helps me into another. Words float around me like fog all the way home. I spend the trip staring out the window, but I can't remember a single thing we pass.

Adrian asks me some questions. I don't answer. His hand rests on my arm.

Grace is dead, but I'm alive.

It hurts, remembering her face. Like she was sleeping, or pretending to sleep, and any minute she could burst out laughing and open her eyes.

But I'll never hear that laugh again. Or see her smile or tease her about peppers or braid her hair. I'll never get to do anything with my sister ever again.

Because even though I'm alive, Grace is dead. Grace is dead. Graceisdead. Graceisdead.

Grace.

We stop. Someone opens the car door.

Mom and Dad run out. Arms around me. Mom says something. I don't know what. Dad talks to the officers.

My legs apparently carry me into the house, but I can't feel them. It's like I'm floating.

Mom ushers me to my room and guides me to my bed—*my* bed. Not Grace's.

My head hits *my* pillow.

A chasm opens within me. The pain cracks me in two and all that escapes is a stream of tears.

Grace.

I fall asleep whispering her name, knowing it is *hers,* but also knowing she will never answer to it again.

May 6

I sleep. A lot. Practically the whole day. It's as if the entire time I thought I was Grace, Maddy was still living in my sleep, never letting me rest properly. I was so convinced Grace couldn't be dead, that I made it a reality. Every conversation, every interaction, from the moment I saw her smiling face on the screen of the hospital's TV up until last night . . . it all plays through my head like the movie of someone else's life. When sleep no longer puts it on pause, I climb out of bed.

My footsteps creak on the steps, and in an instant, my parents appear at the foot of the staircase, Fizzy bounding up with them.

"Maddy?" Mom asks, and I know she's not only questioning if it's me or if I'm okay. She's asking if I know it's me.

I meet her eyes and nod, and she pulls me into her arms with Dad.

We stand in the middle of our foyer, a family of three, knowing we will always carry room in our hearts for four.

We move to the living room couch, and I tell them about the caves, about the water rushing in, about trying CPR, but I can't say any more.

Dad picks up when my voice fails. "Detective Howard told us last night. Someone from school told them the group was supposed to go to the caves the next day. They found your names on the wall of that tunnel. With the rain, they realized what happened."

He mumbles about the idiocy of the school for taking kids to a culvert.

"Robert," Mom says, placing a hand on his knee. "We've talked about this."

"So," I ask, "Detective Howard didn't come to the house to arrest me for Grace's murder?"

"No, nothing like that," Mom says. "He never suspected you. In fact, he was the one who first told us you might need a psych evaluation. You mentioned Maddy in your first interview when I left to go get a pop. He's the reason why we signed you up for appointments with Dr. Cramer."

"You . . . you knew I thought I was Grace?"

"We didn't know what to believe," Dad says. "In the hospital, you seemed to know who you were. The doctors wouldn't have released you otherwise. Even after Detective Howard told us his concern, we mentioned Grace to you directly, by name, and mentioned her death. You never showed any reaction that made us suspect anything. We told the school Dr. Cramer had concerns, but nothing specific. We didn't have anything official. It wasn't until last night that we knew everything Dr. Cramer was telling us was right."

They told the school . . . Principal Avery mentioned my "mental struggles," but I assumed she was referring to my memory loss. And my fight with my parents in the kitchen, how they froze when I mentioned playing volleyball, how they tried to get me to settle down, to make sense. How Mom called me Maddy.

But that seems like years ago, not two nights. I can't remember any other conversations where they called me Maddy. Only headaches. More memories that tipped into the void following the accident.

I remember staring at Grace's face on that TV screen under the word *Missing* and knowing with every piece of my soul that I'd give *anything* for my sister to be okay—even myself.

"We knew you were struggling to accept what happened,"

Mom says. "We all were . . . are struggling. At home, you never gave any indication you were . . . confused. You were already going through so much, we were afraid talking about it might . . . make it harder."

If I learned anything from Sabbatical, from Jade, from Dr. Cramer, from Grace, it's the importance of being direct and honest. No more suffering in silence. No more pretending. "We need to talk about it," I say.

"I know," Mom says, exchanging a look with Dad. "We do."

"You said you didn't suspect anything," I begin. "But . . . Detective Howard thought I killed her?"

Dad shakes his head. "Detective Howard noted the injuries on you and your sister and suspected foul play. He wanted to be thorough, but that meant he wasn't viewing the case as an accident. He didn't believe you intentionally hurt your sister, but he did believe you knew more than you were telling."

"The way he was questioning me . . ." I filtered his questions through Grace's reality, not mine.

Who left the lodge first? Was it her? Was she still upset like she was in this letter and you went after her? What did you say to her?

The conversation is twisted now, wavy like a fun house mirror with more distortions the further back I step.

"He thought you might've been there when Grace . . ." Mom hesitates. "He thought that she might've attempted suicide. He also wanted to personally apologize for suggesting it and upsetting us at the station."

Suicide. Her notebook. I thought it was my notebook. I thought she wrote a letter for me in my notebook.

You're the older sister. You're supposed to set the example. That's what Mom always says. Accept who you really are and be happy for it. Stop pretending to be something better.

Sincerely,
The Stoll Daughter No One Sees
When You're Around

Those were Grace's inner thoughts, her fears, the ones she never wanted anyone else to know. She wrote the letter to herself, showing all the imperfections she tried so hard to keep hidden. Detective Howard believed she was angry with herself enough to attempt suicide, thought she might have acted on the emotions of that letter, thought I might have tried to stop her. That's the secret he thought I was hiding.

"So you never believed I . . . that I could have . . ."

"Maddy, we know you did everything you could to save her." She's crying now, and I am, too, but neither of us tries to hide it. "We could never blame you."

Those words break open a safe where I've locked up and hidden away the question that scares me most. But I have to ask. I have to be brave enough for the truth.

I spent the last several years of my life comparing myself to her. I focused on her perfection with sports, school, and friends, and I equated that to my failures. Grace was everything I thought I could never be. I thought the world would want her more than me.

But maybe it wasn't the world I needed reassurance from. Maybe it was only these two in front of me.

"You don't—" My voice cracks. "You don't wish that it was me instead of her?"

My dad breaks and pulls me into his chest, like I'm five years old. His arms lock around me, securing me in the present. Mom presses in on my other side, a small *no* breaking through her gasps of tears.

"We always loved you both," Dad says firmly. He's crying, but he no longer tries to hide it. "Never one more than the other. Never."

This is the answer I've been searching for. I never wanted to be brighter than Grace or better. I simply wanted to shine in my own way, a way that made them look at me too.

Maybe they were looking the whole time, and I wasn't.

May 7

The next day Dr. Cramer sits across from me in her muted purple chair. The couch isn't as stiff as I remember it. More people sat here besides me. I'm not the only one.

"The last time we spoke, you were discovering who you are without your sister. How has that been?"

"I now know I'm *not* my sister, if that's what you mean." I say it more dryly than I should.

"I'm glad you've accepted that."

"You knew I was confused," I say. Her words from our last

session play back to me with new meaning. *You can change how you view yourself now. You can accept who you are. . . . As you try to get to know your sister, I want you to settle your consciousness on also getting to know yourself.*

"I knew you needed to accept what happened to Grace before you could accept your own identity."

"My parents said they mentioned Grace to me, called me Maddy, but I don't remember."

Last night they told me they didn't know what to believe when Dr. Cramer first shared her concerns. They were still struggling to accept one daughter had died; they couldn't truly process that another might be mentally broken, believing she was someone else. No one else knew.

Nicole didn't know in the police station parking lot, but that's why she didn't hug me; not because she was afraid of my injuries, but because I wasn't her best friend.

And that's why Erica *did* hug me at school, because she was supposed to be mine.

And Ryan Jacobs. I texted him "This is Grace Stoll." No wonder he blocked my number. He must have thought someone was impersonating his dead classmate. I guess, in a way, I was.

Then there's Adrian. I don't know what he must think of me now.

"Your parents were"—Dr. Cramer searches for a word—"reluctant to accept that you were suffering enough to cause delusions. Like you, they wanted to deny a truth that was undeniable."

Delusions. The word sounds too formal, clinical.

"Sometimes," Dr. Cramer says, her voice soft and gentle, "when our brain is trying to protect us from a memory or a truth that will hurt us, it does funny things. There were times during our sessions I mentioned Grace to you, and you acted as if you couldn't hear me. I believe you couldn't, not really. Your brain wouldn't allow you to."

She says it calmly, logically. It takes away some of the shame. It's embarrassing to admit how broken from reality I was, like I should have been able to control those thoughts. But no one could've convinced me of the truth until I was ready to accept it. It wasn't a choice I made. It simply was.

"Have you considered why you thought you were Grace?" Dr. Cramer asks, prodding me back to the present.

She waits without moving, wielding her sword of silence again.

"I missed her. A lot." The words feel true, but they aren't the reason. Not completely. "I wanted to bring her back. I felt responsible for not being able to save her."

I think back to the last hour we had together. Her laughter. Her honesty. Our names written on the wall. Together, forever.

"I didn't feel like I deserved to live more than she did. I didn't feel worthy of this second chance at life when hers was stolen. I wanted her to keep living, more than I wanted to live myself."

"That's a lot of reasons."

"There was no reason for her to die. I have hundreds for why I wanted to bring her back to life."

May 10

The day has come to select the items to bring for Grace's memorial at school. Mom wanted to help, to keep things organized, but I told her I had to do some of it myself, to say goodbye to Grace the way I didn't get to before.

I take down her stuffed purple bunny, the one from when she was five that she hid up on our closet shelf but never wanted to get rid of. I give it a hug, a big one, in place of the one I wish I could still give her.

Then I move to her shelf and pick up each of the trophies she won. I make sure to read each inscription, to remember all she sacrificed to achieve her goals, to honor the dreams she never got to accomplish.

I pick up the book from her nightstand, the one with a bookmark three-quarters of the way through. Grace will never know the ending.

I remove her pictures from the bulletin board hanging on the wall, memorizing her smile and the soft freckles dotting her cheeks from spending so much time at Nicole's lake house. I never want to forget those details, the things about her that make her different from me. Those are the pieces I want to remember forever.

These items will be set out on a table, a small attempt to capture her spirit and heart. The room is bigger, empty, only mine. But I know, even without her things here, she will always be with me.

The police have returned our Sabbatical notebooks. At Dr. Cramer's encouragement, I go through both. Alone in my room, curled up on my bed, I find the real letter I wrote to Grace.

Dear Grace,

When I look at you, all I see is your beauty. Not from your features. We share the same blue eyes and slightly rounded nose. We have identical cheekbones and chins. But I'm not beautiful like you are.

Beauty really does come from within, and you laugh like you don't care who's listening. You talk as easily as you make friends. You glow with confidence. When I look at you, it's like looking in a mirror of everything I want to be instead of who I already am.

And it hurts.

I keep staring at my beautiful sister and only seeing my failures. That jealousy has come between us. If I could take a knife and cut it out, I would. But I don't know how. It's become part of me, a secret that I carry.

I don't know why I haven't told you any of this before. Maybe for the same reason I've never told you I tripped Mateo at the dance.

I'm too ashamed of the truth. Lying to you—to myself—and pretending that none of it matters is easier. If I shatter this mirror, I don't know who I'll see.

It might be an even uglier me.

I wish I could look at myself the way you look at your own reflection. You're everything I wish I was and will never be. I hope one day you'll forgive me for all the pain you never knew I caused.

Maddy

What would've changed if only she'd read this letter when I wrote it? If I had confessed to her instead of to Jade? If I'd been brave enough to tell her way back during eighth grade?

No one will ever know the answer to any of those questions, and Dr. Cramer says it isn't healthy to dwell on them. She also supports my decision to take a year off from school. After finding a steady job, nothing too stressful, I'll probably submit more poems to some scholarships or for publication.

That's what Grace would want me to do.

I set the notebook on the bed and run my hand over the page. Some words at the end are smeared from the few tears that fell while I was writing it. In the mirror, my own reflection stares back at me with bright, clear eyes and a rounded nose. It's the same face I've always seen but different now. I no longer see a friendless girl with mousy hair or sadness tucked in the corners of her smile.

I see a girl loved by her broken parents, who don't always know how to help, but at least know to get her a professional who can.

I see a girl who fought her hardest to save Grace and is slowly accepting it's not her fault.

I see a girl who may not have a sister anymore, but who will always carry her memory with her.

I'm finally looking in the mirror and seeing who I truly am on the inside.

CHAPTER 30

Maddy: May 10

The school holds the memorial on the front lawn in the evening. The parking lot is packed. Many people from the area are here, ones who didn't even know Grace personally. I was right: our story did reach more people than I could've imagined, but unlike all the critics, snoops, and gossips from the comment sections online, these people gather with heavy hearts to honor the true story, the one of tragedy and a beautiful soul gone too soon.

As a community, we are healing. A lengthy article was published in the local paper this week, stressing the danger of open culverts and storm drains. The owners of the lodge are making plans to restrict that area from the public. What happened to me and Grace isn't as rare as I expected. A few times a year, people are sucked into drains following heavy rains or flash floods, even if they never step inside the pipe as we did.

And I will forever wish we never had.

But there are pieces of Sabbatical I will cherish forever. I don't know if Grace and I would've gotten close without the trip bringing us together. It's hard to find the line between gratitude and regret. I try not to spend too much time deciding where I fall.

"Mr. and Mrs. Stoll, here." Tori hands each of my parents a small candle. "We've all lit one for Grace." Her explanation is unnecessary, because the beauty of the sight before us is enough.

All along the sidewalk, hundreds of little lights blaze, casting a warm glow around Grace's senior volleyball picture and a floral wreath from the school. The trophies from our room are displayed next to poster after poster of pictures. Principal Avery told Dad earlier that Grace's friends have been working on the display for weeks in study hall.

Mom and Dad are still discussing whether to take legal action against the school, despite the waivers we signed to attend the trip. The school's already announced that Senior Sabbatical will never happen again. Regardless of the legal ramifications, the individual staff members have shown nothing but compassion.

Many of their faces appear in the crowd. Not all of them had me or Grace in class, but they're not here only for us. They're offering encouragement and comfort to other students who are mourning too. Mr. Gutter lingers near the back, alone.

"I'll be right back," I tell my parents, and head over to him. "Mr. Gutter?" He jumps at his name. "I wanted to thank you. For finding me that day and getting me help."

"Oh, Maddy." His face softens. "Of course I—"

I give him a hug, and after a moment he pats my shoulder. Awkwardly, of course, but this time it makes me laugh. He was only guilty of lacking social skills, not of any inappropriate interactions with students. Rather than return to school, he's retiring early.

"You're both such good girls," he says.

I thank him again and head back through the crowd. No one seems to know if Holtstof was officially fired or if he resigned first, but he no longer works for the school, and it's clear Gutter selflessly volunteered to chaperone the trip because Holtsof was suspended while the school investigated.

Nicole and her friends—Grace's friends—sit near the front. "Maddy," she says. "There's room over here with us." She motions for everyone to scoot down, even standing, as if she'd give up her seat for me.

"Thanks, Nicole." And I mean it. Ever since the police made it clear she wouldn't be in trouble for anything that happened on the trip, her lawyers and parents have set her free to talk to me. She's been stopping by the house and messaging me regularly to see if I want anything or if I need to talk. Sometimes she's the one who needs to talk. She wasn't Grace's sister, but she loved her almost like one, and I understand her pain. I'm not sure whether or not Nicole realizes how wrong Holtsof was to try meeting her outside of school, or even messaging her "as a friend," but losing Grace has changed everything about her perspective on life and she's growing as a person.

With a warm hug of appreciation, I decline Nicole's offer

and sit with my parents. The three of us need to be together tonight.

One face is conspicuously absent from the crowd, but maybe it's for the best, for her own sake. Since Jade's actions weren't illegal, the police aren't charging her with anything, but while newspapers never printed Jade's name or how she was involved with the events of that night, social media has spoken. Jade's name and face are everywhere. She's deleted all her accounts, but it doesn't matter. People blame her as much as they blame the school, as much as I blamed myself.

Dr. Cramer says Jade likely made Grace her target because it was easier than accepting that her father was too selfish to prioritize Jade's best interests. Grace didn't deserve Jade's wrath for being a good friend and reporting her, but I understand the temptation to assign blame to the wrong person if it means avoiding a hard truth.

Someone told me Jade's not going to college next year because they rescinded her acceptance once they saw the public backlash online. Someone else told me she's not going because her therapist is checking her into a long-term care facility. I told them both I know what it's like for guilt to consume your life and alter your reality, so I hope she gets the help she needs before it costs her as much as it cost me.

Gossip and blame hurt Grace during eighth grade, and they are part of what led us outside that night on Sabbatical. Enough lives have been ruined. Jade doesn't need to be added to the list. Her own conscience will probably tear her apart more anyway.

I know mine did.

A hush falls over the crowd, with a sense the memorial will begin soon. I twist in my seat, trying to take in the hundreds of faces gathered here for Grace.

Erica sits with her parents on one side and a boy I don't recognize on the other. He drapes his arm around her shoulder, and Erica leans over him to say something to Zoey. Erica has apologized more than once, so I don't think she believes I've forgiven her for everything she wrote. She doesn't understand that my forgiveness does not grant her my friendship. I know I'm worth more than that now.

Like a magnet, my eyes are drawn to Adrian's, as if he's been watching me since we arrived. He waves with a sympathetic smile. In the days following Nicole's party, he sent me some messages asking to talk. I thanked him for his help that night, but told him I needed time.

Of course, he's respected my request, but I don't know how to have that conversation. Rationally, I know what needs to be said, but my heart wants to delay it as long as I can.

Dad squeezes my knee. "You okay?"

I squeeze his hand back and face the front podium. "I will be."

The next hour is filled with kind words from school staff and coaches, funny stories from friends and teammates, and a beautiful song by our choir. Tears and laughter dance together in the pleasant spring air, and by the time Principal Avery closes the evening, it's clear: no one will ever replace Grace, but her eighteen years on this earth were filled with enough love and joy to last us a lifetime.

"Stoll, wait." Adrian jogs to catch up.

I keep moving. I don't want to do this tonight. Too many hearts are already broken.

"Maddy, please."

It's the sound of my name that keeps me from running to the car. He always called me Stoll, on the trip and after. My brain blocked out anyone calling me *Maddy*, but I always heard Adrian call me by my last name. At school, he said, Mrs. Miller, the secretary, was calling my name, but I couldn't hear her.

How many other times did people say my name the last few weeks and I didn't hear it? How often do we say the name of the person we're talking to?

And then he's next to me. His hat covers his dark hair and shades his brown eyes. He waves to both of my parents.

"I'll meet you at the car," I tell them. Mom nods, and Dad wraps his arm around her shoulder when they walk away.

"I know you need time, but I want to know if you're okay," Adrian says. "I care about you."

"Do you?" The words sting in the back of my throat. I don't know if I can do this.

"Yes, of course. I know I have a lot to apologize for, and I want to do it in person." Adrian takes off his hat and twists it in his hands. "First, I promise I didn't know you were . . ."

"Delusional?" I supply. I can't blame him for being uncomfortable about the word. I was, too, before it applied to me.

"I was worried about you after Sabbatical, but once I heard you were okay, I assumed you wouldn't want to speak to me again after sharing your poetry, and I didn't know how to talk to you about it when Grace was still missing."

I remember seeing him on the walk with Fizzy, his uncertainty about how to act when I approached. I assumed he was uncomfortable with how to be supportive, but really he was expecting me to scream at him like the last time he'd seen me and my sister.

"I should have told you right away that I'd shared an entry from your notebook and you were mad at me, but it seemed like such a stupid thing to bring up when you were worried about your sister. You were hurting so much already, I didn't want to hurt you all over again."

His own pain is set in his jaw, firm and strong. He's only making this harder for me. I don't want to hurt him all over again either.

"I was going to tell you about it when we were at breakfast, but then you smiled. And I . . . I love seeing that smile, and I didn't want to do anything else to make it disappear."

A breeze pushes my hair across my face, and he tucks it back behind my ear, his touch gentle and uncertain.

"When did you know?" I ask, ducking my face away.

"That you thought you were Grace?"

I nod. "When?"

"Not until your dad told me. At the party I could tell something was wrong, but I didn't know what. If I'd known, I swear I would have tried to help, tried to tell you."

I shake my head. "Even if you had told me the truth, I wouldn't have been able to understand it."

From what Dr. Cramer says, I might not have heard it at all. One of the worst headaches I got was when I was looking for my journal in our bedroom, when I tried to see the room with

Maddy's eyes. Dr. Cramer was right. I had to accept my memories before I could realize the truth of my identity.

"I could have tried," he says.

"My own dad tried to make sure I knew I wasn't Grace, and it triggered psychosomatic headaches that blocked his words. So yeah, you could've tried, but it wouldn't have worked."

Adrian tucks his hands in his pockets. "I'm still really sorry for what I did on Sabbatical. I never should have taken your notebook and read it. I should have apologized to you in person on the trip instead of writing that letter."

It's embarrassing that I read it in his trunk and assumed he was with my sister, when he was, in fact, only ever with me.

"There were times when you seemed . . . different, but I chalked it up to dealing with the loss of your sister. Who wouldn't be a little distracted? But I meant everything I said on the playground. I want to be here with you through it all. So . . ." He waves his hand back and forth between us, and asks, "Can we try this again?"

"I—" I want that to be enough, but I have to be honest with him. Adrian might not have known I was delusional until Nicole's party, but it doesn't change things for me. It can't. "I don't think so."

His dark brows draw together in confusion. "I'm really, really sorry for reading your poem, for not telling you about it," he says again, and the sincerity lingering in his voice nearly breaks my resolve.

"I know, but it's not about that."

"Then, what is it? Are you embarrassed about your

confusion? Because I know what trauma can do. I know my mom sometimes woke up forgetting she didn't have a baby anymore."

"No, it's not that." I don't know how to say it.

"Then tell me what it is," he says earnestly. "Is it because you're afraid it will happen again, that you'll forget? Because I'll be here for you if it does. I'll—"

"Adrian, stop."

It hurts more that he's so understanding, so kind.

His eyes search mine, begging me, pleading with me. "Stoll, talk to me. I care about you."

Those last four words are so, so hard to hear. Because I want to believe them. I want to believe *him*.

"You care about Grace," I say, admitting the fear that's been festering over the last few days. "She's the one you got to know. She's the one who flirted with you and opened up and . . . and kissed you. It wasn't me. That's not who I am. I thought I was her, and that's who you fell for."

As much as I want the waffles to be ours, or walks with Fizzy, they're not. They're Grace's. I thought I was confident, outgoing Grace. I—*Maddy*—I would have never done those things. Not without someone pushing me. Not without awkward silences. Even if I'm able to accept that my parents loved us both the same, I can't deny we were still different.

"No, that's not true." He reaches a hand out for mine. It's as warm and gentle as it was on Sabbatical, as it was on the slide. "You may have thought you were Grace, but you were still acting like you. I didn't start liking you after the accident. I liked the girl who smiled at my stupid Speedo jokes freshman year, the girl who could twist her arms into messed up contortions and laugh at Ryan Jacobs instead of with him. That's the same girl who joked with me about dating a rake. And that girl who wrote that incredible poem, that's the same girl who opened up to me over waffles. Don't you see? You thought you had to be Grace because she was better than you, but honestly, you brought out the best in each other, and she still does. Her good traits are still living within you, not because she's gone, but because they've always been there."

"You sound like my therapist."

He smiles, so big and so pure that it makes me smile too. "Not what I was going for, but I'll take it."

He pulls me in for a hug, and I go willingly. I press my face against his chest and sink into his arms. He wants to be with me. Despite everything, he's still choosing *me*.

"Do you really mean it?" I ask, just to hear him say it.

"Every word, Maddy."

He says my name at the end clearly. Emphatically. Significantly. He sees me for who I am. Not who I should be or could be or would be.

If he can see it, I can too.

May 31

By the end of the month, I'm still visiting Dr. Cramer every week. Mom and Dad are seeing a therapist of their own.

Today, after giving Fizzy extra pets and scratches since she couldn't come with us, Adrian drives me to the cemetery. I'm still learning new ways to say goodbye.

"You ready?" he asks, taking my hand. He indicates a notebook poking out from under my lap and asks, "What's that for?"

"It's from Sabbatical," I tell him, and open it. "I was flipping through it again last night, but I felt like she should have it." So many of the words I wrote in here belonged to her all along. The regrets, the pain, the jealousy. It's time to let them go. "I'm ready," I tell him, bringing my notebook with me.

The sun shines brightly, without a single cloud floating in the sky. Her grave is a few rows in. I twist the small bouquet wrapped in plastic. It crinkles loudly, louder than our footsteps on the soft grass. And then we're there. Her full name, birthday, and death day are inscribed in stone, marking her place in time forever but missing the fullness of her life.

"I brought a card for you," Adrian says, as conversationally as if Grace were standing next to us. "It's nothing special, but I hope it makes you laugh."

"I hope it does, too," I say. I'm glad they were friends on Sabbatical. They're both important to me, and she'd be happy knowing we're together.

I fold back my notebook and place it next to his card. The sun shines on my poem, the one Adrian read aloud on Sabbatical. Except, he read it wrong. Or rather, he didn't finish it. Because when you get to the end, you have to look back and keep going. You can't stop when you're convinced it's over. You need to read it from bottom to top.

this is who i am
i've accepted what i tried so hard to deny
i will always be different
it's easy to see that
even if we look the same
only one attracts every eye
you can't convince me
i'm worthy of love
i know the truth:
i was a mistake
and i'll never accept
i can be loved the same
i'm second-born and second-rate
in my heart i will never believe
someone could still want me
when i reflect my true identity

But both versions are true. Sometimes. It's not a before and after. Sabbatical was simply the first time I felt the reverse was real, too. I know my struggle isn't over. These emotions will come back and want to consume me again. But maybe they won't be as strong, or last for as long. Then eventually, someday, I'll only be able to read it in reverse. Forever.

The lessons from Sabbatical are still with me. Open the first, remember the second, act the third, and forgive the fourth. But the fifth day, the one I missed, is important too.

Breathe the fifth.

Adrian says Mrs. Sanderson told them the last day was

supposed to be focused on how we should take everything we've learned the first four days, breathe it in and exhale it out, pouring the lessons onto others.

I need to be open to new people and experiences. I need to remember the past. I need to put my boundaries into action. I need to forgive, myself and others. But I also need to breathe, to keep living.

Not instead of Grace, but because of her.

ACKNOWLEDGMENTS

I have so many people to thank for getting this book into your hands. First, glory to God for creating a better story for my life than I ever could have written.

Thank you to:

My agent, Molly Ker Hawn, for being more than I could ask for and better than I had imagined. May your career be as thrilling as a slip and slide in the rain.

My editor, Kelsey Horton, for making my dreams come true and pushing me at each step along the way. May your life be as satisfying as a s'more made with a perfectly roasted marshmallow.

The rest of the team at Penguin Random House, including Beverly Horowitz, Tamar Schwartz, Natalia Dextre, Cathy Bobak, Trisha Previte, Joey Ho, Kate Keating, Elizabeth Ward, Kim Langus, Becky Green, and Joe English. May you win every game of hot lava you ever play.

The team at the Bent Agency, including Martha Perotto-Wills and Victoria Cappello, for all you do behind the scenes. May you never be locked in a room with a broken doorknob, but if you are, may you be rescued quickly.

My Pitch Wars crew, especially my mentor, Jamie McHenry, for first seeing this story, taking a chance, and pouring in hours of work. May you never have anyone throw up on your bed after a skating party.

My There or Square Stabby Bears: Aimee Davis for watering the first seed of this story, and Laurie Lascos, Sana Z. Ahmed, Christine Arnold, K. A. Blaser, Emily Charlotte, Valo Wing, Lally Hi, Sul, Elle Desamours, and P. H. Low for helping me grow. May you have an unending supply of waffles. Always.

My Mystery Mavens: Paula Gleeson for reading a truly terrible first draft, and Gabi Burton, Karen Jo, Mariann Evans, Jessica Hogbin, and Shante for reading a marginally better one. May you never have to picture a man in an orange Speedo.

Morgan Watchorn for traveling this journey with me. May you never have a notebook stolen and read aloud.

Detective Adam Johnson for letting me pester him with questions. May your cars run as well as Betty White.

All my early readers and encouragers, especially Nancy Haines, Ann Carboneau, and Overbooked Book Club. May you always travel with someone who likes the same music.

My family, especially my parents and in-laws for loving on my kids. May you always know how loved you are.

My husband for more than I can express in words. May you never eat food with peppers in it.

My kids for being you. May the anagram of your life always spell out *HOPE.*

And finally, my readers. May you never forget who you are and how much you're worth.

EDUCATORS' GUIDE

Before Reading

Anticipation Guide

Decide if you agree or disagree with each statement. Discuss your opinions and be prepared to explain your thinking behind each one.

1. Real friends never lie.
2. Once someone has broken your trust, they are unlikely to earn it back.
3. When something goes wrong, it's important to know who to blame.
4. Making friends is easy.
5. Sometimes being a good friend means doing something that could hurt the other person.
6. For the most part, people never really change. You are who you are.
7. Who people see on the outside is an accurate representation of who I am.
8. Being well-liked is more important than being right.
9. My actions mostly affect my own life, not anyone else's.
10. Schools should focus on the mental health of students.

Discussion

An unreliable narrator is one the reader cannot always trust to provide objective information. This can be because of bias, keeping secrets, being mentally unstable, or having memory problems. Discuss other stories you have encountered (in short stories, novels, or TV and movies) with an unreliable narrator. How does this storytelling device affect the reader? In what ways do all books written in first person have an unreliable narrator?

During Reading

Poetry Analysis

The poems at the end of Maddy's chapters are connected to her emotions in the pages preceding them. Pick one poem and explain its message. Use examples from the poem to explain your thinking. Now return to the chapter before, and use examples from the text to explain how it reflects what Maddy is going through.

Extension: Some poems mirror Grace's emotions in the next chapter. Review the chapter after the poem and explain how this poem could connect to Grace's point of view, too.

Mentor Text—Poetry

Choose one of the poems and take note of the topic, word choice, structure, patterns, contrasts, and anything else you find interesting. Use that poem as inspiration to create one of your own. It can be about a similar topic or have a similar structure. Then write a short explanation of how the original poem inspired your own. How is your poem different?

Grammar Analysis

Several times throughout the story, the narrators use incomplete sentences. Find two or three examples and explain the effect of breaking the "proper" rules of grammar. What is being emphasized? How does it add to the character's voice?

Likewise, run-on sentences are used in chapter 28. What is the effect of these sentences? What would be lost if the entire novel was written in run-on sentences or sentence fragments?

Mentor Text—Punctuation

Find a sentence that ends in a period, one that uses a colon, and one that uses an em dash. Make some observations about the sentence patterns and compare with a partner. Experiment with the structure of these sentences by writing a sentence of your own.

Vocabulary and Diction

Identify and track specific words used in the book. These words might be new, important to the story, or connect with you in a personal way. Arrange these words in an artistic display, on paper or digitally. Include quotes that feature the words.

Thought Log

At any point in the book, write down your thoughts about your reading. Make connections to other points in the book, your own life, or other books you have read. Cite specific sections of text that sparked the connections and support your ideas. Share your thinking with others.

Here are some questions to prompt your thinking:

1. What have you noticed coming up again and again? Why might this information be important for the reader? For the narrator?
2. What changes have you noticed in a character? What caused that character to change? How is the change affecting their relationships with other characters?
3. What connections can you make between Grace's chapters in the present and Maddy's chapters in the past? What is being emphasized in those connections?
4. Writers can create suspense using a variety of techniques, including withholding information or foreshadowing information or events. Identify a place in the text you feel is especially suspenseful and explain what elements create that effect.
5. What do you like or dislike about the book? Which characters do you connect to and why?

After Reading

Title Reflection

This book was not always titled *Silent Sister.* If you had to choose a different title for the book, what would you choose and why? Use details from the text to support your answer.

Theme Development

Theme can be developed using a variety of strategies, such as those in *Notice and Note* by Kylene Beers and Bob Probst. One strategy is repetition. What ideas come up in the book again and again?

Sometimes the author reveals a theme by contrasting things within the book. Which characters contrast each other? What do their differences highlight? Do any characters at the end of the novel contrast themselves from the beginning? What has changed?

Other times a wise mentor character can subtly reveal the theme. Dr. Cramer and Mrs. Sanderson both serve this role. Return to some of their scenes and record their advice for the main character. What message is being sent through these characters?

Similarly, when a character has an epiphany, or moment of realization, there can be a connection to theme. In the last few chapters, Maddy has several epiphanies and asks some tough questions. Summarize the questions Maddy asks and the epiphanies she has.

Theme Statements

The following themes can be found in *Silent Sister.* Choose one and discuss how it is developed over the course of the novel through repetition, contrast, mentor characters, and epiphanies. What message is delivered about this topic? Use specific details from the text to support your answer.

1. Reality versus perception
2. Identity
3. Forgiveness
4. Honesty

Extension: Once you've written a theme statement, write a brief paragraph about your own experience with this theme.

Point of View

In chapter 23, the narrator has a fight with Adrian. Return to this scene and write it from Adrian's perspective. How does the tone change? What does Adrian understand? What is he unaware of?

Personal Connections

Maddy struggles with her identity and accepting herself for who she is. Create a visual representation of your own identity. How is the outward appearance the same as or different from what's going on inside?

Discussion

Use the following questions to lead a discussion after completing the novel.

1. Describe the Stoll sisters. In what way is their relationship unique? In what way are they like most sisters?
2. Who is to blame for Grace's death?
3. Discuss the title. In what ways does it accurately apply to the novel?
4. How does the author's use of poetry at the end of Maddy's chapters affect the story?
5. Compare and contrast the way Maddy and Grace interact with those around them. In what ways do others influence them? How do they influence others?
6. Was the ending a surprise, or did you see it coming? Return to earlier passages in the book, including the opening scene, to find instances of foreshadowing.
7. What does Maddy learn about herself at the end of the novel? About the world?
8. What five words would you use to describe the book?

Text Pairings

Fiction (Unreliable Narrator)

Monday's Not Coming by Tiffany D. Jackson

Allegedly by Tiffany D. Jackson

Everything, Everything by Nicola Yoon

We Were Liars by E. Lockhart

A Danger to Herself and Others by Alyssa Sheinmel

Fiction (Multiple Perspectives)

Looking for Smoke by K. A. Cobell

The Cousins by Karen M. McManus

Promise Boys by Nick Brooks

An Ember in the Ashes by Sabaa Tahir

Salt to the Sea by Ruta Septys

Short Stories

"The Tell-Tale Heart" by Edgar Allan Poe (unreliable narrator)

"The Yellow Wallpaper" by Charlotte Perkins Gilman (unreliable narrator)

"Fish Cheeks" by Amy Tan (identity)

"The Landlady" by Roald Dahl (reality versus perception)

"The Story of an Hour" by Kate Chopin (reality versus perception)

"The Wife's Story" by Ursula K. Le Guin (reality versus perception)

"A Retrieved Reformation" by O. Henry (forgiveness/honesty)

Poems

"Heart to Heart" by Rita Dove (trust/vulnerability)

"Identity" by Julio Noboa (identity)

"Jabari Unmasked" by Nikki Grimes (secrets/vulnerability)

"Chemo Side Effects: Memory" by Elise Partridge (memory)

"Momentum" by Catherine Doty (friendship)

"Remember" by Joy Harjo (memory/life)

Nonfiction

"What Your Most Vivid Memories Say About You: How self-defining memories shape your identity" by Susan Krauss Whitbourne, PhD

"Nature vs. Nurture Debate" by Commonlit staff

"Self-Concept" by Saul McCleod

ABOUT THE AUTHOR

Megan Davidhizar grew up moving around the Midwest and graduated summa cum laude from Purdue University. She now spends her mornings wishing she liked coffee, her days learning from the students in her English classroom, and her evenings reading stories to her three children while her husband tries to convince them the movies are better. Miraculously, she is still happily married. *Silent Sister* is her debut novel.